Praise for the work of Verónica Gutiérrez

As You Look

A finely crafted 'whodunnit' private eye style mystery, *As You Look* showcases author Veronica Gutierrez's remarkable talent for creating memorable characters, embedding them into an inherently compelling plot, and creating a gem of a read for dedicated fans of mystery and suspense.

-*Midwest Book Review*

As You Look is a thrilling P.I. procedural, an uplifting window into an aspirational QPOC relationship, and a wonderful debut from a promising talent.

-*reviewingtheevidence.com*

The book is a true whodunit, not a romance. Yolanda and Sydney are happily married from the beginning of the tale, and although we do get to see some of their life together, the focus of the book is on the mystery. I'm happy to see that this is the beginning of what may end up a series of "Yolanda Avila Mysteries." I will be looking forward to seeing more from this author and these characters.

-Betty H., *NetGalley*

It's great that more mystery and thrillers with a diverse cast are being published, and I keep finding wonderful new authors and characters to follow. Yolanda Ávila, a LA PI, as written by Verónica Gutiérrez is one. Yolanda is still laboring with the guilt she feels over her mother's recent death and is reluctant to see the bad dreams she has as anything but dreams when her godson is kidnapped. A former LAPD officer, forced to quit the force, she can ask questions and go places that the cops can't go, and they're not very happy that she seems to get the answers before them!

Great characterization and insight into the world of labor and unions in LA, I look forward to more stories starring Yolanda.

-Roxanne S., *NetGalley*

BURIED SEEDS

Other Bella Books by Verónica Gutiérrez

As You Look

About the Author

Veronica Gutiérrez is a former community organizer, civil rights attorney, and corporate executive. She was born and raised in Boyle Heights, the East Los Angeles neighborhood that her protagonist calls home. Her first novel, *As You Look*, was published in 2022. Veronica lives in California with her wife, Laura. They provide mixology-lesson-themed fundraisers for small nonprofits and host frequent get-togethers for a close community of family and friends of all hues.

BURIED SEEDS

VERÓNICA GUTIÉRREZ

Acknowledgments

There are so many people I can't thank enough.

My parents, Ricardo J. Gutiérrez and Juana B. Gutiérrez came to Boyle Heights when my dad joined the U.S. Marines in 1954. They were among the founders of Mothers of East L.A.-Santa Isabel, one of California's first environmental justice organizations. They adopted their community in a way that instilled in their children a deep love for it, and a strong commitment to social justice.

My siblings, the Lokas, and the Roomies, have all provided great inspiration and, sometimes, great material, including the great cover photo by my brother Abel Gutiérrez and niece Izel Gutiérrez. A special thank-you to Dr. Joella Castillo for the original encouragement. Thank you all for always being there.

My beta readers make me a better writer. All errors in this novel are my own, but you all helped me keep them to a minimum. Thank you to Laura Genao, Wes Fukuchi, and Frank Abe for your great feedback.

The hardest part about doing research for this novel was putting down the great books I came across. I am grateful to the authors listed in the bibliography, and especially to Frank Abe who provided information on multiple resources, and Naomi Hirahara, whose historical fiction and nonfiction hooked me from the very beginning. The Japanese American National Museum provided invaluable information through its exhibits and events.

I am forever grateful to Jessica Hill and Linda Hill of Bella Books for taking a chance on me with my debut novel *As You Look*, and for encouraging me to finish *Buried Seeds*. Thank you also to my ever kind editor, Heather Flournoy. A special shout out to the Bella Books authors, the Golden Crown Literary Society, and the Crime Writers of Color whose encouragement never wanes.

And finally, Laura, thank you for this wonderful adventure. I love you!

Dedication

To Mom and Dad. Your inspiration and love for our
community were boundless.

"Quisieron enterrarnos,
pero no sabían que éramos semillas."
Dicho de activistas

"They tried to bury us, but they didn't
know we were seeds."
Activist saying

CHAPTER ONE

Thursday, September 1, 2022

"So much blood. I didn't think there'd be so much blood." Kinji Abe shook his head, unable to turn his eyes away from the sidewalk slathered in thick, gelatinous goo. Under the dim streetlight the black plasma seemed to suck the last bit of light from the sky. Kinji blinked, but even behind his eyelids, all he saw was blood.

"What's that, old man?" Gamaliel looked up from his squatting position next to the body.

Kinji stirred slowly at the sound of Gamaliel's voice and turned to look at him but could not bring himself to answer. The shock had rendered him speechless.

"Come on, let's get you back to the house. There's nothing we can do for him now." Gamaliel stood and reached out to turn the octogenarian away from the scene.

"Frank's dead," Kinji said. "I can't believe Frank's dead."

"I know. Neither can I, but the cops are on their way. Maybe they'll be able to figure out what happened." Gamaliel steered Kinji through the small crowd that had started to gather. He guided him around the corner store to his house next door. Kinji let Gamaliel help him inside. For the first time in forever, Kinji felt his full eighty-three years. No. Older. So old. Everything ached and exhaustion swept over him. So tired. He breathed in deeply, precipitating a yawn. But how could he sleep? Surely the death of Frank Vásquez would not let him sleep. Maybe he'd just rest his eyes for a few minutes. He ambled to his worn recliner and fell into it, waving a hand in dismissal.

"I'm okay, son. Go be with your cousin. He shouldn't be alone out there." Kinji reached for the throw blanket on the back of his chair. "Here. Take this and cover him." He leaned back and closed his eyes. Gamaliel took the blanket and headed back out. Kinji knew he'd come back to check on him later. He was a good boy. Frank, not so much. But no one deserves to die that way, bleeding out on the sidewalk. Kinji shook his head and leaned back in the chair, his hands going to the growing tightness in his chest. A tear escaped his right eye. How could it have come to this? Kinji squeezed his eyes shut, slowly relaxing his eyelids, exhaustion and sleep overtaking him.

* * *

Gamaliel approached the body tentatively, still in a daze. He shook the blanket open to extend it over his cousin when a police officer he hadn't seen shouted for him to stop and get away from the body. He was the first officer on the scene and was tying yellow tape to Mrs. Barba's chain-link fence, trying to establish a perimeter, telling people to back away. Gamaliel froze next to the body. He held the blanket up to his chest, unsure what to do.

"I said, get away! *Move!*"

Gamaliel took hesitant side steps away from the body.

"He's my cousin," he said.

"Okay. Stand over there and don't go anywhere," the officer said, pointing to the fence where he'd tied the yellow tape. He wrapped it around a signpost at the curb. Gamaliel walked around the body and the signpost and then sank to the sidewalk, still holding Kinji's blanket to his chest, his back against the fence. Mrs. Barba wouldn't be happy about this scene if she were in town. She kept her sidewalk and curb as clean as old Mrs. Ito used to when Gamaliel was little. He and Frank knew not to litter in front of either house. No, Mrs. Barba would not be happy at all.

Gamaliel stared at his cousin. He looked like he did when he slept on his stomach. He'd done that since he was a kid, one leg straight and the other bent at the hip and knee, one arm bent under his head and the other nearly tucked under his chest. Kinji was right—there was so much blood. Gamaliel had tried feeling for a pulse but found none. Another LAPD SUV arrived, its headlights lighting up the body in an eerie glow. The blood went from matte to shimmering. Gamaliel blinked at it and looked at his cousin more closely. Frank's hands were bloody, one with an index finger at attention. He'd probably tried stemming the blood with his hands.

Everything after that was a blur of shouted questions. Was that blood on his hands? On his pants? On his shoes too? How'd it get there? What had he done? He remembered he'd tried feeling for a pulse. But now, his own pulse raced enough to trigger a warning from his smartwatch, the only luxury he allowed himself other than his phone and camera. He stared at the red letters indicating something about a heart rate above a hundred beats per minute after more than ten minutes of inactivity. He'd been told not to move, and he'd obeyed, but now an officer with a pockmarked face rested a hand on his gun holster and ordered him to stand, drop the blanket, and face the fence, hands behind his head. Another officer patted him down, handcuffed him, and had him sit again. He couldn't bring himself to answer any questions.

"Fine," the acne officer said. "You'll talk to Homicide."

Gamaliel startled at that. He was having trouble thinking straight, and now he felt the blood drain from his face. His mouth went dry. It was a good thing he was up against the fence because he might have face-planted otherwise. How had he gotten himself into this mess? How had Frank gotten him into this mess? His mom had conditioned Gamaliel to avoid the police at all costs. She'd given him "the talk" about his immigration status one day when he was little and had tried to take candy from the Abe Grocery.

"They'll turn you over to La Migra and they'll send you back to Mexico because we don't have papers," she'd warned. Most kids his age were afraid of El Cucuy, the boogeyman who hid under children's beds. Growing up, Gamaliel was much more afraid of La Migra. And now, here he was in handcuffs, detained by the LAPD, who could turn him over to the green-uniformed agents.

By the time detectives arrived, a larger crowd had formed and had followed instructions to move farther back. His wrists and shoulders ached, but Gamaliel was more concerned about his mom seeing him like this. Good thing tonight was one of her church nights. He worried he needed to check on Kinji. The old man seemed to have a hard time with Frank's death, and it wouldn't help if they took Gamaliel into custody. But he hadn't done anything. He'd been on his way back from photographing a protest at Mariachi Plaza. He'd whizzed by the spot on his bike and had seen what he thought was a homeless man on the sidewalk. After storing his bike, he'd run his camera and backpack up to the apartment he shared with his mom above the store. He'd seen Kinji sitting on his porch and had told him he was going to see about the homeless man because they didn't want him panhandling near the store—maybe give him some food and water and send him on his way. When he'd discovered it was Frank, he'd felt for a pulse and, feeling none, had run back to alert Kinji while tapping out 911 on his cell phone. They'd both returned to the body together, Gamaliel on hold.

But now, two detectives directed a forensic technician to take swabs from Gamaliel's hands, pants, and shoes, and take photos as well. He had recovered enough from the shock to know he was in trouble. He tried to explain that he'd found the body, that he'd bent down to feel for a pulse, that he'd been away at a protest. No, maybe he should stop mentioning the protest.

"Get a lawyer, ese!" someone shouted from a porch across the street. The veterano cholos, former gang members, had a front-row seat to the spectacle. Other onlookers had moved farther down the street when detectives arrived. When he drew laughter from his friends, the guy repeated his suggestion. He made a good point.

"I want to speak with an attorney," Gamaliel said.

"You aren't even under arrest yet," the Latino detective said.

"I want a lawyer," Gamaliel tried again.

"Fine," an Asian detective said. He helped him up and walked him to a black, unmarked sedan that cried out "undercover police car."

"You can answer questions at the station, then," the Latino cop said. The other detective read him his Miranda rights. He was under arrest, after all.

"Mijo!" Gamaliel's mom shouted for her son from the other side of the yellow tape.

"Llámale a Jesse!" her son shouted back before feeling a hand on his head as he got into the cops' car. His mom would know to call his friend Jesse Ávila for help.

CHAPTER TWO

Friday

She had the unfortunate name of Gumercinda Campamoche. No one could go through life with a name like that, Yolanda thought. Yet, here she was, sitting across from Yolanda, rolling the tissue in her hands into a soggy lint ball. The private investigator had established that the woman's son and Yolanda's own brother, Jesse, were friends, but an accident of geopolitics had determined their very different fate—one the undocumented "dreamer" and the other a US-born citizen.

"Señora, I can't help you if you don't tell me more," Yolanda said in Spanish, hoping to make the middle-aged woman feel more at ease. She hadn't been able to get much more than sobs from her since she'd shuffled in. All Yolanda knew was what Jesse had told her. The mother and son lived above a Boyle Heights corner store where they worked, and the LAPD had arrested the son.

Mrs. Campamoche stared into midspace through tear-rimmed eyes. A self-conscious frown fought with tight lips in a struggle to maintain some dignity. The expression reminded Yolanda of her own mother's never-let-them-know-what-you're-thinking determination. Mrs. Campamoche was not as good at it as Yolanda's mom had been.

Then, thinking her new client might feel intimidated by the formal office setting, Yolanda stood and motioned her to the brown leather couch opposite her desk. The woman followed and took more tissue—two this time—from the box Yolanda offered.

Mrs. Campamoche sat. Her shoulders dropped an iota but remained filled with tension. Sinking into the worn cushions always helped Yolanda relax—never mind that the couch lacked any aesthetic appeal. She'd inherited it from the previous tenant and agreed with her wife, Sydney, that she should replace it, make the space more homey, less *Mad Men*. The only addition so far had been a gift from Sydney, a Synthia Saint James print on the wall above the couch. The *Sisters of Courage* needed company, maybe a new, cream-colored sofa with pillows in the primary colors of the print to offset the wood paneling—and maybe a floor rug, and plants too. No, she'd probably kill the plants. The office in the historic Bradbury Building had been a lucky find, but the grand atrium, with its ornate balconies, intricate tile work, and white oak paneling, might intimidate a grocery worker from Boyle Heights.

"Gracias, Señorita Ávila," she said, sitting next to Yolanda, who might have looked young to the woman. The few gray hairs on Yolanda's head were hidden well in her dark, spiky hair. She liked to think of them as highlights. But Yolanda was no señorita. She let it go. This wasn't the time to discuss her marital status.

"Yolanda," she said.

Mrs. Campamoche nodded, took a deep breath, and continued in the singsong Spanish of northern Mexico, Yolanda's own parents' birthplace.

"Gracias, Yolanda. I don't know anything. When I got home last night, the police were putting Gamaliel in a car. The other police wouldn't tell me anything. The last thing Gamaliel told me was to call Jesse. So, I did. And Jesse told me to come here. I still don't know where my son is."

Yolanda wondered where her brother was, too.

"Señora Campamoche…" Yolanda said.

"Gumer."

"Sí, Gumer. Jesse should be here soon. We'll help you find Gamaliel." Yolanda had never heard the name before Jesse had asked for her help. She'd been about to look it up when she'd mentioned it to her officemate that morning.

"Wow, that's a blast from the past," Jane Stern had said. She'd turned from the doorway of her bright, ultra-modern, tech-filled office. Her yin to Yolanda's yang. Both were private investigators, each with their own agency, but Jane focused on cybersecurity and cyber sleuthing, work Yolanda barely understood. "Gamaliel was a big deal in the Talmud. Sanhedrin and all. I didn't know your people used the name."

"Neither did I. I must have missed the day they covered that part of the Bible at school."

"Catholic school teaches the Old Testament?"

"Some, but mostly the New Testament, I think. Didn't pay much attention in any case."

The phone on Yolanda's desk rang, bringing her back to the present. It was the guard downstairs, announcing Jesse's arrival. The security was a nod to the tenants upstairs, LAPD's Internal Affairs Division. Yolanda avoided them as much as possible, her fruitless dealings with them still fresh after nine years. She'd now been a former cop longer than she'd been a cop. Time flies when you try scraping by as a PI. She was lucky her lawsuit against the LAPD had given her start-up cash and funds for the townhouse she shared with Sydney. The money had come in handy, especially while Sydney was still an intern. She was an attending doctor now, earning more, but Yolanda wanted to carry her own weight when it came to household expenses. The rush of cases following media coverage about her godson's kidnapping and rescue three years ago had waned after a year. The pandemic hadn't helped. This case wouldn't help much either, if she was taking it on as a favor to her brother.

Yolanda informed her new client that Jesse was on his way up and took her seat next to Gumer again. The vintage wrought iron cage elevators were faster than they looked.

"Sorry I'm late," Jesse said before greeting Mrs. Campamoche with a solemn handshake and an earnest Spanish, "I found him. They're holding him at County."

LA County Jail was a horrible place, but in Gamaliel's case it was better than being held by ICE, the Immigration and Customs Enforcement agency, formerly known as the Immigration and Naturalization Service, or INS. The name change from Service to Enforcement was all you needed to know about the agency's focus—and the country's politics, for that matter. Gumer's son, Gamaliel, was one of thousands of "dreamers" who'd crossed the border as children and lived in a legal and cultural limbo, unable to work legally in the only country they knew and unable to live in the country of their birth. Some had qualified for the temporary protection of DACA, Deferred Action for Childhood Arrivals, administered by the Department of Homeland Security. With multiple judicial appeals, the program seemed to hang by an ever-fraying thread every year since its inception. But Jesse had said that Gamaliel was still undocumented. Yolanda wasn't sure what made him ineligible for DACA.

Gumer and her son had to be careful not to come across ICE and risk deportation. But in Los Angeles, you could make a living by getting paid under the table or using an Individual Tax Identification Number. Given their time in this country, Yolanda assumed they used an ITIN. Like many others in their situation, they'd pay taxes and would contribute to Social Security and Medicare without being able to take advantage of either in their old age. Most undocumented immigrants wouldn't even need to be fluent in English to navigate the paperwork. His mother's preference for Spanish told Yolanda that Gamaliel was bilingual, or at least understood Spanish. Gumer wouldn't require more English fluency than she'd acquired over the years. Yolanda imagined their home was much like her own growing up. Spanish only—at least until school came along. Then, even the immigrant parents picked up some English.

Jesse stroked his trademark goatee, much neater than the black, untamed curls that Yolanda envied. He pulled up a guest chair and sat across the chipped and stained coffee table. Yolanda thought she'd have to get rid of that too, then wondered why she felt distracted and tried to focus.

Jesse continued in Spanish.

"I found his booking number online, but they wouldn't let me see him. Because of Covid, they have all kinds of new protocols. We have to schedule a visit online and take proof of vaccination and a negative Covid test. Maybe we can get those things today and visit tomorrow. But they only allow one person per visit."

Gumer frowned, as if not sure what to make of the news.

"Let me make some calls," Yolanda said. "We'll see if we can bail him out before ICE gets hold of him." That much, Gumer understood. A little hope returned to her eyes. They followed Yolanda to her desk. Jesse's eyes examined the parquet floor with more gloom than hope.

Yolanda dialed her best friend but kept her eyes on her brother. Carmen Ochoa was a labor lawyer who would know good defense and immigration attorneys, and maybe a decent bail bondsman. She took the call right away. Yolanda asked about her godson, Joey, before filling her in on Gamaliel. Joey had almost fully recovered from his kidnapping ordeal and had grown less clingy. It hadn't hurt that he'd been instrumental in his own rescue. And staying home for school during the pandemic had helped rather than hurt him, as it had so many other kids. Yolanda wondered how he'd do now that everyone was emerging from isolation.

Carmen provided a couple of referrals and offered to make introductory calls. She also said the cops wouldn't turn him over to ICE right away but might eventually, depending on the charges.

"What are the charges?" Yolanda asked Jesse.

"Murder," he mumbled, barely audible.

Shit.

"Que?" Gumer asked.

Yolanda swallowed. How do you tell a mother her son possibly took a life? When Yolanda was a cop, springing something like this on a mother and watching closely for her reaction was all part of the investigation. But this was her client, so she tried taking a compassionate tone, watching her just the same, the phone still to her ear.

"Señora," she said in Spanish to make sure the message got through. "These are very serious charges. We don't know why yet, but they arrested Gamaliel for murder."

"Asesino? Como que asesino? Mi hijo no es un asesino!"

No mother thinks her son capable of murder. But now Yolanda knew he wouldn't face deportation. Yet. Carmen, still on the phone, acknowledged as much.

Yolanda never thought she'd think of a murder charge as a silver lining, but here they were. Carmen suggested the second attorney but cautioned that he would be expensive and perhaps a public defender might do if Yolanda helped with the investigation. Yolanda thanked her and relayed the information to Gamaliel's mother. Relief and concern struggled for control on her face.

Yolanda's stomach faced a similar struggle. What was she getting herself into? A murder suspect was one thing, but an arrest meant there was plenty of probable cause. She wasn't sure she could do much to help this unfortunate family.

"Learn anything else?" Yolanda asked her brother.

"I swung by the store. Mr. Abe, the owner, said they found Gamaliel's cousin, Frank, dead on the sidewalk. Looked like he'd bled out."

Yolanda returned to the couch next to Gumer. Seemed like an important detail Gumer hadn't mentioned, but then again, she hadn't mentioned much in her state.

"Tell us about Frank," Yolanda said, placing a hand on Gumer's knee, hoping it would help the traumatized woman relax.

"Dead," she answered, staring vacantly at the floor. "He is dead."

"That much we know. But how? And why do the police think Gamaliel did it?" Sometimes, asking questions in English helped get concise answers, without embellishment, from predominantly non-English speakers.

Gumer rubbed her eyes with the heels of her palms and shook her head as if trying to wake from a nightmare. Yolanda waited. When Jesse leaned forward to help prompt an answer, Yolanda held up a finger to stop him, letting Gumer gather her thoughts.

"Kinji say someone stab Frank."

"Who is Kinji?"

"Mr. Abe. He owns the store. Lives in the next door house."

"Do you know who could have done it?"

Gumer shook her head and blew her nose before breaking down into sobs again.

"Did Frank live with you too?"

"No, he move away with my sister, but sometimes he visit."

"Visits you? Or Gamaliel? Or Mr. Abe?"

Gumer paused before saying, "More Mr. Abe now. He want to buy property."

"Frank wanted to buy Mr. Abe's property? The store and the house?"

"Sí."

"Was he there to discuss buying the property last night?"

"Maybe?"

"Were you home when this happened?"

"Church?" It was more of a question again, but Yolanda let it go. The woman had experienced enough trauma.

"I'd like to speak with Mr. Abe, then. Come on, I'll give you a ride home."

CHAPTER THREE

Gumer continued to cry softly during the fifteen-minute drive to the center of Boyle Heights—Yolanda couldn't tell if for Frank, or her son, or both. Probably more for her son. She was able to get more out of her about her undocumented status and Gamaliel's DACA status. By the time they drove past the historic Evergreen Cemetery, Yolanda had learned that Gamaliel was too old for the program even though Gumer's sister had brought him across the border as her own when he was only a few months old. In doing so, she'd rescued mother and son from an abusive relationship. Yolanda wondered why the woman had not applied for legal status, but figured that, like many others, Gumer probably either didn't know her rights or found it too difficult to prove the abuse. And, like many others, she and her son had slipped into the community unnoticed and unbothered, living a mostly normal life.

The two women and their sons had lived together upstairs from the store where they worked. Gumer worried that her son's arrest would subject him to deportation. Yolanda tried to reassure her that she'd help as much as she could, but she didn't sound convincing, even to herself.

Jesse drove his own car, a "new," beat-up VW van that rattled to an uncertain start every time he turned on the ignition. It had replaced his old jalopy, which their mechanic father had convinced him to sell for parts to the shop where he worked. Yolanda couldn't figure out what Jesse saw in the red heap. She glanced at it in the rearview mirror and considered that at least his name for it fit. Chapulin Colorado, the hapless superhero, was a Mexican icon that everyone in the neighborhood watched on TV and quoted often growing up. It matched her brother's idealism and made her wonder if all philosophy doctoral students were as idealistic as Jesse. Actually, he wasn't a student anymore, Yolanda reminded herself. He was an adjunct professor teaching introductory philosophy at Cal State Los Angeles and East Los Angeles Community College, or ELAC, for short. The "adjunct hustle," he called it. Yolanda wondered if he still messed with people by pronouncing his given name, Jesús, in English like he had as a student at UCLA. His had been the only name the nuns hadn't anglicized in elementary school, and this was his way of making up for it. She still thought of him as a student. He lived at home with their dad after all. And his ascetic lifestyle was something that Sydney understood more than Yolanda did.

Yolanda's black Jeep and the red van slowed on Evergreen Avenue before both turned onto Malabar Street. The neighborhood didn't differ much from the one less than two miles away where Yolanda and Jesse had grown up. The streets were wider, with more apartment buildings, but like Yolanda's old neighborhood, the houses were mostly war-era bungalows, some of them hanging on to their original wood siding but many having succumbed to the stucco era of the seventies. Some houses wore the bright yellow, fuchsia, or blue paint more common in Mexico, while others stuck to beige or light gray. Most had chain-link fences. The horizontal wood slats known as "gentrification" fences had not yet replaced them. Some houses had wrought iron bars on the windows. The homes that didn't have well-tended lawns had vegetable gardens or had cemented over them to make room for parking space to accommodate multigenerational households. Dusty loquat trees, ubiquitous in Boyle Heights, dotted the street. Most yards had rose bushes, and a few had makeshift grottos with statuettes of the Virgin of Guadalupe.

The corner store was typical of other tienditas in Boyle Heights. Hand-painted block letters above the entrance read *Abe's Grocery*. The walls sported signs advertising milk and beer on sale alongside a mural of the Virgin of Guadalupe. The absence of graffiti meant that the Virgin kept the taggers away, Yolanda thought. Unlike most other tienditas, a service window faced the side street. A menu board listed sandwiches, biónicos—the popular fruit and cream bowls—licuado smoothies, and snow cones. Also, unlike most of the others, the property behind it had yellow crime scene tape flapping in the breeze from a chain-link fence. Dried blood marred the otherwise clean sidewalk. It had run down to the curb, where a congealed puddle remained in the gutter. Someone had placed orange cones on either side of the stain. Yolanda wondered if they were the kind the store used when mopping up spills. Someone had started a memorial against the fence with a votive candle, a wooden crucifix, and some flowers. Yolanda knew from experience that the memorial would continue to grow.

Gumer glanced at the blood when she emerged from Yolanda's Jeep but looked away with a shake of her head as if trying to blot out the sight.

To Yolanda's surprise, the store was open for business. Gumer led the way in and immediately reached for an apron behind the counter. On a stool behind the cash register sat an elderly Japanese American man with excellent posture. He wore a blue surgical mask over what looked like a nicely trimmed, white beard matching a thinning but still full head of short-cropped hair, both offset by dark eyebrows. He was impeccably dressed in a white collared shirt and a Dodger-blue cardigan sweater-vest. Gumer waved the man around the counter to make the introductions. Yolanda noticed the man's neatly pressed khaki pants with the slightest of wrinkles from sitting.

His white sneakers were spotless. His lanky, six-foot-three frame surprised her. He cut a handsome figure, even with dark bags under his eyes and an array of skin tags on his lower lids—the kind that Sydney once explained telegraphed high cholesterol when Yolanda developed one of her own. An unwelcome change in diet had ensued but had ebbed away, much to her relief.

"Hi, Jesse," the man said with a half-smile of recognition.

"Hi, Kinji."

"The investigator, Yolanda Ávila," Gumer said, indicating with an open palm.

Yolanda and Kinji shook hands. They all confirmed their vaccinations before Kinji removed his mask, their new, postpandemic normal around high-risk people like the elderly, especially in places with lots of public interaction.

"Let's go talk over there," he said, pointing to four stools across the way in front of a deli case. "Gamaliel's planning to build a counter here, so we're testing out the space for stools." The space seemed too crowded for that, but they all pulled up the stools and sat, blocking the narrow chip-and-candy aisle between the deli and the cash register.

"Our condolences, Mr. Abe," Yolanda said. "I understand Frank grew up here with Gamaliel."

"Thank you. Please call me Kinji." Kinji looked at the floor in obvious sadness. "Such a terrible waste of a life. His mother is taking it really hard, of course." He didn't seem to take it much easier. For all his neat appearance, he looked like he hadn't slept in days.

"Looks like everyone is taking it hard." Yolanda looked from Kinji to Gumer and back.

"Frank and Gamaliel are like grandsons to me." He shook his head, his eyes downcast. "Well, Frank…was."

"Didn't think you'd be open today." Yolanda changed the subject at the awkward pause.

"Yesterday was the first of the month. Lots of our families need some basics about now. Bread, milk, eggs." He waved his arm toward the dairy section at the back of the store. Yolanda understood. Most families with children on government assistance receive their EBT funds on the first of the month.

She'd bet he also provided credit without interest to some of these families. The tiendita near her own childhood home had done the same. That might explain the lack of graffiti as well. Kinji and the community likely held each other in mutual respect.

"I see," Yolanda said. "Well, we're trying to help Gamaliel. Anything you can tell us about last night would help."

A young woman with a toddler in her arms walked in trailed by a preschooler, all three wearing what looked like hand-sewn, cloth masks. Yolanda wondered where she'd bought the child-sized ones but figured they made a good side hustle for some entrepreneur.

"Buenos días," the woman said, looking curiously at the assembled group.

"Buenos días," they all responded in unison before Gumer put on her mask and went to help her. Sure enough, milk, eggs, bread, and tortillas appeared quickly at the register. The preschooler carried an enormous block of Monterey Jack in both arms and chanted, "Que-sa-di-llas! Que-sa-di-llas!"

"You know your customers well." Jesse smiled and pointed with his chin over to the young family.

"I've owned this place for eighty-some years."

"You mean it's been in your family all that time?" Yolanda asked.

"No. Well, yeah. But I mean me." Kinji walked over to the shelves behind the register with only a hint of his age in his slow gait. He pulled down two framed documents from an upper shelf and walked back to his stool, dusting off the frames before handing them to Yolanda. "Take a look."

One frame held what looked like a photocopy of a title deed dated 1940. It listed Masaru Abe and Kinji Abe as the owners. She looked up at him. "But you would have been, what? No older than those kids, right?" Yolanda pointed her chin at the departing customers while Gumer retook her seat.

"A year old. My brother, Masaru, would have been fourteen at the time. Look at the other document. I keep the originals in the house."

Yolanda passed the framed deed to her brother and looked at a framed affidavit attesting to the American birth of both Masaru and Kinji, signed by Max Edelman and Judith Edelman.

"I don't understand."

Kinji sat down to explain.

"Back then, Japanese nationals couldn't own land in California. Japanese farmers couldn't even lease land to work. Not legally. But my father picked up a brochure at the produce mart that explained how Japanese farmers could use loopholes in the law to own or lease land. The way to do it was to put the land in the name of their American-born, US-citizen children. The Edelmans sold the store to my dad this way. They signed the affidavit that the brochure recommended. Wish I still had a copy of that brochure, but I'm sure you can find one at the Japanese American National Museum in Little Tokyo. The guy who wrote the brochure was a lawyer who couldn't practice law because he was Issei, Japanese-born himself. I can't remember his full name, but we called him Mr. Fujii," he said, pronouncing both i's. "He was a nice man with one of those big handlebar mustaches. Not a lot of us can grow one of those." Kinji stroked his beard, and Yolanda could see that he was proud of it. "Most stick to a goatee like Jesse here." He patted Jesse's leg and smiled. "But we Nikkei owe Mr. Fujii a lot."

"I thought your generation was Nisei," Yolanda said.

"It is. Nikkei is all of us across multiple generations—or a state of mind like your Aztlán, right, Jesse?"

"So you've said." Jesse chuckled. Yolanda looked up from the framed document in her hands.

"So putting you and your brother on the title ensured that the property stayed in the family," Yolanda said, understanding.

"Yes, but my sisters didn't make the title."

"Why not?"

"Sexism?" Kinji ventured. "I don't think women, much less girls, could buy property back then anyway, but my dad wouldn't have added them to the title in any case. I may be an old coot, but my father was even more steadfast in his old ways. Fancied himself a descendant of samurai. At least, he tried to convince us we were. Those were his swords up there." He pointed with his chin—a characteristically Latino gesture, Yolanda thought—to a shoulder-high shelf behind the cash register. Three swords sat horizontally on a wooden stand, displayed in a column from shortest to longest, with the shortest on top. "Anyway, he probably figured the girls would leave to be with their husbands' families eventually. I think I made the title only because he wanted to make sure if anything happened to either of us, the other would still own the property. As it turns out, my brother passed some years ago and I'm the sole owner now." Kinji's shoulder twitched in what looked like slight irritation at the mention of his brother.

"But your dad never had the title updated to put his own name on it?"

"I guess he could have, eventually. Mr. Fujii took a case to the California Supreme Court that finally did away with the Alien Land Act. I don't remember much of that except a lot of handwringing by folks at the weekend Japanese school. And then a lot of celebration once the state decided not to take the case to the US Supreme Court. But I think my dad figured if they could take away your freedom because of your race, they could take away your land, too. Many Japanese, even US citizens, did lose their land. He didn't want to call attention by messing with the title."

"I understand, then, why you framed these documents. That's a great story. I'd like to hear more of it someday. But, for now, can you tell us anything about last night?"

The glow from the trip down memory lane evaporated from Kinji's face and he set his jaw, his eyes downcast.

"I don't know. I was supposed to meet Frank and his friend Hector. They were interested in buying my property. Young fools," he said, looking up at Jesse. "Foolios, the kids say now, right, Jesse?"

Jesse smiled before Kinji continued.

"But I was going to hear them out—out of respect for Frank, see?"

"And did you?" Yolanda asked.

Kinji's gaze stopped at midspace. He shook his head slowly.

"They…They never showed," he said, focusing, but then hesitating again. He took a deep breath and looked away toward the deli case before continuing, "After I closed the store, I saw Frank's car across the street. Figured he was visiting friends and would be over in a bit." He turned back to Yolanda. "Next thing I know, Gamaliel gets home from one of those protests where he takes pictures and says there's a homeless guy on the sidewalk at the side of the store. He was going to deal with it, but he came running back. He was so shocked he could barely get out that it was Frank, and that it looked like he was dead. We both went back to take a look. Gamaliel said he didn't have a pulse and squatted down to confirm that. My god, there was so much blood." Kinji went silent, his eyes staring into midspace again.

"Does Gamaliel use his phone or a camera for his pictures?"

"Both," Jesse answered.

"Did the police take his phone and camera?"

"His phone," Gumer said. "I think camera is upstairs."

"Good, I'll need to see it," Yolanda said before turning back to Kinji, who continued to stare vacantly.

"And then what, Kinji?" Yolanda tried to snap him out of his reverie. It worked.

"Um, Gamaliel walked me back to the house." Kinji hesitated, thinking. "I…I gave him a throw blanket to cover his cousin. Then I felt so tired. I closed my eyes, but I must've fallen asleep, because next thing I know, Gumer is shaking me awake and telling me that the police took Gamaliel. That boy wouldn't hurt a fly!" He went from being in his own head to Papa Bear mode when talking about Gamaliel. He turned to Jesse. "Do you think we can bail him out soon?"

"We don't know yet," Jesse said. "Yolanda's trying to get him an attorney now."

"I'll call the attorney as soon as I'm done looking around," Yolanda said before turning to Kinji. "Did the police get a statement from you?"

"No."

"What? Damn. Means the detectives on this case are lazy. Okay, we need to get them to take a statement from you." She turned to Gumer. "And from you too, Gumer."

Gumer stood, eyes wide, her arms crossed over her chest and her hands formed into fists as if in double protection from her fear of the police.

"I have to talk to police?" She uncrossed her arms and twisted the front of her apron in her hands. "No, por favor," she pleaded.

"It will help get Gamaliel out of jail," Yolanda said.

Gumer swallowed hard, a worried look on her face, but nodded as if deciding just then to do it.

"Good. I'll make some calls and find out who the detectives are. Kinji, you'll need to think about the times involved. What time were you supposed to meet Frank? What time did Gamaliel get home? Can you do that?"

Kinji met Yolanda's look with one similar to Gumer's, but with a bit more resolve to talk to the police.

"We were supposed to meet at eight when I closed the store. It was my turn to close because Gumer leaves early to go to her church on Thursday nights. Let's see." Kinji's eyes turned up to the ceiling in thought. "I think Gamaliel came home around nine."

Yolanda noted the details in a pocket notebook with a small pencil. She'd upload the information to her notes app later. She looked at Gumer.

"You'll need to remember too," Yolanda said. "What time did you leave and what time did you get back?"

Gumer looked from one face to another, her arms crossed again.

"I leave before Kinji lock up. Took bus to church." She paused.

"Which church?" Yolanda asked, trying to get her to continue. The Church of the Assumption up the street would not have required a bus.

"La Iglesia Espiritualista."

"Por la Boyle?" Yolanda asked. Could this be her own godmother's church on Boyle Avenue?

"Sí," Gumer said, her eyes registering wonder at how Yolanda would know it.

"My godmother goes there, too. Mercedes Rodriguez." Yolanda smiled at the mutual connection. Her godmother went to the storefront spiritualist church on Thursday nights. "Do you know her?"

"Sí. Buena señora." Gumer smiled back, seemingly more at ease.

But Yolanda wanted to get back to the timeline.

"When did you get back?"

"Ten, maybe?"

"That's right," Kinji said. "I think you woke me up just after ten."

Gumer nodded, staring at the floor, her hands going back to working the apron.

"It'll be okay," Jesse said, placing a hand on her shoulder. "The police won't care about your papers. They'll just want to know what happened."

Yolanda was glad for her brother's empathy and hoped Gumer could hold it together to help her son.

"No se apure," Kinji reassured the woman, telling her not to worry. His perfect Spanish surprised Yolanda, but then she realized that it shouldn't because he grew up in the neighborhood and probably watched his customers become more and more Latino over the years.

"Now, I have to ask something sensitive," she said, trying to ease into more questions. When she had their attention again, she asked, "Did Frank have any enemies?"

Both frowned, thinking. Yolanda caught Jesse giving a slight nod, but he kept quiet. Kinji spoke first.

"Well, he was always getting into trouble as a kid, but he seemed to have straightened out after college. After he dropped out, anyway. I tried to hire him here, but he threw in my face that even I didn't want a job here when I was his age." Kinji shrugged. "He was right. I went to work for the postal service after the Army, much to my parents' disappointment. I was lucky they liked the work of Frank's grandparents more than mine."

"They worked here too?" Yolanda asked.

"Sure. Saved the store for us when we got shipped out to Heart Mountain in Wyoming. Ran it for us that whole time."

"I'd like to hear that story too someday, but you were telling me about Frank…"

"Oh, sure. Frank was trying to do this real estate thing now, and I was hoping it wasn't just temporary again and he'd stick with it."

"What do you mean?"

"Aw, you know. Kids these days have a hard time committing to a long-term job or career. Not like in my day. I may not have worked here at the store all my life like my father wanted me to, but, heck, I put in a good forty years with the postal service. Kids now, they hop from one thing to another." He raised an index finger. "If they have a choice, that is. Gamaliel doesn't, but he keeps trying to modernize the store. You know, change things up." Yolanda noted a tinge of pride in Kinji's comments about Gamaliel. "Anyway, Frank always hopped from one thing to another, but he seemed to be settling down."

"Turi," Jesse said. "Turi had it in for Frank."

"Who's Turi?"

"He's an anti-gentrification activist," Jesse said. "Lives across the street on Malabar." He pointed with his thumb over his shoulder. "I think that was his wife who came in earlier with the kids."

Kinji confirmed with a nod.

"Anyway," Jesse continued. "Turi didn't like that Frank was trying to be a real estate speculator. Said some nasty things about him at rallies and protests."

After establishing that neither Gumer nor Kinji had seen Turi or Frank's friend Hector in the area last night, Yolanda asked for contact information for them. Jesse had a phone number for Turi, and Kinji had Hector's information. Yolanda understood why they'd be interested in the large double lot for new development. Apartment buildings were going up all over

Boyle Heights, squeezed into lots that used to have single family homes. Elderly owners or their adult children couldn't resist the increase in land value, and developers couldn't resist the allure of high rents or condo sales.

"Okay," Yolanda said. "I'm going to have a look around, and then I'll come up for the camera. Please let me know if you think of anything else." She directed her request to all three.

Jesse followed Yolanda out to the sidewalk.

"What do you think?" he asked.

"Not much to go on unless Gamaliel's pictures have a time stamp that places him at the protest. What do you know about Frank and this Turi guy?"

"From what Gamaliel has told me, Frank was a bit unfocused, ran from one thing to another, like Kinji said. Apparently, he was a wannabe gang member with Turi when they were kids, but neither of them really got into a gang. His mom would have killed Frank, and Turi's dad is a reformed gang member. They both ended up at ELAC before transferring to Cal State LA. But they had some kind of falling out when they both dropped out. Not sure what happened there, but their animosity seemed to grow when Frank went into real estate. We'll have to ask Gamaliel more about it if those pictures don't clear him."

They had arrived at the bloody scene, and Jesse stopped short.

"Shit, that's a lot of blood."

"Dude definitely bled out."

"That needs to be washed down. I'll ask Kinji for a hose. Probably not a good idea to leave it for them to handle."

"Thank you," Yolanda said, appreciating her brother's thoughtfulness. She stepped away to get a better view of the scene and moved in a slow semicircle. "What does that look like to you?" She pointed to a spot a few inches above the pool of red where two short lines of blood seemed to intersect to form a crooked cross. Another line next to the cross mark seemed to fade away.

"Looks like someone made a mark with the blood. What is that? A cross? An X?" Jesse turned his head sideways for another view. "Maybe a T and the beginning of another letter? Or part of an H? Or a K? Or some other letter?"

They looked at each other without commenting more on the letters, but it was not lost on either of them that a T could stand for Turi, and, as unlikely as it might seem, a K could mean Kinji. An H could mean Hector.

"Could be something. Could be nothing," Yolanda said, raising her phone to take pictures of the mark and the larger pool of blood.

"Do you think Frank made that mark?"

"Or someone who came on the scene. Hard to tell."

"Should I leave the blood, then?"

"No, go ahead and wash it off. I got pictures, and I'm sure the techs did, too. But which house is Turi's? I'd like to talk to him."

Jesse pointed to a white bungalow with chipping paint directly across the street. Like most of the others along the street, it had a small front yard with a well-tended lawn behind a chain-link fence. Rose bushes bordered the yard and the walkway up to the porch.

"Let's check it out," Yolanda said, leading the way to the house. She shook the gate after glancing at the sign on it that read *My dog can eat your dog*. They walked in when no dog appeared, but at the porch they were greeted by what sounded like two barking dogs inside the metal screen door. Yolanda was glad the door looked sturdy. She looked closer and saw a pit bull and a Chihuahua. The pit bull stopped barking, but the Chihuahua kept going.

"Killer, shut up," a woman's voice said from inside.

The woman Yolanda had seen at the store earlier picked up the chihuahua and bent to reach for the pit bull's collar.

"Junior, come and take Baby," she said, calling to the preschooler who had also been with her that morning. She turned back to Yolanda and Jesse when Junior pulled on the pit bull's collar.

"Sorry about that. They're harmless."

"The pit bull is Baby and the Chihuahua is Killer?" Yolanda asked. She couldn't help but smile.

"Yup. Junior named the pit bull, and my father-in-law named the Chihuahua."

"I'm Yolanda Ávila, and this is my brother, Jesse Ávila. We're helping the Campamoches and Mr. Abe. Looking into what happened last night. May we come in? We're vaccinated."

"Oh, sure. Me too," the woman said, unlocking the bolt and opening the door. "Come on in. The kids aren't, but they don't go anywhere except my mom's, and she doesn't go anywhere either. I'm Maya Luna. Saw you this morning at the store. So sad. Here, have a seat," she said, moving toys off a couch covered in a striped Mexican blanket. She handed a dog toy to the Chihuahua under the coffee table, which was covered with scraps of cloth and pieces of elastic.

"You make masks?" Yolanda asked. "They're pretty cool patterns, and they fit your kids well."

"Had to when we couldn't find any their size. People seemed to like them." Maya beamed with pride. "But they don't sell so well now that people are getting vaccinated. At least most people still wear them around older folks like Kinji, over at the store." She took a seat in the armchair next to the couch, both facing a television screen mounted above a fake fireplace. "We're lucky not to have too many Covid and vaccine deniers like in other parts of the country."

Yolanda agreed but wanted to get down to business. "Just wanted to know if you or anyone else here saw anything last night."

"We might have if it had happened earlier or later, but I think they got Frank during the boys' bath time. My father-in-law and I were busy with them. Then we saw all the commotion with the cops later."

"How about Turi?" Jesse asked.

"You know my husband?" Maya asked, raising an eyebrow.

"Sure, from the anti-gentrification protests."

She looked closer at Jesse as if trying to place him.

"You know, I used to be more involved before the boys, but I really can't anymore. Turi's still fighting the good fight. But he was at a Harley-Davidson event last night."

"Where was the event?" Yolanda asked.

"Pasadena. The Rose Bowl."

"He rides?"

"No. He's a tattoo artist. Got approved as a vendor for their events. He's pretty popular at them, so he usually stays late."

"What does he think about what happened?" Yolanda asked.

"We were all shocked. Turi said it was probably a good thing he was away because he'd probably be a suspect otherwise."

"Really?"

"Well, ask your brother," she said, pointing her chin at Jesse. "They hated each other's guts, especially with Frank going over to the dark side. I hope Kinji holds out and doesn't sell. Our neighborhood needs the store. It's the only place we can buy food on credit when we need it. And we don't need no big apartment building with crazy rents, or god forbid, a McMansion."

"Do you know anyone else who could have done it?"

"Well, I saw they arrested Gamaliel, but I don't figure him for it. Too straitlaced," she said. "But you never know what triggers people."

"He was at the protest at Mariachi Plaza taking pictures. Hopefully, we can prove that."

"I hope so too. I didn't grow up with those guys like Turi did, but I know he's a good guy, running the store for Kinji. And he made all those changes so we could order from them during the pandemic."

"And Frank?" Yolanda asked.

"Well, he had his issues, besides being a vendido," Maya said, using the term for sellout. "He and Turi used to be tight, but Frank went his own way, I guess." A cry from the back of the house had her on her feet. "Sorry, trying to get the baby to nap. Gotta go."

"Thank you for your time," Yolanda said, handing her a card. "Please call me if you can think of anything that can help Gamaliel."

"Sure thing," Maya said. She locked the screen door behind them before heading back to her baby. Yolanda and Jesse crossed the street back to the store.

"What do you think?" she asked.

"Dunno. If he was away, he has a good alibi."

"The Rose Bowl's not far. Could've been here and back in less than an hour. Of course, Gamaliel could've done the same. I'll need to check on both events. Could he have put someone up to it?"

"Turi? Not his style. Dude's an artist. His dad's the one who's the veterano, but he hasn't been part of the gang life for a long time, unless he's helping kids go straight. I think he's a gang counselor with a nonprofit now, but I don't know which one. No. I could see Turi losing his cool in an argument, but I don't think he'd plan a murder."

Yolanda took that in but did not rule out Turi as a suspect. She and Jesse went back to the store. Gumer took her upstairs to get the camera. On their way to the back stairs, Yolanda heard Jesse asking Kinji about a hose.

Upstairs, she noted a tidy, quaint two-bedroom and the floral scent of Fabuloso, a brand of cleanser popular in many Latino and Black households. Her own mother had used it, as did her dad now. Even Sydney's mom used it. Gumer and Yolanda went into Gamaliel's bedroom. It also appeared orderly except for an unmade bed and what smelled like laundered clothes in a basket atop a dresser. On a small, homemade desk in the corner sat an open laptop and a stack of photography and business books. A digital camera with what looked like a retractable lens lay on top of two other books, one on carpentry and the other on basic electricity. Next to them, a small notepad listed numbers under a date from the previous week and the heading "BH Bridge Runners" in block letters. A second column contained brief comments like "Mariachi Plaza," "Skyline from C. Chavez & Pleasant," "6th St. Bridge," and other Boyle Heights streets. Other pages in the notebook listed more dates, numbers, subjects, and locations, including "Hollenbeck Park" and a list of birds, as well as "Boyle Heights Scenes" and those of other

Los Angeles neighborhoods. Several listed protest photos but none from the night before. Yolanda checked a backpack that hung from the back of the desk chair. She looked for other dated notebooks or camera memory cards but found none. She breathed a sigh of relief when she checked the camera and saw the most recent pictures. She'd have to download them to be sure, but it did look like Gamaliel had been at a protest the night before.

When they got back downstairs, Yolanda told Gumer and Kinji that she'd get back to them but that the pictures should help. She put the camera in her car and walked over to update Jesse. He was pulling a hose from the house behind the store.

"Kinji's water hose doesn't reach, but he said Mrs. Barba wouldn't mind us using hers," he said.

Yolanda helped her brother pull the hose out to the sidewalk.

"Thanks," he said. "But I think this is going to need some bleach to really get it out."

"Try hydrogen peroxide," Yolanda suggested, then explained its merits.

"Well, what have we here?"

Yolanda cringed at the sound of a familiar voice.

CHAPTER FOUR

"Officer Rios," Yolanda said, turning to face the detective and his partner. She knew Rios hated not having his promotion acknowledged. "What hole did you crawl out of to grace us with your presence? Good morning, Detective Chan." She didn't have anything against Chan, but she'd hoped the team hadn't caught the case. Henry Rios ignored the insult. Elton Chan gave a curt nod and stood silently to the side.

"You sanitizing a crime scene, Ávila?" Rios asked.

"Scene's been released, as far as I can tell." She indicated with her hand to the remnants of yellow tape flapping in the breeze. God, she hated the guy. Never liked his know-it-all arrogance as a colleague. Hated him more since she suspected he'd been part of the retaliation against her for reporting overzealous round-ups years ago. Of course he'd made detective. Too bad he wasn't a very good one.

"Well, you can save yourself the trouble of getting involved. It's a pretty open-and-shut case."

"You ever count how often you say that and end up being wrong, Rios?"

Rios tightened his lips and brought his thumbs to his belt buckle, rocking on his heels. Her jab had hit the intended nerve.

"Perp with the victim's blood on him?" He scoffed. "Stay away from this, Ávila."

"Sorry," she said with upturned palms. "Now that I know you're involved, I know I'll have to clean things up again."

He turned away from her in a rather unsuccessful attempt at a crisp about-face and headed to the store entrance, his off-the-rack sports jacket fanning out and twirling with him.

"Is that the guy who arrested Carmen?" Jesse asked.

"The very one." Yolanda sighed, recalling the detective jumping the gun and accusing Carmen of killing the man behind her son's kidnapping. She'd cleared Carmen, but now she worried that he'd jumped the gun here too. "I should go in case Gumer mentions Gamaliel's camera. I'd rather give the pictures to the assistant DA than that asshole."

With that, Yolanda headed back to her office. When she arrived, she asked Jane for help printing out a couple of copies of the pictures with their time stamp. The computer whiz did it in a tenth of the time it would have taken Yolanda. While she waited, Yolanda caught herself daydreaming. Or rather, Jane did.

"Something on your mind?" she asked. "I mean, besides trying to solve a murder?"

Yolanda snapped out of it and turned her attention back to Jane.

"Nah, don't know where my mind went." Yolanda blinked. "Gotta get myself to focus on this case. Don't know why my mind's slipping lately."

"You do seem preoccupied. Not like you. Left the door unlocked last week, remember? Good thing there's good security in the building. Maybe take it easy?" Jane handed her the prints she'd made of the photos.

"Yeah. Sorry about that. Maybe I'll take a break after this case. Oh, shit, forgot I was gonna call to find out which ADA has the case." Yolanda walked back to her office telling herself to focus. If she could convince the assistant district attorney to release Gamaliel, she wouldn't have to enlist the help of an expensive attorney. She called a friend from her days as a cop, who'd helped her more than a few times.

"Now what?"

"Nice to hear your voice too, Celine."

"Running to a hearing. What's up?"

Yolanda liked Celine Cueva's no-nonsense attitude. She could be fun, but when she was all business, she was all business.

"Just need to know who's assigned to a murder case from last night. I have something for them."

"You're not compromising evidence, are you?"

"What? Me? No, this evidence should help get this guy off and, hopefully, released today."

She heard Celine moan on the phone before she responded. "Name?"

"Gamaliel Campamoche. Some name, huh?"

"What? Damn, chica, that's my case!"

Yolanda pumped a fist on her end of the line, but she couldn't disguise the excitement in her voice.

"Great! I have some pictures for you. He took them last night. They place him away from the scene at the time of the murder. Can I drop them off?"

"Sheegh. Okay, meet me at the courthouse."

"Awesome. I'll get you your next drink at Mel's."

Yolanda couldn't believe her luck. The least she could do was buy her friend a drink at their favorite dive bar. She got the court department number from Celine and walked the four blocks to the courthouse at a fast clip. It beat trying to find parking. She didn't waste any time approaching the slim woman sitting on a bench like others in the hallway. Her straight black hair shined down past her shoulders, a nice complement to the fitted, light-charcoal jacket and pencil skirt.

"How'd you get this?" Celine asked when Yolanda sat and placed the camera and an envelope between them.

"Nice to see you too. Got them from Gamaliel's bedroom. He's innocent. Fucking Rios got the wrong guy. Again."

"Easy, esa. I gotta work with the guy."

"You may want to check his phone for pictures too. He had it on him. Save you the trouble of an affidavit for these." Yolanda hoped she was being helpful, but Celine merely grunted in response while opening the envelope with the pictures, so she tried again.

"The guy's squeaky clean. Has to be, because he's undocumented. You know the type."

Celine grunted again, focused on the photographs. Both women looked up when a bailiff opened the courtroom doors for the first hearings of the afternoon. Celine took the camera and envelope and walked to the courtroom along with other attorneys. She turned back to Yolanda at the door. "I'll take a look at these and call you later."

"Thanks, mujer." Yolanda called all her women friends "woman."

A stomach rumble reminded her she hadn't eaten, so she headed back to the garage where she'd parked her car, then home for leftover fettuccine alfredo, one of her favorites, and one of the few dishes she cooked. The fifteen-minute drive from downtown was one of the significant benefits of living in Northeast LA. Being fifteen minutes from her dad's house in Boyle Heights was another plus. When she walked in from their garage, Yolanda saw Sydney sitting in her favorite swivel chair, staring into space. Yolanda liked the modern take on the armchair, but something was off. That was Sydney's reading chair. Staring into space was unlike her unless she was meditating, but she usually did that on the deck or facing the deck.

"Hey, love, what's up?" Yolanda asked. Sydney took a while to come out of her inner thoughts and turn to acknowledge her wife.

"Um, what? Hi."

"You okay?" Yolanda leaned in with a kiss that Sydney barely returned. Something was definitely not okay.

"Yeah, sure. What are you doing home so early?"

"I was going to ask the same of you." When Sydney didn't respond, Yolanda continued, "How about we polish off that fettuccine alfredo from last night?"

"Not hungry."

"Okay," Yolanda said, sitting on the ottoman opposite her wife. "You weren't hungry last night either. Hence the leftovers.

What's wrong, love? Can I help?" She placed a light hand on Sydney's knee.

"Nah. Work stuff I'm trying to noodle through."

"Okay," Yolanda said, leaning in for another quick kiss and tapping her wife's temple gently with a bit of concern. "You let me in there when you're ready, okay?"

Sydney gave her a weak smile, standing to go upstairs. Yolanda knew to give her space. She had planned to return to her office after lunch but decided to stay and check in on Sydney instead. She ate her pasta in silence, staring out at the deck. Not bad, but could have used more mushrooms to soak in additional flavor. She stared at her empty plate, not even realizing she'd finished, when she remembered to call Celine Cueva. The assistant DA answered after three rings.

"I'll see about releasing him today if similar pictures show up on his phone," Celine said, skipping a greeting as usual, "but I can't promise. And he still needs to be questioned as a person of interest or as a potential witness. That's all I can tell you."

Yolanda pumped a fist in the air.

"Hey, that's great! Gracias, mujer. But what can't you tell me?"

"Yolanda…" Celine's tone told her it was better not to ask any more questions. Like many of her close friends and family, Celine usually called her Yolie. Using her full name meant she was serious, and maybe a bit annoyed.

"Okay, okay. Appreciate your help. Hope you find the guy who did it."

"On it."

"See you tomorrow at Mel's? I owe you a drink." The Friday night hangout would be a good place to probe further.

"Rain check." Celine hung up before Yolanda could respond. She could have sworn Celine was trying to brush her off, but her friend was always curt when working, so maybe Yolanda was overthinking it. Still, she was glad the matter had resolved quickly. She started to dial Jesse before calling Gumer, figuring he'd probably give the woman a ride to pick up Gamaliel whenever he was released, but her phone rang first. It was Jesse.

"Hey, I was just about to call you. They may be releasing Gamaliel today."

"Great," he said, not sounding great. "But I think they're going to arrest Kinji."

"What?" Yolanda stood and paced, her phone to her ear. "That nice man wouldn't hurt anyone. Tell me what happened."

"Well, after you left, the detectives went into the store. I didn't hear the first part of their conversation because I was hosing down the sidewalk. It took a while because most of the blood had dried and a lot of it had pooled in the gutter. And the storm drain's another fifty feet away."

"Jesse…" Yolanda said, impatience in her voice.

"Right. Right. So, when I went in to ask Gumer for some hydrogen peroxide, she wasn't there. I guess she had gone upstairs when the cops showed up. She's so afraid of getting deported. The Latino cop, Rios, was asking Kinji about the samurai swords, so I waited a bit before interrupting. It was more like a conversation, not really an interrogation. I asked Kinji for hydrogen peroxide, but he didn't have any. Told me to go ahead and grab some bleach from the bathroom in back. Then I went back out, and it took me a while to finish up. By the time I got done, the cops were still there, but something had changed. Rios was on his phone outside the store, and he was pissed. He called Chan outside and I couldn't hear what they said, but their tone had changed when they went back in. Chan asked Kinji if he could look at the samurai swords. Kinji hesitated a little. He said he never let anyone else handle them because they were very sharp. But he told Chan to come around the counter to check them out. Chan told him to move to the other side of the counter while he put on some gloves and examined each of the swords. Rios asked Kinji to repeat where he'd been last night. He said he was home waiting for Frank and that other guy. Saw Frank's car across the street, so he figured he was in the area, but they never showed. Figured they'd dropped in on friends. Then Rios got on his phone again. I think he requested a forensics team. At that point, Chan kicked me out of the store, but it looked like he was holding the smallest sword. That's all I know. But it looks like they're holding Kinji and may arrest him."

"Shit. Be there in fifteen minutes."

Yolanda ran upstairs to find Sydney sitting on their bed with her head in her hands. She couldn't leave now. Yolanda sat next to her wife and put an arm around her shoulder. She so wanted to ask again what was wrong, but she didn't say a word. She knew Sydney would share what was happening when she was ready. It took a while before Sydney spoke, staring at the floor.

"Ever feel like you really fucked up? Not like made a mistake, but, like, made a bad moral decision?"

Yolanda stopped caring about poor Kinji Abe and focused on Sydney. She leaned her cheek onto Sydney's tight Afro.

"What do you mean?"

"You know, like something that you regret, that eats at you."

"Oh, love, don't beat yourself up. We all have regrets."

"What are yours?" Sydney pulled back out of the embrace with a strange, accusatory look in her eyes. "You've never mentioned any."

"Well, I…I…" Yolanda stammered, thrown back by the unfamiliar hostility.

"See? No regrets."

Yolanda tried to control the confused and hurt look on her face. Tried to understand where Sydney was coming from.

"Where's this coming from, love?"

"Oh, never mind. I'll work it out." Sydney got up and went to the restroom, closing the door.

Yolanda sat, her mouth agape with unasked questions. What the hell was that? Sydney was usually the calmer, more even-keeled of the two. Grounded and centered. That's what best described her. They rarely argued because Sydney, especially, thought it was a waste of time, and Yolanda welcomed their good communication. She thought a while and decided she needed to meet Sydney wherever she was, and considered her question. Did she have any regrets? Two came to mind, but she wasn't sure if they were the kind of thing Sydney was after. Still, having something to share was better than nothing.

"I have two regrets, " Yolanda said when Sydney came out of the bathroom.

Sydney stopped, her hands on her hips, as if ready to listen, but the side tilt of her head told Yolanda she might not be ready to listen too closely. She tried anyway.

"My mom and I never talked about why she was so pissed at my uncle Bobby. About his dabbling in psychic stuff and her denial of her own gifts. It would have helped so much with those crazy dreams I used to have if we'd talked about it."

Sydney straightened and tilted her head to the side again, as if the example had come up short, so Yolanda continued.

"The other regret was when I roughed up that gangbanger when I was a rookie. I've told you about that. Trying to prove myself to the guys." Yolanda shook her head, still disappointed in herself after all these years.

Sydney let her hands fall from her hips in a Gesture that said *So what?* "The thing with your mom posed no moral quandary. And the thing with the gangbanger didn't really have a lasting impact, did it?"

"Well, maybe not for me, other than guilt, but maybe for him."

"Oh." Sydney waved a hand as if swatting away a thought. "Whatever. I gotta head back to the hospital."

"Wait." Yolanda stood and wrapped her arms around Sydney. "You are not leaving like this. Please, tell me what's wrong."

Sydney's eyes turned down to the hardwood floor again. As upset as she was, she seemed ashamed of the conversation, or maybe ashamed of whatever bothered her.

"Please," Yolanda said again.

"I will," Sydney said, stepping out of the embrace.

It was Yolanda's turn to look at the floor, crestfallen. That seemed to catch Sydney. She lifted Yolanda's chin with a finger and looked her in the eye.

"I promise. I will as soon as I figure things out." She pulled away with a barely audible "Sorry" and walked out of the room.

What the hell was that all about? Yolanda had been distracted lately too, but Sydney more so. What was up with them? Were they both stressed and in need of a break?

On her way back to Boyle Heights, Yolanda couldn't help but worry about Sydney. Not even a goodbye kiss. She'd never seen her that preoccupied and noncommunicative, not even during her exhausting hours as a resident. Their friends didn't believe they rarely argued, but even when they did, it was never a tough conversation. This was different. What was going on? Was it about them?

Yolanda thought for a minute. Sydney had seemed preoccupied for the last couple of weeks. Or was it longer? She did that sometimes when she dealt with difficult cases at work, but it usually didn't last more than a day or two. This time, Sydney had been a bit quiet, distant, not her normal self. Yolanda had been busy working long hours on surveillance. She'd wrapped up a workers' comp case only a couple of days ago. Had she missed something? Was Sydney's distraction giving rise to her own distraction recently?

She tried to replay their interactions of the last couple of weeks, but nothing stood out. They'd both been busy and tired, seeing each other mostly before bed and upon waking. Last night was their first dinner together in several days—rare, but not unusual. Yolanda thought they'd make love, but they were both tired. Wait. When was the last time they'd made love? Was it really three weeks ago? Damn. Was it really because they were too tired? They were too young for the dreaded lesbian bed death, she thought. Yolanda wasn't the jealous type. She was secure in her relationship with Sydney, but something nagged at her. She'd have to get to the bottom of it. Maybe tonight over a glass of wine or a cocktail. They could both use a drink.

CHAPTER FIVE

"Bad traffic?" Jesse asked at the curb when Yolanda pulled up alongside Abe's Grocery.

"Something like that," she said, getting out of the car. Gumer was standing next to Jesse, her hands in her apron pockets, a bit calmer than earlier in the day. Yolanda raised her chin in greeting and glanced at the small group of onlookers across the street from the store.

"They won't let us go into the store," Jesse said. "The techs are dusting for prints, or whatever they do. They won't let us go into Kinji's house either. But Gamaliel called. He just got out. I'm taking Gumer to go get him. Getting her away from here will be good."

Yolanda agreed, but before she could respond, all three turned to the movement at the corner and walked toward it. Detective Chan led Kinji out of the store in handcuffs.

"Noooo!" Gumer let out a mourning wail, bending at the knees and doubling over as if in pain. Yolanda and Jesse both bent to support her and help her stand. "No! No!" she kept repeating.

They all stared, speechless, when the detective's car pulled away from the curb. Kinji looked back at them with a sad, resigned look on his face. He gave a slight shrug of one shoulder as if in apology. Well, that was a development Yolanda had not expected.

The three followed the departing police car with their eyes before Yolanda gathered herself. She leaned forward, trying to look into the store, then turned back to Jesse and Gumer.

"The techs will be here and probably in the house for a while. Why don't you go ahead and get Gamaliel? I'll see what I can find out. Which one is Frank's car?"

Gumer pointed to a blue Honda Civic across the street.

When Jesse and Gumer got into Jesse's red van, Yolanda joined the onlookers there. All of them knew about Frank's murder and Gamaliel's arrest, but no one seemed to think Kinji Abe capable of killing anyone. One woman suggested, to nods all around, that maybe only in self-defense. None of them had seen anything last night either.

"Try the Lunas across the street from where they found Frank," a woman in her forties suggested.

"Turi's house?"

"Yup, that's the one."

Yolanda figured she'd received the suggestion because she came off as a friend instead of a cop and congratulated herself for the feat.

"Just be careful," a young man said. "You look like a cop." So much for fitting in.

"I'm a private investigator," Yolanda said. "Helping out Gamaliel and Mr. Abe." She received a few raised eyebrows at her bona fides. She handed out her card in case they knew of anyone who had seen anything. Hopefully, the gesture would help with her inquiries in the neighborhood. She peeked into Frank's car, but nothing seemed amiss among the King Taco and In-N-Out food wrappers and paper cups. Well, the guy had had a decent taste in fast food, Yolanda thought.

She headed to the Luna home again. They may not have seen anything, but maybe Turi or his father were home by now.

This time, a squat, middle-aged man answered the door. He stood all of about five feet and maybe three inches. His buzz cut didn't seem to go with his thick mustache.

"Hi, I'm…" Yolanda started.

"I know who you are," the man said with a smile.

"Of course, you do. May I come in, Mister…?"

"Luna. Emilio Luna," he said, opening the screen door wider and wiping his hand on his white T-shirt before offering it to Yolanda in greeting. "But folks call me T." When Yolanda looked a question at him, he explained, "For Tachuela. You know, thumbtack. I guess I was short before my teenage growth spurt." He laughed at his own joke. Yolanda forced a smile, thinking of the possible letter written in blood.

Inside the small living room, Maya and her two boys sat on the couch watching a children's program on television.

"You've met my daughter-in-law, Maya, and my grandkids, Junior and Eddie," T said. The women greeted each other before Maya shooed the kids into the kitchen with the promise of cookies.

"You know Kinji, then," Yolanda said when she'd settled onto the slightly worn couch and T sat on the recliner. He looked even smaller in the enormous chair, but the brilliant white of his T-shirt somehow made it seem like he was in formal wear.

"Ken Abe? Sure, I know him. He owns the Quién Sabe store."

"Quién sabe? As in 'Who knows?'"

"Sure. Just a play on words. You know, Ken Abe, Quién sabe?"

Yolanda thought the wordplay was a bit of a stretch but didn't say so.

"He also goes by Ken?"

"Started going by his full name, Kinji, when he got older, but some of us still remember him as Ken."

"You've lived here that long, Mr. Luna?"

"You can call me T, or Emilio, if you prefer."

"Okay, T," Yolanda said, thinking he preferred it, although she preferred Emilio after seeing the blood mark on the sidewalk.

"Lived here all my life. Mom left the house to me and my brother when she passed, rest her soul." He paused to make the sign of the cross. "My brother's away, so it's just me and my son and his family now. Turi's a tattoo artist. Smart kid. Not like his old man and his uncle."

Yolanda wondered if being away meant his brother was in prison but didn't ask that either.

"Did you see that they arrested Kinji just now?"

"No shit!" His bushy eyebrows raised in genuine surprise. "Wait. They arrested Gamaliel last night."

"They did, but they just released him. They took Kinji a few minutes ago."

"Well, damn. Wouldn't have pegged him for it."

"Do you think he did it?"

"Been around long enough to know you never know about some people. What is it the neighbors always say after a murder? 'He was such a nice guy.'"

"Why would he, though? Wasn't Frank like a grandson to him?"

"Sure. But Frank was an asshole."

"How so?" Yolanda tried to hide her surprise at his blunt characterization.

"Didn't appreciate what he had. Everything Kinji did for him and his family. Was always getting into trouble. Hung out with my Turi when they both went through their wannabe stage. No way I was gonna let Turi get jumped into a gang. And the local gangbangers wouldn't have Frank. He was too much of an asshole, even for them. Disrespected his mom when Kinji wasn't around too. Would yell at Chata when she called him Panchito or Frankie. I would have bopped him if he'd pulled that shit on me. But shit, that was before I gave up booze and became a counselor. It was a lot harder than some people think. Even my wife thought I couldn't do it. Rest her soul." He made the sign of the cross again.

"My condolences." Yolanda continued after he bowed his head solemnly, "And what about now? I heard Frank made enemies with the anti-gentrification folks when he showed an interest in real estate."

"Dude ain't got no interest in nothing but himself and easy money. He could never become a real estate agent. Wasn't disciplined enough to study for that license. Tried college but dropped out. Not like my Turi. I mean, he dropped out too, but to dedicate himself to his craft and later his family. He's worked hard at both. And he's stuck to both, too. Not like Frank, jumping from scheme to scheme. No, Frank just wanted a cut of the commission if Kinji sold, then he'd stock up on coke before moving on to the next thing."

"He was on cocaine?"

"Off and on for the past year, depending on how much money he had. I think that real estate buddy of his got him into it. Coke's a tough thing to kick, but at least it's not meth. That shit'll fuck you up. 'Scuse my French. I'd feel for the guy if he wasn't such an asshole. I mean, I kicked booze after my mom died. It was hell, but being sober helps me help others now."

"And Frank wasn't worth helping?"

"Listen, I tried with the vato. He just blew me off. But I kept trying, mostly for his mom. Known him since he was a little escuincle," he said, using the term for the Aztec dog breed that many used to refer to children. "Liked him when he would sneak me and my carnales some forties back in the day, but then he kept disrespecting his mom and thinking he was some big shit because he was going to college. Lorded it over his cousin because he's undocumented. But Gamaliel is a lot smarter than Frank, and a better man. He probably could have gone to college after DACA, but I guess he felt obligated to keep running the store for Kinji after Frank and his mom moved away. She remarried or something. Anyway, Frank just liked to run his mouth. Like he was angry at the world for something even though he had a good life, better than a lot of others in the hood. A lot better. But it was like it wasn't enough for him, you know? Like he thought he should be handed more. Didn't want to work for it, though."

"I see. When was the last time you spoke with him?"

"You an ex-cop? You sound like one."

"A lifetime ago." Yolanda shook her head, not wanting to get into it. "So, when did you last see him?"

T squinted at Yolanda as if trying to picture her as a cop, but then let it go.

"I don't know. Maybe a month ago. He was hanging out at the store talking to Kinji about selling. Sniffing and rubbing his nose like he'd just snorted some coke. Kinji was being nice, but I could tell he wasn't happy with him. I put my arm around Frank and tried to be friendly, right? Get him out of the store and talk to him. But he pushed me off and called me a puto. A younger me would have flattened him right there, but I thought 'fuck it.' He ain't worth it. But it got him to leave Kinji alone. Walked out calling me 'Pinche Puto Tachuela' under his breath." T shook his head.

"How'd you let that go?"

"Like I said. I'm too old to get into it with a loser like him."

"Anything else you can tell me about last night?"

"Nah. Maya and me were bathing the kids. Didn't see nothin' until they were questioning Gamaliel on the sidewalk. Dude looked scared shitless. Some of the guys came over when the cops shooed them away. I yelled over to him to get a lawyer. Guess he did if he's getting out."

"Didn't see anything suspicious earlier in the evening? Frank hanging around?"

"No. And nobody saw nothin'. I mean, nada. Sometimes people just don't wanna get involved, but you still hear rumors about what happened. Haven't heard anything on this one. And I'm pretty sure I'd hear about it if there was anything."

"Okay," Yolanda said, believing that he'd hear. She offered him one of her cards in case he had any other information and thanked him for his time. At the door, she turned back.

"By the way, do you know of anyone other than your son who may have been at odds with Frank over the gentrification issue?"

"Everyone! But, hey, leave my kid out of this. He didn't even get home until all the barullo was over last night." The hard look on his face seemed to bring out his old gangbanger days. A dark shadow appeared under hooded eyes and sent a chill up Yolanda's neck. Then, like the flip of a switch, the affable smile was back. "I tell you, he was an asshole. Rest his soul." This time he didn't make the sign of the cross. The hard look didn't come back, but Yolanda sensed coldness behind his eyes.

"Well, thanks. Please let me know if you hear anything that might help Kinji."

"Sure thing." His smile disappeared again.

Yolanda stood on the porch after he locked the screen door. She stared out at the street. How could no one have seen anything? If T did it, did he intimidate people into silence? He seemed jolly enough and like a truly reformed cholo—until the end of the conversation. Like he said, one never knew. Killer, the Chihuahua, yapped at the screen door, jolting Yolanda out of her thoughts. She stepped down and started to head back to the dwindling crowd on the corner but decided to check for security cameras at the houses within view of the store first.

Yolanda walked up and down Evergreen and Malabar and spotted only two homes with cameras. One on Malabar and another on Evergreen had doorbell and driveway cameras. They wouldn't catch anything at the store, but they might have recorded passersby. She tried both. An elderly man on Malabar Street invited her to sit on his porch but said his security cameras sucked and proved it by calling up an app on his phone and showing Yolanda that neither his porch nor driveway cameras had recorded anything for a couple of weeks, not even the mailman. She listened to him complain about how hard it was to get out of the security company contract and how his daughter hadn't done him any favors recommending it. He was thinking of removing the security company yard sign so his neighbors wouldn't be fooled into trying it, but the bad guys didn't know his cameras didn't work, so he kept it out there. Yolanda stood and stepped off the porch, eager to move on to the house on Evergreen. That house would be a replica of the Luna house, except that the siding had been covered in bright-yellow stucco. Like the Luna yard, this one had roses bordering the lawn, but it also had a huge loquat tree to one side. No one answered the door. She'd have to come back.

By the time she returned to the corner across from the store, only three people stood watch, but Yolanda saw curtains move in a couple of front windows when Jesse's van pulled up in front of Kinji's house. She noted the well-preserved craftsman architecture, one of only a few on the street. She also noted a uniformed officer on Kinji's porch and another at the open door of the store. Gumer and Jesse exited the van and Jesse opened the side door to let out a man with a goatee like Jesse's. He looked a few years older than her brother, maybe in his thirties. Crime scene tape across the picket fence gate blocked their way to the back stairs that led to the Campamoche apartment above the store. They stood on the sidewalk as if uncertain what to do. Yolanda approached, and Jesse introduced her and his friend.

"Thanks for your help," Gamaliel said. "Any idea when we can get back into our place?" He gestured to the stairway.

"Let me see," Yolanda said, glancing at the officer on the porch before heading to the store. Gamaliel and the others trailed behind. She stood back from the uniformed officer and peeked into the store. She didn't see any detectives inside but saw a young tech packing up his equipment.

"Your warrant cover the upstairs, or just the house and the store?" Yolanda asked. "These folks would like to get back into their home."

"Damn. Rios didn't say anything about upstairs. Let me see. The others are already in the house." The uniform moved aside when the young tech walked out and closed the door. "Can't release the store until the detectives say so."

"Chingado," Gamaliel said, having glanced at the dark powder over many surfaces inside. "It's gonna take forever to clean up that mess."

"Use a vacuum and dust cloths instead of liquids," the tech said, "but not until the detectives release the scene." Yolanda thought this helpful advice meant he was still green and potentially more helpful than more seasoned techs. She walked next to him on the sidewalk toward the house.

"Any blood in there?" she asked.

"Can't say." Well, maybe not so helpful. He waved at his colleague who'd stepped out of Kinji's house and joined the uniformed officer. The three conferred on the porch, glancing a few times toward the four on the sidewalk. The older tech with salt-and-pepper hair got on his cell phone, then turned to speak with the uniformed officer. Finally, the uniformed officer approached them.

"You can go upstairs, but stay away from the house and the store."

Yolanda noted that there were no evidence marker cones in the small front yard but could not see if there were any beyond the oak tree that stood off-center. She doubted there'd be any. She hadn't seen any signs of blood on this part of the sidewalk. None on the gate either. Gamaliel led the foursome upstairs and into the small apartment. Gumer motioned Yolanda and Jesse to a worn but clean maroon couch that looked like it had a sofa bed inside. She offered coffee or cinnamon tea or water. When they both declined, she took a seat in a modern-looking armchair covered in a crocheted blanket. The spot near the window provided good northern light and a view of Kinji's house and the oak and loquat trees in the small yard. Gamaliel pulled over a chair from a dinette set and sat on the other side of the couch.

"Thanks again," he said, sounding almost embarrassed by the whole ordeal. "I can't believe it." He rubbed his face with the heels of his palms, a gesture similar to his mother's in Yolanda's office that morning. He probably hadn't slept in the noisy, smelly jail last night. Any adrenaline from his ordeal had started to wane. "There's no way Kinji would hurt Frank. You have to help us help him."

"We'll try," Yolanda said, glancing at Jesse. She felt sorry for Kinji. The man seemed to really care for this family. "Let me call the attorney Carmen recommended and see if we can get him bailed out." She got up and walked to the dinette while the others talked. First, she called Carmen to update her on the latest developments and confirm that she still recommended the attorney. His office required a $5,000 retainer upfront. Cash or check. Damn. Yolanda dropped Carmen's name to get them to agree to a credit card over the phone. Then she hoped that Gamaliel had a credit card. He didn't hesitate when she asked.

"Kinji'll be good for it," he said, handing over his Visa. You might not be able to get a green card if you're undocumented, but a bank account and a credit card are no problem. The attorney couldn't promise anything, but he'd at least look into bailing Kinji out as soon as possible, likely not before Monday. A murder charge required an arraignment and bail hearing before release nowadays, and it was too late to get one today. He seemed especially receptive when Yolanda offered her PI services at no cost. Who knew? The connection could lead to paid work down the line. "You gotta give to get," Yolanda's mom used to say. She hoped her mom had been right, but she wasn't looking for any payoff as much as she was looking to help her brother's friends.

"Okay," Yolanda said after she was done with the call. "Let's see where we are now. Correct me if any of this is wrong." She went through what they knew so far, including the possible additional suspects in Turi, his father, and Hector. "Anyone else I should consider a suspect?"

"I don't know. The cabrón pinche guey—"

"Gamaliel!" Gumer was not happy with her son swearing.

"Pero sí era, 'amá," Gamaliel protested before turning back to Yolanda and Jesse. "Frank was always into some get-rich scheme or another. Real estate was just the latest scheme. What's the saying? 'If you can't, teach.' Well, I don't believe that, but if you still can't, go into real estate." He shook his head. "Lent him money once. Just once. Never paid it back. Others may not be as forgiving. Could've pissed off a lot of people."

"Turi's father said something similar," Yolanda said. "He also said he was doing cocaine. Is that true?"

"Definitely seemed like it. Always had this nervous energy, kinda hyper, but it got worse over the last year. I think that Hector dude got him into it. Frank told me once that I should get some from him to loosen up—not in so many words, but..." Gamaliel's voice faded before he continued, "You know, I was always getting him out of trouble when we were younger, but he never outgrew his shit. Damn." He rubbed his eyes with the heels of his palms again. "Fucker never knew how good he had it." He glanced at his mother when he cursed, but she either didn't catch it or decided to ignore it. "God, how I resented him. But he was still family, you know?" His eyes rimmed with tears for the first time.

"Sorry, ese," Jesse said. "In time you'll be able to let go of the negative energy from that resentment, but…"

"No, you don't get it, bro. How could you? You haven't had to live your life wondering if a single misstep will send you across the border for the rest of your life. Shit, and now that I have an arrest record, I'm probably more likely to end up on some ICE list. I don't care what the local politicians say. The Feds aren't on the same page, not with all the anti-immigrant hate out there now. No, Jesse. I'm not like you. I'm not documented. I don't have your privilege."

Jesse looked stunned, then at his hands, chastised. Gamaliel put his face in his hands and rubbed hard at tears he could barely control. He seemed more frustrated than sad now.

"Shit. Sorry, ese," he said, looking at Jesse. "Damn, the guy's dead and he's still getting under my skin. I'm sorry." He leaned back in his chair, staring at the ceiling again, and let out a long sigh. "What is it that Kinji always used to tell me? 'If you define yourself by what you are not or by what you do not have, you will always want and will always be wanting.'" He faced Jesse again. "Says some Black guy from the South used to say that at the post office. Doesn't change what I'm not and what I don't have, but, whatever. Sorry, dude. I know you're trying to help."

"We're good," Jesse said with a wave of his hand. "And looks like you've applied some of Kinji's wisdom. I mean, look at everything you've done with the store."

Gamaliel grimaced as if embarrassed by his outburst at his friend.

"I'll see if we can get the arrest off your record," Yolanda said. She didn't know how she'd do that, but she agreed with his political assessment.

"Thanks," Gamaliel said. Then he scoffed. "Shit, at least now he won't throw his birth certificate in my face anymore."

"He did that?" Jesse asked.

"He was an asshole." He didn't bother to look at his mother, who only shook her head. "When we were kids, he overheard our moms telling Kinji about how my Tía Chata got me across the border with Frank's birth certificate, then waited for word from my mom's coyote before she could pick her up and bring both of us to LA. The only thing that got him to not mention it in public was Kinji telling him that his mom would go to jail if anyone found out. But that didn't stop him from giving me hell privately. God, I think I hated him. I was so relieved when my tía remarried and they moved out."

Yolanda looked from the couch to the two small bedrooms on either side of the dinette set and the restroom door in between. Two women and two growing boys would make for crowded conditions that likely exacerbated any animosity.

"And what do you feel now?" Jesse asked, ever the empath.

"I don't know. Anger, I guess. Poor Kinji is in jail because of him. I don't know that I even care who killed him. It's like he had it coming. If Kinji weren't in jail, I don't know that I'd feel anything at his loss." Yolanda noted that the tears brimming his eyes said otherwise.

Jesse gave a quick nod but said nothing, letting his friend talk.

"Now we gotta help Kinji. Get the store open again and help Kinji." Gamaliel seemed to come out of a depressed stupor with renewed energy, standing up and pacing. "How soon do you think we can get him out? And how soon can we reopen the store?"

"I don't know," Yolanda said. "The attorney said to wait for his call regarding bail. I'll call the DA tomorrow morning and see if you can get into the store tomorrow. I also need to check the house down on Evergreen with the security cameras. The ones on Malabar weren't working."

"You may want to check El Tepeyac up on Evergreen too," Gamaliel said. "They have cameras. Damn, wish I'd finished putting ours up, but I was still trying to figure out the wiring. Let's go check them out now. I can't just sit here."

With that, they got up. Gumer told them not to be long as she busied herself in the small kitchen next to the living room, but Gamaliel told her not to bother cooking and that they'd eat at the popular Mexican food restaurant and would bring something back for her.

Ever the gentlemen, Jesse and Gamaliel stood back to let Yolanda exit the front door. A bit archaic, Yolanda thought, but somehow, she seemed to like the gesture. Up the street, they passed the now-vacant Ciro's restaurant and crossed the street to the iconic El Tepeyac. Yolanda had only been once when she was a cop. Part of her rookie initiation involved polishing off the famous Manuel's Special, a gargantuan burrito for four. She hadn't been able to finish it, but the effort had kept her from having even a normal-sized one for months. She relayed the story to Gamaliel as they walked the half block up to the modest restaurant.

"They have normal-sized food, you know," Gamaliel said. "But there was a time when anyone who could finish a Manuel's Special could win twenty bucks."

He was greeted warmly by a server. Gamaliel explained that he often delivered last-minute produce when the restaurant was in danger of running short. Personally, Gamaliel said he thought that Manuel, the legendary founder who had greeted everyone with a warm "mijo" or "mija," had meant to give business to the Abe Grocery. Gamaliel was glad the practice continued, but he missed Manuel, who'd passed away a few years earlier. He asked about security camera video but was told that the police had already collected it. One of the younger employees offered to pull up some digital backup of what they gave the detectives. While they waited, they ordered dinner.

When the video came up, they all stood at a small monitor to view it, fast-forwarding and slowing it down whenever a car came by. At 8:06 p.m., a dark sedan drove south on Evergreen and back north again, faster this time, at 8:11 p.m.

"I can't be sure," Gamaliel said, "but that might be Hector. Can't tell if that's his black BMW."

"I'll have to pay him a visit," Yolanda said.

They fast-forwarded through the rest of the video but saw no sign of Turi or Frank. Of course, they could have approached from the south. Frank's car was facing north, so that seemed likely. The three sat again to finish their delicious albondigas, enchiladas, and chiles rellenos. Gamaliel ordered a chile verde plate for his mom, her favorite.

"So how is it that you didn't qualify for DACA?" Yolanda asked, referring to the program that allowed some, but not all, immigrants who arrived without papers as children a temporary reprieve from deportation.

"Too old. Didn't meet the 1981 cutoff date because I was born in 1980. Just my luck." He seemed resigned to his fate. "Still pay taxes because Kinji pays me, but he's risking at least a fine, if not jail time, for hiring me and my mom. Good thing ICE hasn't gone after small shops like ours. Yet. But you never know. The fascists out there would love to see raids like when all the bracero workers got shipped back to Mexico in the fifties."

"Fifties? Heck, how about the early nineties?" Yolanda said, turning to Jesse. "You remember when Mom took us to the garment district and ended up helping ladies running away from a raid? Took them home."

"I don't remember," Jesse said. "I was a baby, but I remember you guys talking about it."

"Don't know if it was a real raid or just rumors of one," Yolanda said, turning back to Gamaliel, "but people ran all over the place trying to get away. Mom took us back to the minivan and invited some ladies to join us. Ended up filling the van with strangers. Spent the rest of the afternoon driving them home."

"We all have targets on our backs," Gamaliel said. "No matter who's in the White House. I'll bet the raids will come back. I'm just lucky I don't work where they can catch a bunch of us."

"Might need to enlist my Chapulin Colorado for future raids like Mom did," Jesse said. All three shook their heads at the thought of new raids.

"How'd you and your mom end up working for Kinji, anyway?" Yolanda asked. "He told us something about the Vásquez family, but how do you and your mom come into the picture?"

"My Tía Chata, my mom's sister, married into the family. She got her papers through my Tío Tommy. He was Fernando's son and the grandson of the couple who kept the store open for the Abes when they were imprisoned at Heart Mountain in Wyoming. Tommy died when Frank and I were babies. A stroke like his dad, I think. My aunt asked my mom to come and live with her and work in the store. It was a good way to get away from my father. Don't know the guy, but he was abusive. Kinji hadn't retired from the post office yet, and my aunt needed help. She went for me and brought me across the border with Frank's birth certificate, then met up with my mom after her coyote got her across in a truck with a bunch of produce. A lot of people have it harder getting across now."

Yolanda and Jesse murmured their agreement and dug into their food as Gamaliel continued.

"Then my aunt got married again when Frank and I were seniors in high school. She and Frank moved out to Montebello that year. My aunt kept coming to work at the store for a couple of years, but my mom and I were pretty much running it by then. Then, when Kinji retired, he let us keep running it. It's like his hobby became helping out at the register. I keep telling him to take up bird watching or something, but he says he prefers interacting with people. I'm just glad he can take a nap every day now that he seems to need them."

"So, change of subject. Tell me about Kinji's swords. They seem to be the main evidence."

"Not much to say. He guarded those carefully. No one was allowed to touch them, even when we dusted the shelves. Only him. He was afraid we'd cut ourselves on them and didn't handle them much himself. Except for one time. Some dude strung out on something tried to rob the store. Kinji pulled out the katana, the long sword, and waved it around with both hands, shouting something in Japanese. Scared the shit out of the guy. Us too!" Gamaliel laughed at the memory. "The guy ran out, and we never saw him again. But word got around, and people knew not to mess with Kinji. Called him Yabai for a while after that. Means something like badass. Even the local cholos made sure no one messed with him. I'm sure the credit he provides their families and the occasional free forty help too."

Yolanda and Jesse laughed at the story, but Yolanda worried about fingerprints.

"And he was right about how sharp they were," Gamaliel said. "One time, when we were kids, Frank tried to show them off to Turi. He cut his palm pretty deep. It left a big scar. Kinji was so pissed. And I got in trouble for not stopping him, even though I was nowhere near the register at the time." He shook his head at the memory, then looked at Yolanda, wide-eyed. "Hey, wait. If there is any trace of Frank's blood on that knife, could it be from way back then? We were seniors in high school, just before Frank and his mom moved away."

Yolanda sat up and lowered her fork. "Which sword was it? And who cleaned it?"

"The tantō—the smallest one. Kinji cleaned it, I think. He wouldn't let any of us try. Said he was going to get a case for them, but he never did. Something about his dad wanting them to sit as they were, or something like that. But you bet none of us touched them again after that. Even Kinji never touched them. Just used the feather duster on them."

Yolanda wrote in her small notebook again and tapped it with her pencil, thinking.

"That could complicate things if it's the same sword the techs identified, but you'd be able to provide an affidavit. Who else saw it happen?"

"Well, Turi and my mom, I think. Frank's mom wasn't around that afternoon."

"But that still means someone with a knife got at Frank. Do Turi or his dad or Hector carry a knife?"

"I don't know. We all played with cheap switchblades growing up. They've always been illegal as far as I know, but some people would bring them up from Tijuana. Still do, I think. I don't know if Turi needed a knife for his job or if his dad carried one for protection. Have no idea about Hector."

Jesse shook his head thoughtfully, indicating he didn't know either.

"Worth finding out," Yolanda said, pocketing her notebook.

The restaurant worker came to the table with a small memory card and offered it to Gamaliel. He handed it to Yolanda.

"Hope you can enhance it," he said.

"Hope so too," she said, hoping Jane could.

Yolanda looked at her phone when it chimed with the tone she had assigned Sydney.

"Sorry, guys, I need to run home," she said.

"Something wrong?" Jesse asked, concern crossing his face.

"Nah. Just need to help Sydney with something," Yolanda said before standing. "Maybe you guys can try that house on Evergreen with the security cameras in case we can't enhance the video we got."

"You got it," Jesse said.

"Thanks. Send me Hector's address if you have it. Kinji only had a phone number. I'll try to visit him tomorrow morning, whether or not the attorney calls."

With that, Yolanda jogged to her Jeep, more worried than ever about Sydney. Her text had said simply, *We need to talk. Home in a few.* Sydney never sent messages like that. What the hell was up?

CHAPTER SIX

On the drive home, Yolanda ruminated about Sydney's text. "We need to talk" never meant anything good. Was it really a work thing? Could it be something between them? No, Yolanda could not bring herself to think that she and Sydney had a problem. What was it that the social media posts said about signs of a relationship problem? Emotional distance, noncommunication, secretive behavior. Damn, okay, maybe some of those were true over the past few weeks, but they were mostly due to both of them being busy. Their love life was pretty good. They'd just been tired lately. Yolanda could not bring herself to think that this could be about their relationship. And, yet, what was it that Sydney had asked about regrets? Something about a moral quandary. Shit. Infidelity. An affair could fall into that category. She'd said it was a work matter, but was she just trying to let Yolanda off easy? And she'd seemed almost angry at Yolanda for not having regrets similar to her own. Was that a guilt thing? As much as Yolanda tried to write it off as impossible, a nagging feeling told her that whatever Sydney was going through could be about them. She felt a queasy unease growing in her stomach.

The mounting nausea made Yolanda pull over on Soto Street. She was glad the street grew wider in front of the water district building, giving her plenty of room to open her door. She leaned sideways to spit out an acrid mix of enchiladas and bile. She thanked the goddess for the bottle of water in her car and rinsed out her mouth. A thought intruded that she might be overreacting, but she couldn't help it. She couldn't help a new wave of nausea either. She bent over again just in time. A car slowed next to hers, and a woman asked in Spanish if she was okay and whether she needed to call 911.

"No. Gracias." Yolanda's voice sounded weak, even to her. The woman drove away, appearing unconvinced that Yolanda was okay. She rinsed out her mouth again and closed the door, leaning back in her seat.

"Pull it together, Yolanda," she said aloud, hoping she'd do just that. A few shallow breaths later, she was able to focus enough to take a deep breath, hold it for a few seconds, exhale slowly, and wait a few seconds before repeating. Sydney had shared the box breathing technique she'd learned from some Navy SEALs she'd bandaged up in Afghanistan. Yolanda wasn't sure how they made it work for them. In a much less stressful situation, she could barely make it work for herself. But the nausea abated, and she popped a stick of gum in her mouth before driving on, trying to convince herself that Sydney's text had nothing to do with their relationship. Sydney had remained friends with a couple of her exes, but Yolanda had never felt jealous. She was confident in their relationship, or at least thought she was.

When she arrived home, the house was dark. Yolanda mentally kicked herself for not bringing food from the restaurant for Sydney. She rushed to the upstairs restroom to brush her teeth. It took a while, and she wasn't sure, but after gargling she thought she'd finally gotten rid of the taste of bile. She descended the stairs to see Sydney placing her keys on the tray by the front door. Yolanda glanced out the window and saw Sydney's car on the street instead of in their garage. She ignored the acid reflux bubbling in her chest and tried to sound nonchalant.

"Hey, love. Why'd you park outside?"

"Need to head back to the hospital in a bit."

Yolanda tried not to make too much of the lack of eye contact.

"So, whatever you have to share you have to share in person. That serious?"

Neither rushed, but they moved toward each other and embraced. Sydney pulled back first, sending an ache through Yolanda's chest.

"I fucked up, babe. Really fucked up." Sydney still didn't make direct eye contact but reached for Yolanda's hand, much to her relief. Sydney led them to the sofa and sat down, never letting go of Yolanda's hand. The fear and nausea Yolanda had felt earlier returned for a bit, this time mixed with a deep concern for the woman she loved.

"Whatever it is, we can work through it," Yolanda said, not sure she meant it if it involved another woman. Sydney finally looked her in the eye for what seemed like an eternity. Yolanda's own eyes searched Sydney's, but all she could read was pain. Her heart ached again.

"I'm getting hammered with a lawsuit at work," Sydney blurted out.

"What?" Yolanda looked at her wife, confused. Sydney repeated herself, slower this time. Yolanda's head sank to her chest, and she let out a sigh of relief.

"Oh my god, Syd," Yolanda said, unable to suppress a smile.

"Did you hear what I just said?"

"I'm sorry, love. Really. It's just that I'd spun myself up thinking maybe this was about us. Whatever is going on at work, we can handle. I'm listening."

It was Sydney's turn to look at Yolanda with concern in her eyes. She caressed Yolanda's cheek with the back of her fingers.

"I'm so sorry, babe. I had no idea you were reading me that way. No, it's definitely not about us. It's all about work. But it's pretty serious."

"Okay, I'm all ears, but would a drink help?" Yolanda moved to get one, but Sydney held her hand tighter, and she sat back down.

"No. I really do have to get back. There's going to be a peer review, and I need to keep working on my defense for that. It'll determine how much the hospital stands behind me."

Yolanda let her continue.

"So, remember the motorcycle accident I mentioned a few weeks ago? The one with the grandfather and the kid Joey's age?"

"Sure. You stabilized the kid, but the grandfather didn't make it. He was the guy with the Nazi and KKK tattoos on his chest, right?" Yolanda recalled her wife's description of the horrible accident that slammed the older man and boy into a sound wall, crushing the man's ribs, which pierced his lungs. His helmet had flown off, causing a severe head injury too. The boy's helmet had stayed on, but he'd suffered a concussion and internal injuries. His grandfather's body had protected him from fatal injuries, but he couldn't protect the boy's arm and side from road burn bad enough to require skin grafts.

"Right. Well, I'm under investigation for negligence in his care."

"But I thought a resident took care of him and you took care of the kid. Why would you be responsible for the old man?"

"I was the attending and passed him on to a resident."

"Wait. Someone sued you and exposed you to possible disciplinary action because you saved a kid's life and another doctor couldn't save the grandfather?"

"Because I, ostensibly, refused to provide care to the grandfather because of his tattoos."

"But even if that were true, it's not like you denied him care. And you've treated guys with racist tattoos before, so no one can say that you turned him down for any reason. You just prioritized the life of a kid because you were the most experienced and most likely to save his life, from what you told me."

"All true. But the son is making a big deal about it, and the hospital has to look into it."

"Okay. They'll look into it, but they won't find anything because there's nothing to find. You're a damn good doctor. You saved the life of that kid. You didn't deny care to anyone."

"Didn't I?" Sydney looked so sad that Yolanda had to wrap her arm around her and pull her close to keep herself from crying.

"Love, you can't beat yourself up about this. You didn't do anything wrong."

Sydney stared into midspace, shaking her head slowly, almost thinking aloud in a soft voice.

"Everyone is capable of doing the wrong thing, even letting someone die." She shuddered and wrapped her arms around herself. Yolanda pulled her closer, wrapping her own arms around her wife but letting her speak. Sydney seemed to welcome the gesture, resting her head on Yolanda's shoulder. After a moment, she spoke again. "You know, you work your ass off to be twice as good as you have to be to get half as far as the other guy. And once you do, you're still vulnerable to having it all taken away. It's just so fuckin' unfair." She pulled back from Yolanda and rubbed her face with both hands, as if willing away the hurt.

Yolanda wrapped her arms around Sydney again, both sinking into each other. Neither needed to say anything. They'd both lived the struggle of BIPOC women. Sydney more so, being Black. Neither of them was a stranger to her emotional exhaustion. Yolanda knew just what she needed.

"How important is it to get back to the hospital tonight? Maybe a dose of sisterhood at Mel's will help. I don't know who all will be there tonight, but it is Friday." They knew that at least some of their group of regulars would be there. During the pandemic they had resorted to Zoom happy hour on Fridays, but no one was happier than Mel to see them come back in person when restrictions lifted.

Sydney pulled back from the embrace and held Yolanda at arm's length. Yolanda read that as a no but tried to hide her disappointment, glancing away. Sydney placed a finger under Yolanda's chin and turned her face to meet her eyes.

"You know, you may be right." The smile in her eyes was the first Yolanda had seen in a while, and she smiled back, bringing her wife close and into a deep kiss.

"Or maybe just some 'us time,'" Yolanda suggested when they pulled apart again.

"Not sure I'm up to it, love, but maybe tomorrow morning." Sydney winked at her. "I can use some of that sisterhood you suggest first. Just won't be able to have a cocktail or stay long. Let's go in separate cars so I can take off from there."

When they arrived at Las Adelitas, most of the gang was there and working on their second round, from the sound of their laughter. The group turned to welcome the couple with cocktail glasses held aloft. Mel, the owner and bartender extraordinaire, came up to them and gave them each a welcome hug. He wore a mask, as did Brissa, his partner. Yolanda and her friends were glad they'd finally gotten together, having known Mel since before he transitioned. Brissa was a wiz at tech stuff and helped the business make it through the pandemic with a cocktail delivery service and Zoom mixology lessons for online parties. Her DJ skills were still in demand for Zoom parties with groups of geographically diverse friends that had come together during isolation. And Mel continued to offer online mixology lessons as a fundraiser for local nonprofits, with plans to host them in person soon.

"Thought you weren't going to make it tonight," Roxanne "Rox" Piedras said. She was the "Frida child" of the group, whom Jesse had nicknamed "Stones" due to her full name. He'd dubbed her tall partner, Clara, as "Sticks." Together, they were "Sticks and Stones."

"Almost didn't make it, but we needed some mujeres time," Yolanda said, drawing Sydney closer to the long table with a hand on her lower back.

"Uh-oh," Carmen said. "Whose ass do we need to kick?" Carmen was Yolanda's comadre, Yolanda having baptized her son, Joey. They'd been best friends since elementary school. And Yolanda knew it was not wise to underestimate her petite size. Both she and Sydney were tae kwon do black belts.

"No one's ass," Sydney said, sitting down after asking Brissa for a Diet Coke. "Just needed to be with you strong, beautiful people to forget some work bullshit." Yolanda stood with her hands on Sydney's shoulders and ordered a Mezcalrita.

"Well, sounds like good chisme anyway, so spill," Roxanne said. "Let's hear it." She wiggled her fingers in invitation when Sydney hesitated.

"Let her get her drink first," Angela Abner said. Angela was the beauty of the bunch, benefiting from her Black and Vietnamese genes. She also had a gift for eloquence that brought her much success as a public affairs and crisis communications consultant. She'd eschewed offers to model "thick" women's clothes because she didn't want her body objectified. As far as Yolanda could tell, she was between partners because there was no man or woman looking at her with eyes that said they couldn't believe their luck.

"Well, I can't say much publicly," Sydney said, taking her drink from Brissa, "but I'm dealing with shit at work because a patient's son is accusing me of denying care."

Yolanda interrupted the chorus of "no ways" and "bullshit."

"A racist dude, by the way, and she saved the life of the kid he came in with."

"Don't think we can say more, love," Sydney said, touching Yolanda's hand with her own. "HIPAA and all."

"That is some bullshit!" Roxanne said.

"What can we do to help?" Clara asked.

"Will this be in the media?" Angela asked.

"Could be," Sydney said. "Not sure there's anything any of you can do, but happy for your emotional support." She raised her glass to Clara before turning to Angela. "Depends on how far the son wants to take it and if he tries to fight it out in public."

"Because they have no case," Yolanda added.

"Well, I'd be happy to help if they do," Angela said.

"Thanks," Sydney said, raising her glass to Angela. "I think the hospital will take care of that after they rake me over the coals, but I'll definitely keep you in the loop if it looks like they're turning on me." Sydney craned her neck to stretch it, obviously uncomfortable with the conversation. She changed the subject. "So, what were you guys laughing about when we walked in?"

"Angela has a new boo," Carmen said.

"And she's whipped!" Rox added.

"No, I'm not," Angela said, looking at her Topo Chico water.

"You're taking them to the airport, right?" Rox asked.

Angela gave a slight nod.

"Burbank or LAX?" Yolanda asked.

Angela took the last swig of her water before mumbling, "LAX."

"Whipped!" the group said in unison with more laughter.

"Hey, even Syd and I don't take each other to LAX anymore," Yolanda said. "The FlyAway from Union Station will do."

"Well," Angela said, standing. "Gotta go."

"Me too," Sydney said, surprising Yolanda, who stood up with her wife and her friend and walked out with them. They exchanged goodbyes and promises to stay in touch regarding Sydney's proceedings. At Sydney's car, Yolanda held her wife in a tight embrace, willing her positive vibes.

"Let me know when I can step in to help, okay?"

"I will. Thanks. Love you." A quick kiss later, Sydney was in her car.

Yolanda watched her drive away before stepping back into Mel's under the sign that read *Las Adelitas*. Yolanda couldn't think of anyone who called Mel's by its official name.

"She gonna be okay?" Carmen asked, more concern on her face than earlier.

"I'm sure she will be," Yolanda said, "but she's taking it pretty hard. Thanks for cheering her up, guys." Yolanda took a sip of her Mezcalrita to encouraging words all around.

"Better not talk about it too much in case it goes to court," Carmen said, "but I'll take fifty cents to provide legal advice if you need it."

"Thanks. I've asked her to let me help too." Yolanda sat staring at her drink. She must have sat like that for a while because Carmen reached across the table and tapped her hand a couple of times. Yolanda blinked and roused. When she looked around, her friends all looked at her with varying degrees of concern.

"You okay, mujer?" Carmen asked.

"Dang," Yolanda said. "Spaced out for a bit. Been doing that lately. No idea why."

"Could be stress," Clara said. "Sydney's case too."

"Maybe," Yolanda said, shaking her head. "Didn't know what was bothering Syd until she told me tonight. Thought we were having a problem for a bit, but glad it's nothing like that. Now I wonder what else I'm missing, fading out like that."

"No way," Carmen said. "You guys are solid." Rox and Clara chimed in to agree.

"Whatever," Yolanda said, not wanting to discuss it. "I need to focus. Have a new case, but I can always do some legwork for Sydney."

"What's your new case?" Clara asked, much to Yolanda's relief. She'd rather get help solving other people's problems than her own.

"Stabbing death in Boyle Heights," she said. "Evergreen and Malabar. Jesse got me to meet with the mother of the first guy arrested."

"First guy?" Clara asked.

"Well, Jesse's friend was arrested, but he had a good alibi, so they let him go, but then they arrested the old man who owns the tiendita where he works. Now I need to help the family. Can't imagine the old guy doing it unless he was defending himself, but there's no evidence of an altercation that I can tell. Plus," she said, turning to Carmen, "your old buddy Rios is on the case, so you know he won't give up even if he's wrong."

"Chingado," Carmen said. "That asshole?"

"Fill us in from the beginning," Clara said.

Clara had a friend at the morgue who Yolanda had asked her to contact in the past. She wasn't sure she needed help from him this time around, but she started from her meeting with Gumer and filled in her friends.

"Sounds like that Tachuela guy or his son may be good for it," Rox said. "Or the other guy who was supposed to meet with the owner of the store."

"Maybe," Yolanda said, "but I may have to prove it to get the old man off the hook."

"Maybe Celine can help you where Rios can't," Carmen said.

"I don't know. You know her ethics. She gave me a bit of a brush-off after telling me they were going to let Gamaliel go. Probably won't see her here for a while either." Then, thinking aloud, Yolanda added, "Unless I can bring something to her again that she may not already have. Just don't know what. Hopefully Kinji will give me something when I see him tomorrow." She turned to Clara.

"May help if your buddy at the morgue can confirm that Frank had cocaine in his system, or anything else they may have."

"Sure," Clara said. Yolanda knew she'd call with any updates.

"To solving this case," Rox said, raising a glass with the others.

On their way out, Carmen and Yolanda stopped at the curb.

"You know," Carmen said, "maybe you and Sydney need to get away together. You're both stressed out. Don't let that get in the way." When Yolanda said nothing, she continued, "You guys have better communication than most couples, definitely better than Luis and I ever had before we split up. You guys aren't us. Like I said, you're solid. Don't lose that."

Yolanda held her friend in a long embrace. Had it been anyone else, Yolanda would have dismissed the advice. But this was her comadre, the woman who knew her best other than Sydney. And Carmen was close to Sydney too. She had introduced them and knew they were in love before they did. Yolanda swallowed hard.

"Damn, okay. Maybe a trip up the coast like old times. Nothing like a nice bed-and-breakfast to take care of relationship problems."

"You do not have a relationship problem, torpe." Carmen smiled and playfully slapped the side of Yolanda's head. "You guys are just stressed from work."

Yolanda hoped she was right.

When Sydney got home, she seemed more exhausted. Determined, but exhausted. Her review prep had gone as well as it could have, but she had more work to do. When they got ready for bed, Yolanda mentioned Carmen's suggestion about taking time off. Sydney was all ears, asking what Carmen had noticed.

"Well, I kind of spaced out, but that's not unusual when I'm focused on something. It's just that I've been doing it a bit lately. She thinks both of us are stressed out and need a break."

In bed, Sydney placed an arm around her wife.

"That sounds like a good idea." Yolanda could feel her wife's smile on her shoulder. "Like Carmen always says, it's a good idea to take care of yourself when taking care of others."

Yolanda had to agree, but both tossed most of the night, and Yolanda had a nagging, anxious feeling that something wasn't right. But at least she hadn't woken up at 3:23 a.m. like she had three years ago with warning dreams. She'd told herself she'd be careful in any case and had finally slept soundly. Until 3:23. It wasn't a nightmare or an anxious feeling, but a strong smell of onion and cilantro. At first, she thought that maybe Sydney had brought food to bed, but then she realized it was just a dream. At 3:23.

The last time she'd woken like this was when she was working to rescue her kidnapped godson and fend off a stalker going after Sydney. It took a while, but her own godmother had helped her realize they were warning dreams sent by her deceased mother and uncle, and that she should pay attention to them. But she felt only unease. Were these weird dreams starting to mess with her concentration while awake? Was that why she felt she was missing something? Or was it her preoccupation with her case? The smell of onions and cilantro told her nothing other than to be careful of Mexican food. Not helpful at all, she thought. She tried some deep breathing to get back to sleep. It seemed to work.

All seemed better by morning. Sydney didn't have to go into the hospital until late afternoon, so they took their time making love. Still, as much as their intimacy reaffirmed their love, Yolanda couldn't help the nagging feeling of something being off. She'd think about it after visiting Kinji Abe.

CHAPTER SEVEN

Saturday

Yolanda knew conditions at the county jail were horrible, but the feral nature of the place always surprised her. She'd arrived later than she'd planned, but Kinji wasn't going anywhere any time soon, she thought. Yolanda got in line with suited lawyers, crying mothers, and people who looked lost and scared, out of place. Others acted like routine visitors who could have been in line at the airport. She checked her vaccine card. She hoped that her sports jacket, khaki pants, and Birkenstock dress shoes were conservative enough to get decent treatment. She hadn't finished breaking in the shoes Sydney had given her for her birthday months ago. She would have been much more comfortable in her usual sneakers but thought the green suede shoes might make her look more respectable.

At the metal detector, she learned that the sheriff's deputy didn't care about her shoes as long as she took them off before entering. She waited for what seemed like an eternity before she heard her name called. The envious looks from others waiting told her that perhaps forty minutes had not been too long after all. She felt lucky until she learned that she could not see Kinji. Apparently, an "official" meeting was in progress. That meant he was meeting with his lawyer. Either he had bumped her visit, or the post-Covid online system still had glitches. Well, it wasn't a bad thing that the lawyer had made it, but she wished she'd been able to identify him when she'd arrived. She stepped outside and called the attorney's office, hoping they'd be open on a Saturday. The phone rang a while, but someone finally answered. All she could get from the receptionist was that they closed at noon and that she had to go and did not know when the attorney would be available. She'd send him a message.

Yolanda was able to get the receptionist to describe the lawyer so that she could identify him coming out of the jail. While she waited for him to emerge, she dialed Celine's cell phone to get the DA to help give Gamaliel access to the store. She had to leave a message but hoped Celine would call back soon. Then she called Jane to let her know she'd go by the office later to drop off a memory card with the security video from El Tepeyac. Jane probably wouldn't be able to get to it until Monday, but that should not be a problem. It meant Yolanda would owe her another stakeout. Jane hated doing them, but Yolanda was glad to trade her in-person sleuthing for Jane's cyber sleuthing any day. Next, she thought of calling Hector Garcia to schedule a visit but thought better of it. Giving a suspect too much time to think before being questioned made for a more difficult interrogation. A surprise visit to the man who was supposed to have met with Kinji would be much better. Fortunately, Kinji had given her his number. The boys hadn't come up with his address, but she'd been able to find it online. Jane wasn't the only one in their office who could do a background check.

Yolanda had been waiting half an hour outside the jail and had started pacing with impatient energy when her phone buzzed in her hand. It was Gamaliel's number.

"Hi. Hey, thanks for getting the cops to let us back into the store." Yolanda could hear the relief in his voice. "Just got off the phone with the detective. He didn't seem too happy about it, but I'll take it. Shit, it's a mess in here, but at least Mom and I can open the store today. Any word on Kinji?"

"I'm outside County right now. The lawyer's in with him. They wouldn't let me in. Our appointments conflicted or something. I'll need to reschedule, but I'm waiting for the lawyer to come out first. Will keep you posted. Glad you can get the shop open today."

"Yeah. Thanks. And let us know about Kinji. Do you think we can bail him out today?"

"The lawyer said last night that Monday was more likely, but I'll ask him again," she said before signing off.

That was odd. Celine had not called her back, but it sounded like she'd called Rios or Chan right after Yolanda left her message. Or was it something Celine had done on her own? Yolanda resigned herself to not knowing until after the case was resolved, if even then.

A man fitting the description of Kinji's lawyer came out of the jail's reception area. Yolanda had to smile at the receptionist's description. When he removed his mask, he did, indeed, look like a young Danny DeVito with more hair and better-tailored clothes.

"Mr. Herrera? José Herrera?"

"That's me."

"You were just in with Kinji Abe, right?"

"Yes, and you are?"

"I'm Yolanda Ávila, the private investigator helping him and the family. We spoke yesterday at the recommendation of Carmen Ochoa."

At that, the attorney smiled, his eyes flashing a Danny DeVito twinkle.

"You might want to talk to our mutual client," he said. "I think I can get him bailed out based on his age, clean record, and business, but not until Monday. Murder and manslaughter require an arraignment and bail hearing. They probably won't let you schedule a visit anymore today," he said, glancing at his Timex watch, "but you can try tomorrow. Sign up as an official visitor and they'll give you greater priority than a public visitor.

I'll send you a retainer so that you can prove we're working together. See if you can convince him to talk."

"Talk? What do you mean? He was pretty chatty yesterday."

"Look, I see all kinds." He sighed. "He was pretty chatty with me too, but mostly he asked questions. I had a hard time getting him to tell me what happened. He was more interested in what I thought the cops knew."

"Is that odd?"

"Not really. Hopefully it means he's trying to figure out how to defend himself, but that's my job. Clients who think they can defend themselves are not the easiest to defend. I think I can get him off on self-defense, but I need his full story. He said he didn't say anything to the cops, but they were with him for almost two hours at the store. We need to know what they discussed."

"Do you know the detectives on the case? Elton Chan is decent, but Henry Rios is the senior detective and he's not very good."

"Even bad detectives get lucky once in a while. I need to know what Mr. Abe told them—even if it seems insignificant to him. It'll make our job easier."

"Got it." Yolanda liked him. She would bet prosecutors underestimated him in their first trial together. There was nothing slick about José Herrera. He didn't dress in expensive suits to impress, but the one he wore looked well-tailored. Yolanda commented on it with admiration.

"I have the best tailor in town," he said. "My mom is a seamstress." They laughed at that, and Yolanda liked him even more. He didn't look like a high-paid defense attorney, but she knew from his up-front retainer for Kinji that he wasn't struggling and could probably pick and choose his cases.

"I'll see what I can get out of him tomorrow," she said. "In the meantime, you should know that there are two other suspects, maybe three." Yolanda filled him in on Turi, the activist; T, his father; and Hector, the real estate agent.

"Yes, Mr. Abe told me about them too. You know who Hector is, right?"

"The real estate speculator?"

He smiled up at Yolanda and shook his head. "Hector Garcia. From *the* Garcias. Former activists turned developers."

"Oh, shit."

"Yup, you may want to do some research before contacting him. If he was involved with the victim, he was likely doing it on behalf of his father or his father's business. If he's involved in the murder, he'll want Mr. Abe to take the blame. And he'll have the resources to see to it."

"Dang." Yolanda shook her head, mad at herself for not making the connection on her own. "Okay, thanks for the heads-up. Will we need more help?"

The attorney looked at her with a raised eyebrow.

"Sorry, didn't mean to offend, but you mentioned the Garcias' resources."

A small smile crept over his lips. "I've gone up against bigger Goliaths. You just get Mr. Abe talking and let me know what you learn about the other suspects."

"Got it," she said again, liking his confidence. "Also, the DA on the case, Celine Cueva, is a friend of mine. She goes no-contact when she's on a case that I'm involved in, but she'll take information from me. It'll all be one-way communication, but she'll be fair if we can find information that exonerates Mr. Abe." She mentioned Celine's response to proof of Gamaliel's innocence.

"Good to know," the attorney said. "She's good. Really good." He stared into midspace, thinking, but didn't comment further on Celine.

They talked about the security video and the blood markings. The attorney took a special interest in those and looked closely at his phone after Yolanda forwarded the pictures. Then she mentioned Frank's old knife injury and the possibility of old blood on one of the samurai swords.

"You're good," he said. He pointed a finger at Yolanda and smiled. "Really good. Even if we can't prove someone else did it, all this may help create sufficient doubt about Mr. Abe being the perpetrator." He bit his lower lip, thinking some more. Yolanda hoped it wouldn't take a trial to clear Kinji.

They traded cards and agreed to keep each other updated. Yolanda headed to her office to drop off the memory card with the security camera video and do some online research. On her way there, Sydney called, and Yolanda couldn't help but smile at the caller ID.

"I may need your help after all. Are you free this afternoon, say around three?"

"Sure, love, what's up?"

"I'm going to visit the kid from the motorcycle accident at Children's Hospital. Wanna go with? Could use the company."

"Sure. Just swinging by the office for a bit, but I can meet you at home or at the hospital."

"I'll be heading down from Pasadena, so why don't we meet there?"

"Sure thing. Should I know anything more before the visit?"

"His mom called to ask me to come by. I'll explain more when we meet there. Thanks. Gotta run."

They exchanged their usual "love you" and signed off.

That was interesting. Yolanda was glad Sydney had called, and especially glad that she had the time free to support her wife. Of course, she'd probably drop anything she was doing in any case.

Once at her computer, Yolanda wished that Jane was there to help with tips on research. Instead, she looked over public documents involving the Garcia business and its social media, as well as the family's personal social media accounts. From what she could gather, the son worked for the father, who appeared to pay him well. His social media posts revealed lots of travel, a black BMW similar to the black sedan in the video from El Tepeyac, and a bright-yellow Ferrari. But from the looks of it, he still lived at home, or at least hosted parties at his parents' house.

Yolanda became bored scrolling through rich people's comments on Hector's social media when she spotted something that piqued her interest. A comment on a recent Instagram post with multiple pictures of a party in Cabo San Lucas said simply *I know how you paid for that party*. What the heck was that? Yolanda tried to identify the person who posted the comment but came up empty. The account was private and had no posts of its own. And the name, "knowwhatyoudid" and a string of numbers, didn't show up on other social media. She really needed Jane's help now. But she had to run to meet Sydney first.

CHAPTER EIGHT

At the Children's Hospital garage, Sydney stood by her car in her white coat, right where she'd texted she'd be. Yolanda made her way into a welcome embrace. They walked to the hospital entrance holding hands, not something they normally did in public. Maybe Sydney meant to reassure Yolanda about their relationship. The gesture moved Yolanda to give her wife's hand a squeeze. She savored the moment before speaking.

"Okay, tell me what we're up to."

"Well, I don't know if this'll work, but I thought seeing the boy and his family might remind them that I helped him survive. His mother called, asking that I come see him because he keeps asking for the 'angel in white' that saved him." She made air quotes. "We didn't talk long, but she's not part of the complaint her brother-in-law filed against me. He just filed one against Connor too."

"Connor…the resident?"

"Yup. My theory is that Brian Jacobs is going after him because he found out he's gay. As far as I know, that's part of what's motivating him against me too."

"Oh, please. This is 2022, for Pete's sake."

"Sure, but plenty of people would love to go back to the McCarthy era, or Hitler's Germany for that matter."

"I guess," Yolanda said. She wasn't sure meeting the family would work, but instead of saying so, she asked how Sydney's defense preparation had gone. Her wife explained that the team in the ER had adhered to proper protocols, but they'd have to be convincing for the peer review.

They donned their masks and walked through the automated entrance doors. Sydney filled in Yolanda on what she would see in little Jack's room. Sure enough, an array of medical equipment surrounded a bed with a boy lying on his side, his right arm, torso, and legs bandaged. He seemed groggy, possibly from the pain medication, but awake. His eyes opened wide when he saw Sydney. A young woman next to the bed turned to welcome them. The dark bags under her eyes and her matted blond hair told them that she'd been at the hospital since her son got there, with very few breaks. What would it have been? Three weeks? Four? She looked like she was in her late twenties.

"Thank you for coming," the woman said. She stood and smoothed her blue T-shirt, placing a lock of hair behind her right ear before wiping her hands on her jeans. She didn't look them in the eye at first but took a deep breath as if deciding just then to go forward, her back straight. She stood tall, about five foot ten, taller than both Yolanda and Sydney. She extended a hand to Yolanda.

"I'm Jack's mom, Christine Jacobs." Yolanda introduced herself. The woman then shook Sydney's hand and turned back to her son. "Honey, this is Dr. Garrett. Do you remember her?"

The boy swallowed and whispered in a hoarse voice, "The angel?"

Yolanda couldn't tell if the medication made it hard for him to speak or if he'd been intubated. His mom went over to him and caressed his forehead.

"Yes, honey. The angel." She turned to Yolanda and Sydney and explained, "He keeps talking about an angel in white who helped him. I wanted him to see you." Christine looked at the floor. "To see that it was a Black doctor who helped him."

"Thank you," Sydney said. "Does the rest of your family know that you've invited me?"

"Heavens, no. But I'm Jack's mom. I know what's best for him, not my in-laws." The resolve in her voice told them that this was only part of the battle with her in-laws. "Only Eric, my husband, knows."

Sydney turned to the boy and leaned down to greet him face-to-face.

"You're a very brave boy, Jack," she said. "Are they treating you well here?"

Jack tried to smile but seemed to have a question in his eyes.

"You can ask me anything," Sydney said. Yolanda smiled at her bedside manner.

"Will I have Grandpa's tattoos?"

"You mean the skin grafts?" Sydney asked. "I think they stay away from tattoos for that."

The boy let out a breath, relieved, and looked at his mom.

"It'll be okay," Christine said.

"They do a great job here," Sydney tried to reassure him. "Does it hurt much?"

"A little."

"You just let the nurse know when it hurts and she'll adjust the medication, okay?"

"Okay," Jack said in a quiet voice.

"Once the grafts take, you'll do some physical therapy so that you can move just like you used to. Physical therapy will be very important. Do you understand that?" When the boy nodded, she continued, "Where did they put the grafts? Do you know?"

"My side and my arm. My legs got tore up, but the skin stayed on."

"Well, there you go. You'll be walking around fine in no time. Just be sure to mind your mom and the nurses."

With that, Sydney straightened and introduced Yolanda.

"This is Yolanda. She's a private investigator and has some interesting stories for you. Yolanda, this is Jack, one of the bravest boys I know."

The boy's broad smile signaled that he'd puff up his chest if he could. But it was Yolanda's turn to look at Sydney wide-eyed. Her wife winked at her and motioned Christine for a private conversation in the corner of the room. Yolanda understood the assignment and relayed the story of another brave boy about Jack's age who helped save himself from a kidnapper. She'd really gotten into her godson Joey's call to 911 and was showing Jack how to unlock a cell phone to make an emergency call when Sydney and Christine approached. Sydney signaled that the boy might be tired, so Yolanda wrapped it up.

"Dr. Garrett?" Jack asked. "Can you tell me when I get to go home?"

"I guess you're not so tired after all," Sydney said. "Let's see, I can tell you about the next steps in your treatment if you'd like, but the doctors and nurses here will know more."

"I think he wants to talk to his angel," Christine said with a smile.

"I'm all ears," Sydney said, pulling up a chair. Turning to Yolanda, she said, "Why don't you and Christine get acquainted?"

With that, Yolanda went back to the corner of the room where Christine filled her in on her interest in seeing Sydney. The young woman spoke in a halting voice, as if she'd practiced what she wanted to say.

"Like I told Dr. Garrett, this has got to stop. I don't want Jack growing up like his grandfather and uncle. I mean, my husband is a good man, but sometimes he can't help but go along with them." She looked down and fidgeted with a silver charm bracelet.

"You mean the racism?" Yolanda asked, trying to make it easier on her.

"Yes." Christine looked up at Yolanda with the determination she'd shown earlier.

"Well, if it's any help, having you as his mother will go a long way, as far as I can tell."

"I wish it were that easy." Christine shook her head, looking around the room.

Yolanda let her gather her thoughts.

"See, Eric grew up poor. His dad and his older brother were construction workers. Eric too. His dad got hurt when Eric and Brian were kids and went on disability. Brian got hurt on the job too, a bad head injury, and now he's on disability too. I don't think Brian was as bad as his dad before he got hurt, but they spent so much time together afterward that all they did was drink beer and talk smack about the Blacks and Mexicans taking their jobs. I think they kind of resent Eric, too, because he got his contractor's license and hires mostly Mexicans." She paused as Sydney neared.

"Jack's going to sleep for a bit," she said. "Would you like to get a cup of coffee in the cafeteria?" When Christine hesitated, Sydney added, "We can bring it back here."

"Thank you. I don't want to be away from him too long. Eric can't be here to relieve me until tonight. But he has to go to a worksite early tomorrow, so I'll come back right after a shower."

On the way to the cafeteria and back, Christine relayed some of the ways she tried to avoid political conversations with her in-laws.

"I mean, they get on my case too because I work for a developer, a Mexican developer, but they're the nicest people. They told me to take all the time I need to care for Jack, and they keep paying me without me having to take family leave or vacation or sick time. My boss says we can talk about family leave when Jack's rehab schedule becomes clearer. And I think they gave Eric extra work after the accident. Brian and my mother-in-law think I should quit and do bookkeeping for Eric only. I mean, I do that on the side, but he's still building his business." She paused and shook her head, annoyed at something unspoken. "His workers are the nicest people. Some of them have been bringing homemade meals to the house. How sweet is that?" She chuckled at herself. "Heck, I think Eric likes their wives' cooking better than mine."

Yolanda thought it was good to see the exhausted woman smile.

"So, Eric is not on the same page as his parents and his brother?" Yolanda asked.

"Oh, heck no. But sometimes he goes along with the talk just to 'keep the peace,'" she said, making air quotes. "Bugs the hell out of me. I can't stand to be in the same room when they get political."

"Have they met your boss, or Eric's workers?"

"Maybe some of Eric's workers when Brian and my father-in-law used to drop by worksites to pass the time and criticize. They've never met the Garcias, but they want me to quit working for them anyway."

"Wait." Yolanda stopped when they came out of the elevator on Jack's floor. "Did you say the Garcias? As in Las Casas Builders?"

"Yes, you know them?" Christine looked surprised.

"Well, not really, but they may be involved in a case I'm working on—or at least one of them might be. I'm a private investigator. Do you know Hector Garcia?"

"Sure." Christine hesitated, looking uncomfortable. "Why do you ask?"

"Well, I think he was trying to buy some property in Boyle Heights with a friend of his." It was Yolanda's turn to hesitate, unsure how much she should reveal. When they reached Jack's room, they peeked in to see him sleeping and stayed in the hallway. "His friend was killed Thursday night."

"Oh, no!" Christine covered her mouth with her hand in genuine surprise. Her eyes darted from side to side. At first, Yolanda thought that she was trying to avoid the conversation, but then she realized that Christine was thinking, trying to remember something. "Was it the guy from Boyle Heights? I think I saw him once or twice, but I don't remember his name."

"That's the one," Yolanda said. "Frank Vásquez. You saw him with Hector?"

"Yes. Right after Hector got his real estate license. They went in to talk to my boss, but I don't know about what." She shook her head as if giving up trying to remember whatever she was trying to remember.

"Well, please let me run something by you." Yolanda waited for Christine to respond.

"Okay," she said.

"Hector and Frank were trying to buy property at Evergreen and Malabar in Boyle Heights. Does that ring a bell?"

"Not really. But there are lots of properties in the pipeline for development. Or at least a lot of properties that the company is considering for development. We have multiple projects in Boyle Heights."

"They were supposed to meet the owner on Thursday night, but they didn't show. Later that night, Frank's cousin discovered his body on the sidewalk. He'd bled out from a stab wound. The police arrested the cousin but let him go because he had a good alibi. Then they arrested the property owner, Kinji Abe. He's in jail right now, but I don't think he did it."

"You don't?"

"No, he's an old man who wouldn't hurt a fly," Yolanda said. Then, mostly to herself, "Unless it was in self-defense, I think."

"And you think Hector did it?" Christine grew more uncomfortable, fidgeting with her charm bracelet again.

"Well, I don't know, but he may have seen something."

"I...I don't think I can help," Christine said, turning to go into Jack's room.

"Please," Sydney said. "Yolanda is good at confirming information through other sources. She just needs to know where to look sometimes."

Yolanda gave her wife a grateful smile. Christine hesitated, her hand still on the door. She took a deep breath and turned to face Sydney while exhaling.

"Well," she said, letting go of the door and fidgeting with her bracelet again. After a moment, she looked up at Sydney. "I have no other idea how to repay you for saving Jack's life. That internal bleeding from the impact could have gone undetected, but you found it and stabilized him. Even the doctor here had trouble keeping it under control for a few days." Her eyes welled with tears. "He wouldn't be here if it weren't for you. I just hope the concussion doesn't do to him what Brian's head injury did to him." She looked from Sydney to Yolanda and back, then turned back to Yolanda. "You can keep me out of this?"

"I can definitely try. Like Sydney said, I just need to know where to look. So let me ask you something." She waited again for Christine to agree with a nod.

"I found an odd comment on one of Hector's social media posts. It was a post with pictures from a party in what looked like Cabo San Lucas. I think Cabo was one of the hashtags, anyway." Yolanda paused to make sure Christine understood. "The comment said something like 'I know where you got the money for that party.' It seemed odd to me, but I don't know what it means or who posted it. Someone with the handle of Know What You Did and some numbers, but I couldn't find that handle on any other social media."

Christine looked pensive for a while before her eyes widened. She looked quickly between Yolanda and Sydney.

"It makes sense to you, somehow?" Sydney asked.

"Well, I don't know if it makes sense so much as…" She paused and leaned against the wall. "Can we sit down somewhere? We can go inside Jack's room if he's still asleep."

"He'll be out for a while, from what I can tell," Sydney said before leading the three inside. "Let's just keep our voices down."

When they were all seated, Sydney on an exam stool and Yolanda and Christine in visitor chairs, they continued their conversation. Christine rubbed her thighs, hesitating, but she continued after some encouragement from Yolanda.

"I don't work with Hector, not really. I work mostly for Oscar, his older brother. Their father is kind of retired, but he still has the final say on a lot of things. Anyway, I keep the books mostly on my own since Mrs. Garcia passed away a few months ago. She worked on smaller but sometimes more complex projects like rehabs and stuff. I work on new construction. After she passed away, I got all of her accounts. I'm training the daughter, Lisa, and I've been turning some of the accounts over to her little by little. But I still have most of Hector's accounts because they're a mess. I need to clean them up before I give them to Lisa."

"Did you see any irregularities in those accounts?" Yolanda asked.

"I'll say. Some of his rehab projects had weird expenses."

"Like what?"

"Well, for some accounts, there are entertainment expenses, mostly when they're trying to get community support. I mean, sometimes they even host community people at their house in Cabo. But that's usually for new construction, not rehabs."

Yolanda bit her lip at the obvious practice of bribing community members to limit opposition to new development, but she let Christine continue.

"Anyway, Hector had a lot of entertainment expenses, but he was missing a lot of receipts too. I mean, it's a family business, but they still want receipts for anything over two hundred dollars. Hector had lots of items on the corporate card over that, a few in the thousands. Some of them into the five figures. And some of it was in company checks that his mom signed before she passed, which I don't understand." She shook her head again. "The expenses and the checks looked fishy to me."

"Did you tell anyone about it?"

"Well, not at work. I mean, I was going to tell Oscar, but he was on vacation. And then the accident happened. I still need to tell Oscar, but with Jack here…" She motioned with a hand to her son.

"Do you think Frank knew about these expenses?"

"I don't see how. I mean, he was probably at some of the parties, but I don't know if Hector told him he was expensing stuff, or how much. I don't know that he'd share that."

"Did you tell anyone else about your suspicions?"

"Well, I mentioned it to Eric. He agreed I should tell Oscar." Christine pursed her lips in disgust. "And that's another reason I want to break this cycle of hate, you know?"

"I don't understand."

"Well, my father-in-law overheard us and went off on one of his tirades. I didn't even know he was in the house, but he had come over to fix the bathroom sink and was working on some caulking without making a sound." She shook her head. "Eric asked him for help like that once in a while to make him feel useful. Eric could have done the work himself. I wish he had."

"What happened when your father-in-law overheard?"

"He went off and said he was going to make life hard for that little, spoiled, rich Mexican. Only, he used harsher terms."

"How was he going to do that?"

"I don't know, but Kyle used to get fixated on stuff, and I was afraid he was going to challenge Hector somehow."

"Kyle? Your father-in-law's name is Kyle?" Another "K" name, Yolanda thought.

"Yes, but I don't know that he'd act on it. He was more bluster than anything. Brian too. But they'd get each other spun up, you know?"

"Was Brian there too?"

"No, but I'm sure Kyle told him. We tried to calm him down, but I don't know that that's really possible."

"Do you know if Frank knew Kyle?"

"I don't know."

"Do you think Kyle was capable of blackmailing Hector?"

"What? Wait…"

Christine sat with her back straight. Her eyes narrowed in thought, shallow breathing building up to deep, rapid breaths. When Yolanda feared she might hyperventilate, Christine stood, her lips pressed tight, and her hands formed into fists before speaking.

"Are you saying that Kyle could have been blackmailing Hector and that Hector could have run him off the road?" She wasn't whispering anymore, but Jack continued to sleep. She paced up and down the small space next to Jack's bed. Sydney went to her and guided her out of the room into the hallway. Yolanda regretted upsetting the already distraught woman.

"Christine," Yolanda said, pacing up and down the hallway with her. "I don't know. I'm sorry this is so upsetting. Let's think of the timing and sequence of events, okay?"

Yolanda summarized quickly, relieved that Christine had stopped pacing. Christine had learned of the possible embezzlement by Hector, she'd mentioned it to Eric, and her father-in-law Kyle overheard her and vowed to make life difficult for Hector. How much time had elapsed between Kyle learning about Hector and the accident? Christine confirmed that it had been three days. Yolanda looked up the social media post that taunted Hector. It was two days after Kyle learned of the embezzlement and one day before the accident. Christine leaned against the wall, her face in her hands.

"That bastard," she said, barely above a whisper. "He could have killed my son." Christine's eyes went from Yolanda to Sydney and back. "Thank you. Thank you for letting me know."

"Wait," Yolanda said. "We don't know for sure that Hector did anything."

Christine looked at her slack-jawed, incredulous.

"We don't know for sure," Yolanda repeated, "but we definitely need to go to the police with this. It happened on the freeway, right? The California Highway Patrol would have jurisdiction and would control the investigation. Let's contact the CHP investigator. If you don't have a contact, I can find one."

Christine moved without a sound, in a daze, back into Jack's room to get her purse. She sat heavily on a chair, hugging her purse and staring vacantly at the floor.

"Christine," Yolanda said, kneeling at the chair to place her face in the catatonic woman's line of sight. When she got no response, she placed a gentle hand on her knee. "Christine, I'm so sorry. I don't know if this means Hector caused the accident, but I'll help you find out."

Christine stared vacantly into midspace. "Brian insisted that Kyle and Jack were run off the road," she said without emotion. "Jack can't remember the accident, so we can't confirm. And no witnesses have come forward. But Brian insisted because he said his father was too good a motorcyclist and too experienced to lose control of his bike, especially with Jack on it too. We tried to convince him that there was no conspiracy. He loves talking about conspiracies and always cites social media posts that back him up. I thought this was just another crazy conspiracy theory. I mean, accidents happen, right?" She seemed to gather herself to look from Yolanda to Sydney and back. Both nodded in agreement.

The exchange seemed to shake Christine out of her stupor. She looked down at her purse, blinking a few times before taking a deep breath and fishing inside for a business card. She offered it to Yolanda, who took a picture of it with her phone. She promised she'd contact the CHP investigator.

"Please don't mention our suspicion of Hector to anyone," Yolanda said, knowing she couldn't keep her from mentioning it to her husband. "The investigators will want to make all of the inquiries on their own." She felt like a hypocrite, knowing she'd be making her own inquiries before calling the CHP.

They thanked each other and hugged. Sydney told the woman that she'd walk Yolanda to her car but would be right back to check in with Jack's medical team. Yolanda knew she'd offer any help she could regarding Jack's recovery.

Yolanda and Sydney walked back to Yolanda's car in silence, both deep in thought. When they turned into the garage, Sydney spoke first.

"Well, that took an unexpected turn."

"I'll say. Sorry. I know this was supposed to be more about your case."

"Oh, don't worry. I'm glad we made the connection. She seemed more worried about the concussion than the skin grafts when we talked. It makes sense now. If her brother-in-law's work injury involved a serious concussion, she may associate it with his racist behavior and paranoia. Doesn't want the same for her son. Who would?"

"Were you able to allay her fears about that?"

"Well, I think so. But I think learning about your suspect is doing more on that front. Creates a distraction. Please call her after you've talked to the CHP investigator. If nothing else, she should know that someone's looking into the accident."

"I will," Yolanda said when they reached her car. They hugged for a long moment.

"Thank you, love," Sydney said. "Thank you." She gave Yolanda an extra squeeze before letting go.

But now Yolanda was really confused. What had she stepped into? Was this now a case of multiple murders? Had Kyle or Brian created the social media account to taunt Hector? Had Frank? Had any or all of them tried to blackmail Hector? Had Hector retaliated by running Kyle and Jack off the road?

In her car, she dialed José Herrera to fill him in. The defense attorney agreed about contacting the CHP investigator and asked that she keep him posted on any contact with Hector Garcia.

"I'll call the investigator after I talk to Hector," she said.

"Actually, I have a responsibility to call him now that I know this. Give me his number, and I'll call on Monday during working hours."

Yolanda did not miss the way the lawyer communicated his legal obligation. It meant she had until Monday to connect with Hector. She didn't want to wait that long anyway.

"Be careful," he said. "I don't want to tell you how to do your job, but you know you don't want to tip him off. And you don't want to become a target either."

"Don't I know it," she said. She headed to the address she'd found for Hector with no intention of becoming a target. But first, her phone rang. It was her brother.

"You'll want to see the security camera video from the house on Evergreen," Jesse said. "Come by the store and we'll walk over."

"On my way."

CHAPTER NINE

The yellow bungalow on Evergreen was on the same side of the street as the store. A four-foot-high tree trunk sat on one side of the yard. Someone had removed the bark and etched or burned an image of the Virgin of Guadalupe on the wood and polished it. In niches around the image, small vases held fresh roses, likely from the rose bushes around the makeshift grotto. Yolanda stopped to admire the artwork.

"My dad carved that years ago," a middle-aged Latina said, coming down from her porch.

"It's beautiful," Yolanda said before Jesse made the introductions, Gamaliel at his side.

Like many of her first-generation neighbors, the woman named Esperanza had lived in Boyle Heights since birth. She took care of her elderly father and, on weekdays, two grandchildren about the age of Turi and Maya's children. Her daughter dropped them off and picked them up every day. She'd been busy with her father's bedtime care on Thursday and had not seen anything until she heard the helicopter and saw the police cars and onlookers at the intersection. On Friday, she'd taken her father to a doctor's appointment.

Most importantly for Yolanda, the house had a camera that faced northeast to capture the front door and porch. It didn't capture any part of the store, but at some distance, it covered the spot where Frank had parked his car. The resolution was decent, but the distance didn't help.

"What are we seeing?"

Esperanza showed Yolanda the screen on her phone. It captured what looked like her porch and the street beyond it, Frank's car visible in the distance.

"Go ahead and play it back," Jesse said.

The woman pressed play and the video showed Frank's car parking at the curb, grainy but identifiable. A white pickup truck turned from Malabar onto Evergreen and slowed down alongside the car and stopped. Its left brake light was out. The people in the car and truck were blurry shadows, the camera unable to capture any movement inside the vehicles. After less than a minute, the truck sped off. The license plate was a blur too.

"Go ahead and fast-forward," Gamaliel said. The woman did, and Yolanda saw a man emerge from the car and cross the street.

"That's Frank," Gamaliel said. "And that's it. Frank arrives around 7:32 p.m., the truck stops alongside him, and he walks toward the store at 7:36 p.m. He doesn't go back to his car, and no one else approaches it later."

"Can you download a snapshot of the truck?" Yolanda asked the woman.

"I think so, but it's pretty blurry being so far away."

"Do you have more video that can show the truck some other day?" Yolanda asked.

"The boys asked me the same thing, but I don't pay for that service. All I have is a memory card that overwrites itself every week. We looked back to Monday and didn't see anything."

"Now forward to 8:05 p.m.," Jesse said.

The woman did, and Yolanda saw a black sedan coming south on Evergreen and turning onto Malabar. At 8:11 p.m., what appeared to be the same car turned from Malabar back onto Evergreen at a high rate of speed. She couldn't tell for sure, but it looked like the car had run the stop sign on Malabar. This tracked with what Yolanda had seen on the security video from El Tepeyac. It was a closer shot, but the lower-quality video still made it difficult to confirm the driver's identity.

"Have you shared this with the police?"

"No, but I can if it'll help."

Yolanda scrolled through her phone, looking for Detective Chan's number.

"Please AirDrop these to me and send them to this number," Yolanda said. She planned on sending them to Kinji's attorney and Celine Cueva. The assistant DA may not respond, but at least she'd have the video in case Chan and Rios ignored it.

Yolanda thanked the woman and walked back to the store with Gamaliel and Jesse.

"What do you think?" she asked. "Know anyone who has a white truck like that?"

"Turi has a white pickup," Gamaliel said, "but I think it may be older than the one in the video. That one looked pretty clean and new."

"Video cleans up images," Yolanda said. "At least, that's what the folks at the Fair Housing Coalition used to say when going after slum lords. We'll need to see if we can enhance it." She considered how much more she would owe Jane. "What I don't get is that Kinji said Frank hadn't shown. If he crossed the street to the store, did he not go in? Did he see someone on Malabar that he approached instead? Did the guy in the white truck come back around the block, or did Hector in the black car get to him first?" She didn't ask whether Kinji had, in fact, seen Frank in the store and gotten into an argument, but the men's silence told her they might be thinking the same thing. She broke the silence at the corner.

"Nice job, guys. I have another stop to make this afternoon, but let me know if the timeline rings any bells."

She walked to her car on Malabar while the two men continued to the store. As she'd expected, the sidewalk memorial for Frank had grown. Several more candles, flower bouquets, and a Roosevelt High School Rough Rider teddy bear had joined the wooden cross and candles from the previous day. When she reached for her car door, she heard a man behind her.

"Heard you were looking for me," he said, both arms crossed and leaning on his front gate. Turi was taller than Yolanda expected, given his father's height. The son was about five foot eight to the father's five foot two or three. Turi's build was similar to Gamaliel's, a bit stocky. He even sported a goatee like Gamaliel and her own brother. What was it with all the goatees all of a sudden? Yolanda couldn't think of anyone else she knew having one, but here were three guys who knew each other. You'd think at least one would want to be different.

"Yes, I have been looking for you," Yolanda said, walking across the street and extending her hand in greeting. He took it and held it while he sized her up. Yolanda let him, while she did the same.

"Arturo Luna," he said. "Turi or Art, if you'd like."

"Yolanda Ávila," she said. "Impressive sleeve." She raised her chin at his arm covered in a colorful, coiled Quetzalcoatl, the winged serpent of Mesoamerican lore. "But I guess you'd know the good tattoo artists."

"Can't do business if you have bad ones," he said. "It's not like we're hairdressers."

Yolanda couldn't think of any hairdressers with bad hair but didn't mention it.

"Would you like to come inside?" he asked.

The house seemed strangely quiet to Yolanda. No kids, no dogs, just her and Turi.

"Maya took the kids to visit her mom," he said. "My dad's walking the dogs, I think."

That explained the silence. She noted that he tried to put her at ease.

"Have a seat. Would you like some water, or a soda?"

"I'll take water, thanks," Yolanda said. It always helps to have something to drink to buy time for questions. She took her water and a seat on the couch and watched him sit on the recliner. He leaned back, comfortable in his own home.

"So, I hear you think I'm a suspect in Frank's killing." He didn't waste any time getting to the point.

"You, among others," she said.

That seemed to surprise him. He sat up, leaning forward in his chair.

"Who?"

"Can't say, but seems like you might have a good alibi in any case. What time did the event end at the Rose Bowl?"

"Around nine, I think. But I kept working until ten thirty or so. Didn't want to turn away good customers."

"I'd be interested in who else you think I should be looking at."

"So, I'm off the hook, just like that?"

Yolanda ignored his question but was glad he thought he was off the hook. Suspects who didn't see themselves as suspects tended to talk more.

"Have the detectives questioned you yet?"

"No. Why? Should they?"

"If they were any good, they would," she said. "By the way, know anyone else with a white pickup truck like yours?" Yolanda had not seen one on the street nor in the driveway, so she had to rely on Gamaliel's description.

"Mine's in the shop for new brakes and a smog check. Otherwise, I'd be at my shop. Was just gonna walk down to get it and head back to work. Can't say I know anyone else who owns a white truck, but there are lots of those around."

Yolanda had to agree. She didn't ask about his brake lights but knew she'd have to find out if the left one was out. Instead, she asked about potential enemies Frank had made, and he gave her the same response his father had. Frank was an asshole and lots of people could have had it in for him.

"Tell me something," Yolanda said. "You've known Frank since he was a kid."

"That's no secret."

"And you and your dad say he ran all kinds of schemes."

"Yeah."

"Do you know if he ever tried to extort money from anyone?"

"You mean like blackmail?"

"Yes."

"Well, let's see. I don't know about actual blackmail, but when we were kids, he was a pinche snitch. He'd get the Catholic school kids up the street in trouble if he saw them smoking. After a while, they'd give him smokes to keep him quiet. Don't know if that's really blackmail, or, what did you call it? Extortion?"

"Anything with bigger stakes as he got older?"

Turi squirmed in his seat, not quite as comfortable as he'd seemed earlier.

"Not that I can think of," he said, taking a drink of his soda.

"Why'd you guys stop being friends?"

"Stupid kid stuff," he said, waving a hand in dismissal. He leaned back in his chair again but looked intently at his black jeans and dusted off some invisible lint.

"I understand you both went to ELAC and transferred to Cal State LA at the same time. Did you drop out at the same time too?"

Turi looked at her, his jaw set at the unwelcome topic.

"That's a sore subject," he said. "That pinche guey double-crossed me. We had the same work-study job at the copy center. I came across a physics exam that a professor had left in a machine. Showed it to Frank, and right away he made a bunch of copies. Wanted to sell them to students in the class. Of course he got caught, but he dragged me into it, saying it was my idea and that I'd given him the document. Fucking coward. We both lost our work-study jobs and got suspended. Lost my scholarship too. Didn't go back because I couldn't afford it anymore."

"Frank too?"

"I don't know why he didn't go back. Probably the same reason, but it's not like school was for him anyway. So, no, I can't say he wouldn't blackmail anyone. It wouldn't surprise me if he did, though."

"What do you know about Hector Garcia?"

He jerked his head back, the change of subject surprising him.

"That cabrón?" he cursed. "Nothing good coming from him and his family with all their gentrification projects."

"Do you know him?"

"Only know that he's some pinche vendido," he said, cursing him as a sellout. "Didn't even have the sense to stop driving his Ferrari in the hood until it got egged on First Street."

"Who egged it?"

"Could've be anybody. You don't drive into Boyle Heights to do business in your Ferrari and expect to get no reaction. You ask me, that guey asked for it. Remember those limos that brought a bunch of people to some opera performance at Hollenbeck Park? Thought they could shut down the Roosevelt High School band practicing there." He shook his head. "Well, they learned you don't pull that shit here. So did Hector."

Yolanda remembered reading about the band incident. The kids drove the pop-up opera performance and audience away in their limousines when they refused to call off their band practice. She noted that Turi became more upset the more he spoke, but he took a breath and calmed himself.

"My dad thinks Hector turned Frank on to coke. Who knows. They deserved each other."

He stood to end the conversation. "Listen, I gotta go get my ride and go back to work. Saturday's my busy day, but I had to meet the damn smog check deadline. Good thing evenings are best. Tattoo social hour, and all that."

"Do you recommend your mechanic?" she asked, hoping he wouldn't recognize her fishing for his mechanic's information.

"Sure. They're pretty good. Can't say they're any better than all the others in the hood." He gave her the name of the mechanic on Cesar Chavez Avenue. She never needed one, not with her dad being a mechanic himself, managing his boss's shop on First Street.

"I can give you a ride, if you'd like." Yolanda wasn't sure why she made the offer to a murder suspect.

"Órale pues!" Turi perked up. "Thanks."

Yolanda drove them the three or four blocks to the auto repair shop across from Evergreen Cemetery. She parked in the driveway and pretended to text on her phone while she spied the white truck, noting the license plate in case Jane was able to enhance the video she'd just seen. The tailgate faced away from her, so she couldn't see the brake lights. She wondered if they'd fix a broken one when they worked on the brakes. An argument to her right drew her attention. Turi and a mechanic rushed to the tailgate. Yolanda couldn't make out what they were saying, but it sounded like someone in the shop had damaged the truck. The mechanic tried to reassure him that they'd fix it. Yolanda leaned out her window.

"Need another ride?" she asked Turi.

He gave the mechanic a few choice words and wagged his finger at him before approaching Yolanda's Jeep with his hands in his pockets, more sheepish.

"Actually, can you give me a ride to my shop? Pendejos backed my truck into some equipment and broke the taillights." He raised his arms in exasperation. "How the hell does that happen?"

"Dang, that sucks," Yolanda said, meaning it. "Hop in. I'll give you a ride to your shop." When they drove off, she tried to be subtle.

"If the taillights were in working order, make sure you get them to do the repair without charging you."

"Oh, they'll do the repair, all right," he said without addressing the prior condition of the taillights.

Yolanda didn't want to push and let it go, for now. She'd have to go back and ask the mechanic herself. She stopped to drop off Turi at his shop on First Street near the popular Eastside Luv bar and the Mariachi Plaza.

"Mind if I ask you about someone else?" she asked.

"Sure. Come on in. Have an appointment in half an hour. We can talk while I set up."

They walked into Boyle Heights Tattoo. It appeared to be a converted barbershop set up for several tattoo artists. Oldies played on a sound system, but not so loud as to inhibit conversation. Yolanda thought it might be a collective that made it affordable for each artist. A woman with two full sleeves of tattoos sat reading a comic book at a station set up for piercing. The other five stations were for tattoo artists, but only two were occupied—one woman and a man bent over their clients.

Turi greeted them, and they all responded, but the tattoo artists went right back to their work. The comic book reader's smiling eyes followed them to Turi's station. Yolanda had gotten used to reading smiles that way since the pandemic. The skill came in handy since people still masked in most Boyle Heights businesses, especially those like this one that required close-up work.

"Gimme a minute to check my stuff," Turi said. He offered her his cushioned work stool while he checked his equipment and ink. Everything was well organized, and Yolanda doubted he'd need to make any adjustments. She was right. He turned to her expectantly, leaning against the wall counter at his station.

"Shoot," he said.

"Need to pick your brain about something. The other night you were at a Harley-Davidson event. Do you ever come across customers at those events who have racist tattoos?"

"Sure, but I don't do them. Don't do any of that MAGA shit either," he said. "But most of the folks at those events are from motorcycle clubs. Pretty good vatos—around LA anyway. Only the losers ask for those tattoos, and they're mostly loners. Guess the other guys wouldn't want them in their clubs. Why?"

"Ever come across some guys named Kyle Jacobs, or Brian Jacobs?"

Turi shook his head.

"Never heard of 'em. But I don't usually get full names if people pay cash. And a lot of 'em go by other names that their carnales give 'em. What's with the Jacobs guys?"

"They're a father and son. The father, Kyle, rides—or did— but I don't know what kind of bike. Just wondered if either of them drives anything else."

"It's bikes or trucks with that crowd. Not much in between, 'cept for the rich vatos who only ride on the weekends and drive fancy cars to work during the week."

Yolanda figured she wouldn't learn anything about Kyle or Brian Jacobs from Turi but tried again.

"Kyle Jacobs had Nazi and Klan tattoos on his chest," she said. "Ever see those on anyone?"

"Seen all kinds, but those dudes don't come to me for work. What kind of images?"

"Three K's and three swastikas encircling a Confederate flag on his chest." Yolanda made a circle with her hands indicating that it would cover most of her upper chest. At least, that's what she thought Sydney had described.

"Shit. Nothing like using ink for a subtle message." Turi paused to think. Yolanda looked around the tattoo parlor and noticed the woman with the comic book now on her lap, actively listening while she gave Turi time to call up any memory.

"Wait. Did the guy have a smaller one high on his biceps, but without the flag?" He cupped his hand over his left biceps.

Yolanda looked up, hopeful that he had more information. But, dang, Sydney hadn't mentioned that. She'd have to ask her.

"Don't know, but sounds possible. I mean, how often do you see something like that?"

"Right? I remember seeing a guy like that. Came by my stand at an event out in Chino a couple of months ago. Showed up kinda early, not long after I set up. But he didn't ask for a tattoo. Just spent some time looking at this." He pointed with his thumb to the wall behind him. A large, white sheet displayed illustrations of typical line tattoos—skulls, birds, flowers, and armbands—as well as more intricate, color tattoos of Mesoamerican images and geometric designs. A few photos of portrait tattoos held pride of place, pinned to the center of the sheet. Yolanda had never considered a tattoo, but if she ever did, she'd want an artist as skilled as Turi. "He was wearing a T-shirt with the sleeves cut off. The tattoo caught my eye because most people aren't that in your face with their shit, you know? Older guy. Old tattoo. Younger guy with him had the same tattoo, but newer. That's why I remember it. Thought maybe it was some new, racist club. I was glad they walked away and didn't put their name on my wait list."

"What did the younger guy look like?" Yolanda asked.

Turi scrunched his face, thinking.

"Same beard, same kind of T-shirt with cutoff sleeves. But you see lots of those at those events. Had lots of ink too." He paused, his eyes looking upward, thinking again. "Oh, wait. Saw the younger guy at the Rose Bowl the other day. He was by himself. Didn't stop at my stand, but saw him checking out knives in the stand next door. Recognized that same tattoo with the swastikas and the three K's. But what caught my eye was a new tattoo. A truck tattoo. Thought it was weird because it looked like something a kid would want. Like one of those temporary tattoos, you know? But this guy's looked like a good artist done it."

The other tattoo artists had paused their work and now listened as well.

"What kind of truck?" Yolanda asked.

"A pickup."

"Any particular make?"

"Probably, but I didn't get that close a look. The reason I noticed it was that it popped. You don't see too many white tattoos." The other tattoo artists nodded in agreement.

"White? Are you sure?"

"Yeah, a white pickup truck. Had a black outline. Usually, guys who want to ink their rides have dark-colored cars. White ink is hard to work with. I don't usually recommend it, especially for guys. You need to do touch-ups to make sure you have full coverage. And you gotta use sunscreen to keep it from washing out, and guys aren't as good about applying it as girls." His colleagues nodded again. "This guy's will just look like a truck outline in a year or so. Probably why the artist used a black outline in the first place. Hey, you were asking about a white pickup earlier. You think this guy's truck is what you were looking for?"

"Don't know. Maybe. But thanks, man. This could be helpful."

"No worries," Turi said, waving to a woman who had walked in. "My appointment," he said to Yolanda. She thanked him and walked out, all eyes on her. She was sure they'd all talk about her questions as soon as she walked out. The barbershop vibe was unmistakable.

On her way to her car, Yolanda thought about the white truck. Was Brian Jacobs extorting Hector Garcia after learning about his possible embezzlement of the family business? What would he be doing in Boyle Heights the night Frank Vásquez was killed? Was he following Hector? Turi himself might have a good alibi with the Rose Bowl gig, but he also had several reasons to hate Frank. Was there anything redeeming about that guy? She'd focused on Brian and hadn't asked more about Hector. Was there anything redeeming about him? She was about to find out.

CHAPTER TEN

Yolanda drove to San Marino, the Beverly Hills of the San Gabriel Valley—without all the high-end shops and traffic. The old money in this bedroom community tolerated the wide avenue of Huntington Drive because the transit-dependent help had to get to them somehow. The Garcias lived north of it, the more "desirable" part of town. A quick glance at her background search app told Yolanda that Hector and Lisa lived there with their dad. The system had not yet recorded the mother's death. Oscar, the eldest son, lived with his own family in nearby San Gabriel, south of Huntington Drive. Yolanda went by both homes to rule out a white pickup truck. Trucks weren't as common in these neighborhoods as in Boyle Heights, unless you counted the gardeners.

She wondered what the old money thought of the new-moneyed Garcias and Asian families moving in. Of course, old money now went well beyond the Europeans who'd married into Mexican land grant families, who had in turn taken the land from the original Tongva-Gabrielino natives. Yolanda and Sydney had once walked through the San Gabriel Cemetery after a friend's funeral. The older tombstones reflected the names of some of the early families—the Roses, the Stonemans, and the Pattons, among others. The most famous Patton had a tombstone, but Sydney had informed her that he was buried in Arlington National Cemetery.

Yolanda parked across the wide street from a stately manor on a block where the green lawns ran all the way to the curb. She didn't find the neighborhood very inviting. Why no sidewalks? She couldn't imagine growing up in a house like this one with its dark-red, brick façade, Doric columns, and tall French windows.

A black BMW in the driveway indicated that Hector might be home. A white Mercedes in front of it meant someone else was home too, probably a good thing. Yolanda decided to approach the house before her black Jeep, the only car on the street, drew the attention of any neighbors or the San Marino police.

At the door, a young woman with dyed, jet-black hair greeted Yolanda. She wore black leggings and a loose black top that made for an odd yoga-goth aesthetic. When Yolanda asked for Hector, the woman shouted toward the back of the house.

"Hey, Hector! Someone's here to see you. My Uber's here, gotta go."

With that, the woman walked out to a silver car pulling up to the curb. Yolanda closed the door behind her. The house was quiet except for the sound of steady, electronic pinging and water dripping, accompanied by somber electronic music. Yolanda recognized the sounds of a video game that Jesse used to play. She walked toward it, through the foyer, past an ornate, oak staircase. She wasn't surprised when she heard the electronic blast of machine gun fire, grunting, and glass shattering. Beyond a modern kitchen that belied the dated exterior of the house, a young man sat on a sofa in a sunroom. He faced a large television screen and punched his thumbs into a game controller, leaning side to side as if avoiding gunfire coming at his avatar on the screen. Yolanda knocked lightly on the doorframe, then harder when he didn't respond.

"Gimme a sec," he said without looking away from the screen. She waited in the doorway until his avatar took a head shot and cartoon blood splattered all over the screen. "Aaagh!" He threw the controller on the sofa, stood, and turned to Yolanda, arched eyebrows and O-shaped lips telegraphing his surprise. He was taller than Jesse, Gamaliel, and Turi. More hormones from more meat growing up, Yolanda thought. She'd bet he ate meat more often than once or twice a week like her own family had when she was a kid. He had leisure time to hit the gym too, judging from the look of his biceps stretching the sleeves of his long-sleeved T-shirt.

"Who the hell are you?" he asked.

"Good afternoon to you too," she said, taking a step down into the sunroom, her card in hand. "My name is Yolanda Ávila. Your sister let me in. At least I think it was your sister heading out to catch an Uber."

"Oh," he said. "You looking for me?"

"Yes, you're Hector Garcia, right?"

"The one and only," he said with a smile, spreading out his arms and turning on the charm. He was a good-looking young man in his late twenties. His smile disappeared when he read Yolanda's card.

"Private investigator?"

"Yes. I'm trying to help Mr. Abe after Frank Vásquez's death. Can I ask you a bit about him and Mr. Abe?"

His breeding got the best of him, and he offered Yolanda a seat, pointing to an armchair next to the sofa, and something to drink.

"Thanks, I'll take a water, please."

He hopped up to the kitchen. He didn't skip leg days either, Yolanda thought, watching his tan calves ripple below dress shorts. He returned with a Perrier for her—of course—and a Diet Coke for himself. She would have preferred still water but thanked him and took the fizzy water instead.

"I heard what happened. So sad," he said, shaking his head while popping the tab of his soda can. He took a long drink before retaking his seat on the sofa and spreading his arms across its back. He crossed an ankle over a knee, a Reef flip-flop exposing the built-in bottle opener in its sole. Yolanda did not want to like the guy, but she noted that she had the same flip-flops, if a bit more worn.

"I understand you and Frank were scheduled to meet Mr. Abe on Thursday night."

"Frank was supposed to call me to confirm, but he never did. I figured it was off," he said, lifting a hand and letting it fall on the sofa back again.

"Did you call Mr. Abe to let him know it was off?"

"No," he said, leaning forward and focusing on the soda he now held with both hands between his knees. "It was Frank's meeting. Figured he'd do that. But don't know if he did. He was a little flaky like that. Good guy but scattered sometimes." Yolanda noted that he was the first person to call Frank a good guy. Why would he deny going by the store? Had he killed Frank? Had he found him and been too freaked out to stay and report it? People did that sometimes, but she'd bet he had more to do with Frank's death.

"How'd you guys meet?"

"At Xela's in Boyle Heights a couple of years back, I think. Before the pandemic. Went to check out the crowd for an LAFC game. My brother took our season tickets for his kid's birthday, but I wanted to watch with real fans, you know? Ever been?"

"To Xela's? Sure. Not to an LAFC game, though. Heard they have quite the fans."

"Best soccer fans in the country," he said. "Wish we had our tickets out in the North End, but Dad wanted a corporate suite." Yolanda had heard that LAFC games were quite a spectacle, but she didn't argue that she thought the newly minted Angel City games were more wholesome and family-oriented. Women's teams did not draw as much beer-splashing as men's teams. Damn, she was starting to feel old.

"So, you and Frank started hanging out after that?"

"Well, I wouldn't say hanging out, really."

"But he was trying to help you buy the Abe property."

"Well, that was more recent. When I told him I'd gotten my real estate license, he asked about commissions and stuff. Said he knew about a property that an older guy might want to offload. Went by a few times, and I thought our company might be interested in developing it. It's a good-sized corner lot."

"Did you ever speak to Mr. Abe?"

"A couple of times, but he didn't seem interested. Then, Frank said the old man was sick and might have a change of heart."

"Sick?"

"Yeah. Said his mom told him the old man had heart issues."

Yolanda thought for a moment. Kinji hadn't mentioned it, but his age would make that almost automatic, she thought.

"Know of anyone who might have it in for Frank?"

"Sure. Those anti-gentrification activists who picket our developments. One of the leaders lives across the street from the Abe property. I told Frank that would make it harder to develop."

"But you were still interested in buying it?"

"Or representing Mr. Abe if he was interested in selling. Or a buyer." He took a last drink of his soda and placed it on the coffee table, signaling the conversation was over. Yolanda sat back and sipped her Perrier.

"Tell me something, Hector. I was going through some social media accounts and came across this. What do you make of it?" They leaned toward each other to see a screenshot of the comment on his account: "I know where you got the money for that party."

"Where the f—"

"Language, mijo." A barrel-chested man with bronze skin and thinning gray hair appeared at the doorway. Yolanda and Hector both stood to greet him. He stepped down into the sunroom, his dark slacks as tight against his thighs as his white polo shirt against his chest and protruding gut.

"Hey, 'apá," Hector said, recovering. He glanced at the business card on the coffee table. "Um, this is Yolanda Ávila, a friend of Frank Vásquez." He motioned to Yolanda with one hand, then to his father with the other. "Yolanda, this is my dad, Rolando Garcia."

"My condolences," the older man said, shaking Yolanda's hand with his fingers instead of his whole hand. She didn't know why, but that always turned her off. It was like they couldn't be bothered with social graces and just went through the motions, dismissive. And Yolanda didn't like being dismissed. She straightened her back.

"Thank you. Actually, I'm a friend of his cousin," she said. "I think your son was more of a friend to Frank."

The man's eyes turned to his son, and Hector came to his side.

"She was just leaving," he said, smiling. The smile didn't reach his eyes.

"Actually, I was just getting started asking about Frank," she said. The older Garcia raised a single eyebrow at his son. Hector swallowed hard when his father motioned them back to the seating area. His father joined him on the sofa. "I'm a private investigator," Yolanda continued. "I'm helping Frank's cousin, Gamaliel Campamoche, and the owner of the store, Kinji Abe. Trying to find out more about Frank's actions before he was killed."

Hector flexed his jaw and reached for his empty soda can but didn't try taking a drink. He turned the can in his hands instead.

"Then, we must help however we can," the older Garcia said, turning to his son.

"Sure," Hector said. "That's why we're talking."

"And what did Ms. Ávila show you that upset you so much?" his father asked.

"A comment on a social media post," he said. "Nothing important, just some hater hating on one of our parties."

"May I see it?"

Yolanda leaned over to show Rolando Garcia the screenshot.

"Just some jealous hater," Hector said.

The older man looked at the post for a moment, frowning. When he looked up, his facial features relaxed, a blank expression on his face, his hands on his slacks.

"Sometimes, it's hard to have friends who don't have what we have," he said. "Envy is a terrible thing."

"Did Frank envy you?" Yolanda asked Hector. He said nothing, but tightened his lips.

"Of course he must have," his father said, answering for his son. "Probably couldn't help it. But he was always welcome in our home. Now, if you'll excuse us, we have a family gathering to attend. Please let us know if there is anything else we can do to help Frank's family."

All three stood. Damn, she hated being dismissed, but Yolanda was glad the father had shown up.

"So where did the money for that party come from?" she asked midway through the kitchen. When she turned back, she noted both Garcias frowning.

"Doesn't matter," the older man said. He opened his hands in a you-never-know gesture. Or was it a shooing gesture to get her to move along and out of their house?

Once she stepped outside, the Garcias couldn't close the door fast enough. Yolanda walked to her car, confused. What the heck was all that about? The father seemed surprised by the question in the social media post, but he wasn't going to allow any more questions of his son. And Hector didn't share anything useful after his father had stepped in. Was the father protecting the son? Did she just tip him off to Hector's embezzlement?

Yolanda sat in her car pondering these questions when a San Marino police cruiser pulled up alongside. The officer in the passenger seat rolled down the window of his spanking new police car. She'd never driven one that clean when she was in the LAPD. Yolanda lowered her own window.

"Can I help you?" she asked.

"I was just about to ask you the same," the officer said.

"This is a public street, isn't it?"

Before she could get into an argument with the officer, Yolanda saw the Garcias exit the house and get into Hector's car. Hector smirked at her before getting into the driver's seat.

"No worries, officer," she said. "I was just leaving." She turned on her ignition, and the officer waved with the back of his hand as if he couldn't be bothered before pulling away. Okay, Yolanda thought, she wouldn't want to be a rich person's bouncer either, but did everyone in this town have to be so haughty?

She pulled away from the curb, looking at the black BMW in her rearview mirror. The car headed in the opposite direction, toward San Gabriel. She drove away and made a couple of right turns before ending up back on Huntington Drive. Oscar Garcia's house was in the middle of a block not far away, so Yolanda was careful to turn onto a side street rather than drive in front of the house. From a spot near the corner, she saw Hector's car parked in front of the house. If there was a "family event" happening, it was a pretty small one. Hector's was the only car parked on the street on that block. She decided to wait to see how long they'd be and was grateful that the growing darkness would give her a bit more cover. The San Gabriel police weren't at the beck and call of its citizens like the San Marino police, but Yolanda sank low in her seat, not wanting to attract any attention. A couple of cars parked across the street gave her some hope that she wouldn't get a visit from the local cops.

While she waited, Yolanda texted Sydney to let her know she might be a while on a last-minute stakeout and not to wait for her for dinner. She'd been doing that more often than she'd like lately. Typing the text made her stomach rumble. She was glad for the protein bars she kept in her car. Even with melting chocolate, they were still good. The warm water in her water bottle was another story.

Fortunately for her and her bladder, she didn't have to wait long. Less than an hour later, Rolando and Hector Garcia walked down the driveway at a fast clip, or rather, Rolando did. Hector tried to keep up, the pretty boy charm gone. His bent head, and hands in his shorts pockets, made him look like a little boy who was in trouble. He took his hands out of his pockets to catch up to his father and get into the driver's seat. Yolanda waited a moment after they pulled away before following. There was no traffic, so she had no car to shield her from the Garcias. Even in the dark, they'd be able to make out her Jeep. Why hadn't she gotten a nondescript sedan instead? She had to let them go and swung around an adjacent street to see if they'd gone home. When she drove by the house in San Marino, sure enough, Hector's car was in the driveway again. She kept driving, thinking there was nothing more she could do there.

Yolanda decided to swing by Turi's mechanic on the way home, hoping he was as hardworking as her dad and would still be open on a Saturday.

"Este pendejo," the mechanic she'd seen with Turi said, pointing with his chin at a younger mechanic sweeping a car bay. He'd told her they were getting ready to close the shop for the day. "I drive stick," the man mimicked. The young man focused on sweeping. "Now he's going to fix the lights."

"Dígame," Yolanda said, trying to connect in Spanish. "Did both tailgate lights work on that truck before they broke? Or was one of them out."

"Quién sabe," the man said, shaking his head. "Can't tell now with the damage this muchacho caused."

Well, that was unhelpful. Yolanda thanked him and was glad he expressed no curiosity as to why she was asking. He was still upset at the cost he'd have to absorb to fix Turi's truck.

On her way home Yolanda received a notification on her phone of a voice mail on her office landline. She loved the feature. It gave her time to check voice mail and figure out if she had to do anything before returning calls. Now that most people preferred texts or email, some considered it rude to leave a voice mail. It meant the rare ones were usually important. She listened to the message.

"This is Oscar Garcia. Please call me as soon as possible…"

CHAPTER ELEVEN

Why call when you can speak in person? That was Yolanda's thought as she turned around and headed back to San Gabriel. But first she called Christine Jacobs to give her a heads-up. The woman didn't answer. Yolanda recalled Christine telling her she was going home to shower. She didn't want to leave a voice mail, but she couldn't text while driving. She figured it was best to be sure and leave a message in case Oscar called her after she met with him.

"Hi, Christine. It's Yolanda Ávila. Sorry to leave a voice mail, but thought you'd want to know that I've met with Hector and Rolando Garcia. I'm about to meet with Oscar. I didn't, and won't, tell them anything about our meeting nor about the account irregularities you found. I'm focusing on the social media post. But I'll tell Oscar Garcia that I'd check the company financials if I were him. That will lead him back to you, but it's up to you whether you want to tell him about our meeting. I won't. Hope Jack is doing okay."

Darkness enveloped the dimly lit streets in San Gabriel. Here it was an aesthetic choice, not the result of copper theft taking out streetlights. Oscar Garcia had the same build as his father, but about thirty pounds lighter. He was several years older than his brother and sister, maybe in his midforties. Yolanda thought he must be the son from a first marriage. She recalled that Christine had said Mrs. Garcia had died recently and had been a bookkeeper with the firm. Yolanda wondered if she'd been the second wife—an employee, no less. Her catty senses told her that the second Mrs. Garcia had stayed close to the office, perhaps with good reason, but what did she know?

Focus, Yolanda thought to herself. She followed Oscar to an overstuffed chair in the living room off a small foyer. Beyond the formal living room, divided by French doors, was a larger family room that looked like an addition. Unlike the well-appointed *Architectural Digest* living room with its antique end tables and tasteful home décor sconces and vases, the family room was full of children's toys around an antique chest that served as a coffee table.

"My wife is putting the kids to sleep," Oscar said. "Would you like a drink? I was just about to make myself a boulevardier."

"Ooh, that sounds lovely," Yolanda said, wondering if the house made her use the word *lovely*—not something in her regular vocabulary. But she loved a good boulevardier. "If you have mezcal, I'll have it with that instead of bourbon."

Oscar, who'd started to walk through the foyer, stopped in his tracks and turned around with a smile—not as charming as his brother's, but more genuine.

"Mezcal? I've never tried it that way. I'll give it a shot. Come on over and we'll make it how you like it."

Yolanda joined him and walked into a formal dining room with a built-in wet bar. They talked about their favorite sweet vermouths and Yolanda's preference for just a little Campari. She explained that the recipe was one of her friend Mel's secrets and that she was always trying to guess the proportions at home. She suggested he visit Las Adelitas in Highland Park. It probably wasn't his kind of place, but it didn't hurt to sound friendly. Back in the living room, they each took an overstuffed chair facing a large sofa and the front windows, their backs to the French doors and the family room. The end table between them conveniently held leather coasters embossed with a fleur-de-lis. Oscar spoke first.

"This is pretty good," he said, raising his glass to Yolanda. After Yolanda raised her own glass in response, he continued, "My father and my brother say you paid them a visit today."

Yolanda savored the first sip of her perfectly balanced cocktail before answering. Maybe she'd finally gotten the proportions right: An ounce and a half of mezcal, three-quarters of an ounce of sweet vermouth, and a quarter ounce of Campari.

"I did, indeed, pay them a visit." What was it with her speech in this house? Indeed? Really? "Did they say what they were concerned about?" It was better to be the one asking the questions than having to answer them.

"They said you are investigating the death of one of Hector's friends. Is he a suspect?"

"You tell me. Should he be?"

"I don't see any reason why."

"Would blackmail be a good reason?"

"Blackmail? Blackmail over what?"

"Mr. Garcia," Yolanda said, putting down her drink.

"Oscar. Please."

"Oscar, in my business, when you come across a taunt like the one on Hector's social media post, you are well-advised to look into the finances of the person being taunted. If they find that threatening, it's generally a good idea to dig deeper. Your brother seemed a bit spooked. And your dad seemed protective of him. Worried, but protective."

"I like that you cut to the chase, Ms. Ávila."

"Yolanda. Please."

"Yolanda, then. My brother was my stepmother's favorite."

Bingo, Yolanda thought. Second wife, indeed.

"Got my dad to give him more leeway than he ever gave me. But tell me, what am I really looking at here? What do you know?"

"I don't know much other than that your brother and his friend were supposed to meet a property owner together. Your brother may have been seen in the area, and his friend shows up dead of a stab wound. Then I find that comment on one of his social media posts. What would you think?"

"Is that all you have?" Oscar put down his own drink and leaned back in his chair. He drew his hands together, his fingertips touching, his brow furrowed in thought. To Yolanda he seemed like a serious businessman trying to figure out what kind of mess his brother had created.

"There may be more, but I'm not at liberty to say. How involved is your brother in the family business?"

"It's more like a hobby to him. Not something he takes seriously." Oscar flipped his hand as if to shoo away the thought of taking his brother seriously and took his rocks glass again.

"Listen, I can't tell you how to run your business, but I'd look into any financials having to do with your brother if I were you. Tell me something else." Yolanda waited for him to look up from his drink. "Did your brother do cocaine?"

"I don't know," he said, pausing a moment. "But I wouldn't be surprised. Do you think he's after money for drugs?"

"Don't know. But his friend may have been into cocaine." Yolanda looked at the man dropping his shoulders. Was that in resignation of trouble from his brother? "And his friend likely could not afford a habit."

"Damn it." He lifted his glass to his lips then put it back on the coaster as if he'd lost his taste for it.

Yolanda, for her part, savored another sip of her own. Both sat in silence, Yolanda giving him all the time he needed to say anything else. She'd taken another sip before Oscar finally spoke again.

"My brother is not a killer," he said. "He may have gotten himself into a mess, and I'll check his accounts, but he's just a spoiled kid who's always had everything handed to him. Dad made him get rid of that ridiculous Ferrari after my stepmother passed. Can't do business in poor neighborhoods flaunting a car like that. She covered for him in the office, and maybe now that she's gone, he's in over his head. But he's no killer."

Yolanda let that sit. Blackmail can make people do unpredictable things, she thought. Oscar downed his drink and stood.

"Thank you for sharing this information with me." He stood and extended his hand, making Yolanda stand to take it, but not before she took a final sip as well. She pulled out a card to hand to Oscar.

"Can you keep me posted and let me know if you see any irregularities in Hector's accounts? Anything he could have been blackmailed for?"

"I can't promise that," Oscar said, thinking. He collected himself and turned to walk Yolanda out. At least he'd admitted that blood may be thick enough to cover for his brother.

At her car, Yolanda's stomach gurgled. She hadn't had much to eat all day and didn't feel like having another protein bar. Didn't go with the cocktail she still savored in her mouth. She'd stop for tacos on the way home. Taco truck tacos were more nutritious than protein bars, according to her brother.

Yolanda headed back down Huntington Drive, stopping at the first taco truck in El Sereno, the first neighborhood within the Los Angeles city limit. Neither San Marino nor South Pasadena would dare allow them on their streets. She got extra tacos in case Sydney wanted some, but she couldn't help herself and ate one in the car before heading home with the rest. The fresh onion, cilantro, and tender meat replaced the taste of the cocktail. She considered her next steps while turning onto Monterey Road and up Via Marisol. The steep street was named after the daughter of the councilman who'd expedited city permits for development of multiple condominium buildings on her hill. It was a good thing her townhouse complex had dealt with landfill subsidence well before she'd bought her own.

Yolanda climbed up the wide arc of the hill. It seemed darker than usual. Had copper thieves hit the streetlights here too? She slowed to study the light posts to her right for signs of broken bases. The dry grass on the slope beyond did not reflect any light.

She heard it before she felt it. Crunching, screeching metal. She tried looking to her left but felt herself thrown sideways in her car. All she could see was the white blur of inflating airbags. She felt her chest compressed by a tightening seat belt and panicked at the continuing screech of metal on metal, then the sensation of tumbling down the embankment.

The Jeep came to a stop on its side, Yolanda on the bottom. She closed her eyes, trying to control her breathing, but she smelled gasoline. She had to get out. She grasped at her seat belt, tried to find the release, but her fingers felt like the hot dog fingers in that crazy movie. Why couldn't she undo the seat belt? A man's voice carried over the buzzing in her ears.

"You okay? Gotta get you out! Gonna break the windshield."

At the same time that her fingers finally found the seat belt release, the already smashed windshield collapsed like wet paper. She could make out a man with a long, dark beard. Two women stood at a distance. One of them appeared to be on her phone. Yolanda tried reaching out to the man with both arms, but her left arm wouldn't budge. By the time she realized she was lying on it, the man had reached in, pulling her right arm while removing the seat belt over her head. She tried to lift herself up, but her legs weren't cooperating. Was she paralyzed? A new wave of panic swept over her. The man managed to roll her onto his back and carried her a few yards, placing her gently on the ground next to one of the women. Yolanda glanced back at her car and saw it propped up against a tree before it burst into flames. It was the last thing she saw before passing out, wondering why her clothes smelled of onion and cilantro.

CHAPTER TWELVE

When she came to, Yolanda pushed away smelling salts, still in a daze. Her left arm was killing her, but at least she could feel it. She couldn't say the same for her legs. She tried wiggling her toes but wasn't sure if she was getting anywhere when she felt a sharp pain up her legs to her lower back. Damn, that hurt. But at least she could feel the pain.

"Ma'am, we're gonna immobilize you," she heard a paramedic say. She glanced toward his silhouette. Beyond him she saw water dripping from the tree that had stopped her car. What was that onion smell? Before she could ponder it any longer, she heard Sydney's voice.

"Stop! Let me check her before you move her."

Yolanda turned to the voice.

"I'm a doctor. She's my wife."

Yolanda tried to smile at Sydney but couldn't see her clearly in the darkness. She saw her face come and go with the flashing lights. Sydney knelt beside her, and Yolanda puckered her lips, thinking she was going in for a kiss. But Sydney was all business, running her palms over her wife's body.

"Broken left arm," Sydney said to the paramedics. Then she turned to Yolanda. "I'm here, love. Any pain or numbness in your legs?"

"Both. My back too. Please tell me I'm not paralyzed."

Sydney's face didn't look optimistic, but she tried to smile and asked Yolanda to try rotating her ankles.

"They work," Sydney said, relief in her voice. "But the paramedics need to immobilize you to make sure. They're going to put you on a board and then a gurney and get you to the hospital. I'll go with you," she said. Then, she shouted to the paramedics. "Cold packs!"

Yolanda's panic subsided. She knew she was in good hands with Sydney. Her forearm hurt like hell, but she was worried about her legs. She bent both slightly at the knee before one of the paramedics tied them down to a board and lifted her onto a gurney, Sydney at her side. A woman came up to Sydney and gave her a cell phone.

"This flew out of the car," she said, pointing up the hill.

"Are you the one who called me?" Sydney asked.

"Yes," the woman said. "We found her driver's license in the phone wallet. She had a sticker listing you as her emergency contact on the back. I should do that too."

"Thank god," Sydney said. She hugged the woman. "Thank you so much. And, yes, I'm an ER doctor. I can tell you it's a good idea to do that." She'd been the one who'd suggested it to Yolanda after her last incident requiring a trip to the hospital. She exchanged contact information with the woman and the man Yolanda now recognized as the one who'd pulled her out of her car.

"Thank you," Yolanda called out before the paramedics placed her in an ambulance. Sydney ran toward her and hopped into the ambulance before it drove away. Then she was Dr. Garrett again.

"Let me check your eyes," she said, blinding Yolanda with a pen light.

"Which hospital, Doc?" a paramedic asked.

"County," Sydney said.

"Wait. Not your hospital?" Yolanda asked.

"They'll have more immediate emergency care for spinal injuries at County," Sydney said. "Just in case you have one," she added. "Try to relax."

"How can I relax with that news?" Yolanda said. She closed her eyes at her wife's raised eyebrow.

At the hospital, one flurry of activity followed another. She was wheeled through hallways, placed on tables with lots of machinery, and in and out of an emergency room bay. Yolanda barely kept track of it all. She felt woozy. Had they given her pain medication? She would have been more alarmed had Sydney not been by her side the entire time. The Sydney shouting orders to the paramedics had settled into the Sydney she knew. Back in the emergency room bay, Yolanda noted the difference.

"That was some take-charge, kick-ass shit with the paramedics." She tried winking at her wife, but it must have come off as if she had something in her eye because Sydney did not respond. "Why so quiet now?"

"You're my wife," Sydney said, looking her in the eye and squeezing her hand. "I wouldn't let a spouse call the shots in my ER either. But don't worry, I'm on top of it."

"Never a doubt. But thought maybe it meant bad news for a while there."

Sydney smiled at that and squeezed Yolanda's hand again. "You know, you really should stop trying to interpret my silence."

"Then don't be. Silent, I mean."

"Fair enough. How about I fill you in on your condition?"

"Perfect."

Sydney ran down the numerous tests they had run on Yolanda. Her left arm had broken in two places, but with fractures that should heal well. Her back X-ray showed a small herniation in one disc that could be treated with physical therapy and rest. Lots of rest. But her back and leg muscles had tensed so much during the impact that she'd need muscle relaxants to unfreeze them. And, again, rest. Lots of rest.

"But I have to get to Kinji Abe tomorrow afternoon," Yolanda insisted.

"Love, your body has been through significant trauma. If

you interfere with your recuperation, you'll only make it worse."

"Do I have a concussion?"

"No."

"Are they keeping me overnight?"

"No, unfortunately. Staying here is probably the only way to get you to rest."

"What if I promise to not do anything until tomorrow afternoon?"

Sydney gave her a side-eye and shook her head, but she didn't say no.

"Okay, I promise. I'm going to nap now. Wake me up when I get to go home."

Sydney leaned over and gave Yolanda a quick kiss on the forehead before raising the blanket over her shoulders and leaving to check in with the medical staff. Where did she get such a warm blanket? Yolanda smiled to herself and tried to sleep. When Sydney returned, she gave Yolanda her clothes and helped her dress.

"What is with this onion smell?" Yolanda asked, sniffing the shirt she wore over her T-shirt. She thought better of it and asked Sydney to help her remove the shirt. She'd go home in her T-shirt instead. Then it came to her: She'd woken up at 3:23 a.m. smelling onions. *Shit, the juju's back and as useless as ever.* She should have remembered the dream when she got the tacos. She would have been more vigilant, more aware of her surroundings, maybe alert enough to avoid being rammed and pushed over an embankment. Damn. She needed to focus more and start paying attention to her dreams again, but for the moment she tried to put it out of her mind, grateful that she hadn't suffered greater injury.

Sydney agreed when Yolanda shared these thoughts with her.

Later that night, Yolanda woke up in a panic, drenched in sweat, feeling pressure on her chest. The sensation went away when she opened her eyes and drew in a deep breath. She would have felt relief, but her body felt like she'd been hit by a truck. Then she recalled her accident. She had been hit, probably by a truck. Her eyes opened wider at the thought that it might not have been an accident at all, but a targeted hit. She recognized that she was in her bedroom but had no recollection of getting there. She glanced at Sydney, who breathed rhythmically, then at the alarm clock. At least it wasn't 3:23 a.m. Meant it wasn't a warning dream, she thought before trying to sleep again.

CHAPTER THIRTEEN

Sunday

Yolanda woke again, feeling groggy. The weight of her cast reminded her someone had run her off the road. Who'd done that? She looked around, recognizing her bedroom, then at the alarm clock. Almost 10:00 a.m. Had she really slept that long? The pain all over her body kept her from dwelling on that. So much pain—some of it a dull ache, but some of it sharp and biting. Even her toenails hurt, but at least she could feel them. Sydney walked in with a tray, but Yolanda was in no mood for breakfast. And what was with the orange juice? She never drank orange juice. Too much sugar.

"Did you drug me so I'd sleep?"

"I didn't give you anything. The nurse gave you something in the emergency room and you knocked out. You were somewhat lucid on the way home. I should have recorded you."

"What did I say?"

"You kept repeating something about a white truck, about having to find the white truck. You kept asking about some Hector guy too. Kept saying, 'Gotta find Hector.' Then you kept listing other names: Turi, T, Brian."

"Dang." Yolanda made to sit up but groaned instead.

"Need help getting to the restroom?"

"I think I'm okay if I roll to my right," she said, trying to make the move look smooth and failing. "This cast is bulky."

"Not bad," Sydney said when Yolanda had sat up. "But let me help you stand up. Do it slowly so you don't get dizzy and lose your balance."

"I'm okay," Yolanda said. "Let me try on my own first." She hoped she looked steadier than she felt. She made it to the restroom and left the door open as instructed. She counted her blessings that it was not her dominant hand in the cast. When she looked at herself in the mirror, she thought she looked okay, if a little loopy, her spiky hair pointing in all directions between flat spots. A growling stomach signaled more hunger than she'd felt a few minutes ago, and she thought that was a good sign. Sydney heard it too and suggested her wife get back in bed and eat from the tray she'd brought.

After Yolanda took a few bites of her breakfast burrito, Sydney laughed.

"I can make you another, if you'd like."

Yolanda paused midbite and looked at the small morsel left in her hand.

"Dish might pothebly be da besh huevo con chorizo I have ever had." She smiled with her mouth full.

"If you say so." Sydney laughed again.

The Mexican sausage had been banned from Yolanda's diet when her cholesterol rose. Before popping the last bite into her mouth, she smiled at her wife.

"Aww, you love me. You really love me"

"I do. But don't get used to the chorizo. Looks like you are recovering better than I thought you would. How are the body aches?"

"Achy. But not too bad, Doc." Yolanda downed her orange juice and felt like a new woman. "Dang, did you put something in the OJ? I feel great! Achy, but great."

"Might be a sugar rush, but if you didn't admit to being achy, I'd be concerned. Glad you feel better. You'll be sore for a few days. And you'll have to watch your back. No heavy lifting, no running. We should get you to the chiropractor soon to start some therapy for that herniated disc."

"I'm glad you're not one of those MDs who doesn't believe in chiropractic," Yolanda said, wiping her mouth with a paper napkin. She started to stand up with the tray, but a back spasm stopped her.

"See? No twisting either. Some anti-inflammatories will help for a while, but you should use a wrap-around brace so that you don't accidentally strain that herniation. Got one for you at the hospital." She reached for it on the nightstand. "Here, let's put it on."

"Got it. Thanks. And thanks for breakfast, love."

Sydney watched Yolanda stand with some caution and helped her wrap the brace under her shirt.

"Okay, so if I can get down the stairs, can I go see Kinji Abe at the jail?"

"Really? You are impossible."

"Please?"

Sydney had picked up the breakfast tray but put it back down and walked ahead of Yolanda down the stairs. She managed to get down slowly.

"Okay, now I'll go back up. A shower should help, right?"

"It should, but if you use hot water, you may increase the inflammation."

"I'll use lukewarm or cool water. How about that?"

Sydney watched her go back up the stairs. It seemed to Yolanda that going up was easier than going down. Sydney came up and helped her undress and wrap the cast in a plastic bag to keep it from getting wet. Cold water triggered muscle spasms. Lukewarm felt best. After a quick shower, Yolanda felt even better and said so. Sydney reluctantly agreed to let her see Mr. Abe but insisted on driving her there for her appointment later that afternoon. Yolanda didn't have a choice with her car wrecked. She probably couldn't get a rental until the next day anyway. Good car insurance was a small blessing. She now considered it another blessing that she hadn't been able to get an early visitor slot to see Kinji. It gave her time to call José Herrera and update him on the latest developments: her meetings with the Garcias, the new video from the house on Evergreen, and the hit-and-run.

"Yolanda, I told you to be careful for a reason," the attorney said. "This is great stuff for Mr. Abe's defense, but I'd rather you stayed alive."

"Me too, believe me."

"I'm going to call the CHP investigator with the latest. I'm concerned that this Hector guy may be escalating things."

"Good idea. I'll call Christine Jacobs and let her know. And I'll keep you posted on anything that comes up in my meeting with Kinji."

Yolanda dialed Christine while pacing. Walking felt better than sitting and was the movement that hurt the least at the moment.

After Yolanda told her that Mr. Herrera was trying the CHP investigator, the woman expressed gratitude and hoped they'd be able to reach him.

"There's something else, Christine. I was hit by a car last night. My Jeep was."

"What? Are you okay?"

"I am. My car's not. But it was a hit-and-run. I didn't see the car, but it had to have been a big one because it pushed me down an embankment near my home."

"Oh, no. You sure you're okay?"

"Just a broken arm and very sore muscles, but I'm okay."

"Do you think it was Hector?"

"No idea, but I'll need to check on the security cameras in the area. It'll involve some legwork." Yolanda knew she had to track down the LAPD officer looking into the hit-and-run but called Celine Cueva first. She tried her on her personal cell phone but didn't get an answer. Before Yolanda could dwell on whether the assistant DA was ignoring her calls, she tried texting her. It was a long text with more information on the meetings with the Garcias and the hit-and-run. A few seconds after she hit send, her phone rang. It was Oscar Garcia.

"Hector's dead," he said. "And my father thinks you may have had something to do with it."

"What are you talking about? What do you mean, 'Hector's dead'? How?"

"Who else did you tell about your suspicions, Ms. Ávila?"

So, it was Ms. Ávila again?

"Wait, Oscar. Tell me what happened."

"I don't know. Some kind of drive-by shooting, but my father and I don't think it was random or a mistake. He was targeted."

"Where?"

"Eagle Rock. Colorado Boulevard and Figueroa, near the entrance to the 134 freeway. I'm asking you again, who else held your suspicions?"

"Oscar, someone rammed into my car and sent me down an embankment near my place last night. I'm banged up but alive thanks to a neighbor who pulled me out of my car before it blew up. What time was Hector shot? And where was he before then?"

"What are you intimating, Ms. Ávila?"

"Oscar, I'm sorry for your loss, but I'm not intimating anything. I'm definitely suggesting that Hector could have had sufficient motive to come after me after I suggested you look into his finances."

"I'm sorry you were in an accident," he said, not sounding like he meant it. "But my brother was obviously targeted."

"What time did this happen?"

"Sometime around nine last night. He'd texted our sister to bring his car to him someplace in Highland Park, and…"

"Wait. He wasn't driving his own car?"

"No. Not before he was shot."

"Was your sister with him? Is she okay?"

"He dropped her off at some bar in Eagle Rock. She Ubered home. May be why he was on his way to the freeway. My family would like your help getting to the bottom of it."

"I would too, but first I'd like to know if he had anything to do with my attempted murder," she said and ended the call. Yolanda's hands shook, triggering a back spasm. She leaned against the kitchen counter, rattled. What the hell did this mean? She paced again, faster this time, but she needed some fresh air. She went out on the deck and paced some more, drawing Sydney's attention.

"You okay?" she called from the living room.

"Sure, just need some fresh air." Yolanda stopped pacing and took some deep breaths before calling José Herrera again. She filled him in on Oscar Garcia's call.

"I'll call the CHP investigator again," the attorney said. "They should connect these cases, the Jacobs' motorcycle accident, your rollover, and the Hector Garcia shooting. Let me have your LAPD contact as soon as you have one for your case. But we also need to figure out how they all connect to Frank Vásquez. More law enforcement eyes usually help, but sometimes they get in the way. My client is Mr. Abe. He's the one we have to exonerate. Any chance you can check on Frank's online activity to see if he was blackmailing Hector Garcia?"

"That was going to be my next step after checking in with Kinji this afternoon," she said, suddenly exhausted again. "But I gotta find out what Hector was driving earlier, and if it shows any signs of a collision with my car. Will call you with any developments."

She wasn't sure she was up to it, but she did have some time before heading over to the Twin Towers jail to see Kinji. She also considered enlisting Jane in this effort now, instead of waiting to see her in the office tomorrow. She went to lie on the couch for what she thought was a few minutes. She relayed the calls to Sydney and promptly dozed off. An hour later, she startled awake from a disturbing dream reliving her car tumbling down the hill, but this time she was in a white truck. Checking her watch, she sat up faster than she should have, triggering her back and glute to spasm. Once she caught her breath, she turned to Sydney, who sat in her chair typing on her laptop.

"Why didn't you wake me?"

"You need rest," she said, closing her computer.

"Well, we still have plenty of time before going to County," Yolanda said, glancing at her watch again.

"You ever consider that your 'County' and my 'County' are very different facilities?" Sydney smiled.

"I'm glad you can smile at that, but have you ever wondered how similar the tragedies are at both?"

"Touché."

Yolanda sat still, staring into midspace, thinking.

"What's the matter?" Sydney asked. When Yolanda didn't respond, she added, "I mean, besides nearly being killed while trying to track down a killer."

"Doesn't make sense," Yolanda said, almost talking to herself. "I get that Hector may be mad at me, but now I wonder if Brian Jacobs would have any reason to go after me too. I don't think so, but I need to find out. Oh, and hey, I just remembered. I think Turi—the tattoo artist—may have come across Brian and his father. Do you know if Kyle Jacobs had a tattoo on his biceps similar to the one on his chest?"

"Don't remember. I was focused on his injuries and the kid's." Sydney looked at Yolanda as if asking *What are you thinking?*

"Hmm." Yolanda's mind was going a mile a minute. "I think we should talk to Christine and maybe Eric about Brian. He's the most likely suspect going after Hector."

"Can you call them?"

"I'd rather do it in person. Can we go down to Children's Hospital now? It's Sunday. Maybe we can catch both of them there." Yolanda knew that her wife wouldn't leave her side this early in her recovery.

Sydney sighed but stood to help her wife stand as well. Yolanda suspected Sydney was interested in seeing her former patient again anyway. On their way to the hospital, Sydney took a call from her own ER, sending a pang of guilt through her wife. Damn, Yolanda thought, here she is, sacrificing her own work. Again. She had to stop letting this happen, but she wasn't sure how. After giving instructions to a resident and ending her call, Sydney explained that little Jack should be released soon but would need lots of rehab and pain management. His concussion and internal bleeding had resolved, but the skin grafts would take time to heal and would likely need more surgeries as he grew.

"Poor kid," Sydney said. "But it looks like his mom is all in. And the staff there is great with follow-up on skin grafts."

When they arrived at the hospital, they donned their masks, but Yolanda realized that they normally wouldn't be allowed in under the Covid protocols. Sydney wasn't wearing her white coat this time, but as soon as she pulled out her work lanyard showing she was a doctor, they waved her in. At Jack's room, Christine looked as tired as before, but her posture seemed more relaxed in a visitor chair. A man in jeans and a very white T-shirt sat next to her and their sleeping son. What Yolanda could see of a nicely trimmed beard behind a mask reminded her of Kinji's, only this one was a mixture of black, brown, and strawberry blond, darker than his full head of mostly strawberry-blond hair. After Christine introduced him as her husband, Eric walked up to Sydney and wrapped her in a warm embrace.

When he shook Yolanda's hand, she had the sudden thought that he might have as much of a motive for hurting Hector as Brian did. She hoped he wasn't involved but made sure to observe him just the same. After Yolanda assured them that she was fine after her accident, Christine told her she'd have to show her cast to Jack when he woke up.

"Just heard that Jack will be going home as soon as tomorrow," Christine said with a bright smile. That explained her more relaxed demeanor.

"That's great!" Sydney and Yolanda said, genuinely happy for the family.

"So, what brings you back?" Christine asked. "Any word from the CHP investigator?"

"Not yet," Yolanda said. "Sorry we didn't call in advance, but there's other news. Right after we spoke on the phone, Oscar Garcia called me. He said Hector had been killed in a drive-by shooting in Eagle Rock." Surprising someone with news like that generally ensured genuine reactions from guilty and innocent alike. She watched as they dropped their jaws in unison.

"I don't have the details yet, but it appears he was heading toward the 134 freeway, probably heading home. We're trying to get ahold of the investigator on that case too."

Nothing about Eric's reaction told her he knew or was in any way involved, but she knew she'd have to reserve judgment until she knew more.

"That's crazy," Christine said, shaking her head. "Did they catch the shooter?"

"Now we'll never know if Hector caused the accident," Eric said, turning to look at his son. He turned back to Yolanda, his eyes pleading for more answers. Her heart went out to him, to his family, but she had to ask some sensitive questions.

"I don't have any more information," she said, thinking the shooter probably got away on the freeway. "I was wondering, though, if you knew where Brian was last night." The husband and wife turned to each other. Sydney raised an eyebrow at Yolanda's lack of preamble, but Yolanda gave her a look that said *I know what I'm doing.*

The Jacobs couple continued to look at each other until Eric took a deep breath. He turned to Yolanda.

"Brian called last night. He never calls, but he called and was very chatty. Not like him at all. Turns out he wanted to borrow money."

"What time was this? And what did he say?"

"Sometime after you called me about your meetings with the Garcias," Christine said.

Yolanda raised her eyes, thinking. That would have been around 7:00 p.m., Eric continued for the couple.

"He started by saying he just wanted to know how we were doing. How Jack was doing. He wanted to talk to him, but I told him he was asleep. Said something about a lead on a job in East LA. Said a friend told him about it and that he was checking it out for me."

"Brian doesn't have any friends," Christine said. "It was weird."

"Did he say where in East LA? And was he at the site?"

"He said something about Boyle Heights and that he was there if I wanted to check it out with him." Eric shook his head like it still didn't make sense to him. "Said he'd been before and thought he'd swing by again. Near Evergreen Cemetery."

Yolanda perked up at that. She wondered if Brian had been trying to set up an alibi, maybe near Kinji's property.

"Does Brian own a gun, by any chance?"

"He doesn't," Eric said, "but my dad had a rifle and a handgun, I think a Glock. They used to go to the range together all the time. Dad was big on gun safety. I can't imagine Brian using them outside of the shooting range." He turned to look at his son. "But if he shot Hector, maybe he did us all a favor."

"Eric…" Christine said, placing a hand on her husband's arm and shaking her head in disapproval. Yolanda let it go.

"Does he drive a white pickup truck?"

"He does," Eric said, turning back to Yolanda. "Did someone see one near the shooting?"

"I don't know, but there was one seen near where Hector's friend was killed. Do you know if one of his taillights might be out?"

"Yeah," Eric said. Then, more slowly, "But I think he's having it fixed."

Bingo, Yolanda thought. Christine and Eric glanced at each other again before Eric continued.

"He mentioned last night that our mom was on him about it, but he said it wasn't a simple fuse thing and was probably a defect and that he'd have to take it into the dealer this week. Asked to borrow money for it if they charged him. I thought that's what the call was really about. But it's a new truck, so I just told him to let me know. I'm sure the dealer would be good for it."

"Still don't know how he paid for that truck if he's asking to borrow money," Christine said. "He mostly drove Kyle's truck anyway."

"When did he get it?"

Eric thought about it and looked to Christine for confirmation.

"Maybe a week before the accident?"

"Sounds about right," Christine said. "With Kyle gone, he might run into problems with car payments now."

Not if he paid cash, Yolanda thought. Especially not if Hector provided the money in exchange for his silence about the embezzlement. But she went back to Christine's comment.

"What kind of truck did Kyle drive?"

"Well, an old red SUV, actually," Christine said. "A Suburban. It's as big as a truck. But Kyle preferred his motorcycle."

Well, that doesn't help, Yolanda thought, but she made note of the two trucks in case either of them came up in surveillance video near the shooting, or near her accident.

Jack stirred in his bed, and his parents and Sydney went to him, leaving Yolanda with her thoughts. She leaned forward, her right elbow resting on the cast and sling. The timing seemed to fit. But if Brian Jacobs was the guy who stopped by Frank's car on Thursday night, was Brian involved in Frank's death? Had Frank been present when Brian squeezed Hector? Was he looking for Hector for more money? Or had Brian and Frank colluded to extort Hector? Had Brian eliminated Frank to keep payments from Hector himself? With Hector and Frank both dead now, they might never know. Had Brian killed both, or had Hector killed Frank before Brian killed Hector in revenge for his father's death? It was all enough to make her head spin. She leaned back in the visitor chair while the others busied themselves with the boy.

Sydney looked over to her with concern in her eyes. Yolanda gave her a thumbs-up, and her wife turned back to Jack and asked him if he wanted to see Yolanda's cast. The boy nodded eagerly. Yolanda stood to oblige him, thinking the poor kid must be bored.

"Will you sign it for me? You'd be the first," she said, removing the arm sling.

"Sure!" The boy tried to sit up but stopped with a wince.

"Whoa," Eric said. "Let's go slow." Jack tried to sit up again, this time with slower movements. The adults in the room cheered his progress. Yolanda was glad he'd be released soon. Christine grabbed a marker from a food tray that contained coloring books as well as math and writing workbooks.

"Just my name?" Jack asked, looking up at Yolanda.

"You can draw anything you'd like," she said, squatting down to rest the cast on a tray table and give the boy a better angle to work with his left hand. Sydney saw her trying not to bend her back and rolled over the exam stool so that Yolanda could sit. Yolanda gave her wife's arm a grateful squeeze and turned back to the boy. "Ah, good thing you're left-handed," she said. "I'm right-handed, so a cast on my left isn't too bad. The bandage on your right won't keep you from using your left hand, so that should help you get around better, just like me."

Her attempt to cheer up the boy seemed to work. He smiled before focusing on his drawing, his tongue sticking out in concentration. It was a kid's drawing, but it clearly depicted the outline of a pickup truck.

"Uncle Brian's truck," the boy said, a proud grin on his face. "He gave me a ride when he bought it. Said he's getting a tattoo of it too. Can't wait to go for another ride. Safer than a motorcycle, right, Mom?" He turned to his mom with a serious face. Yolanda couldn't help but think of the trauma he'd experienced and what it would take to overcome it. A healthy fear of motorcycles was probably not a bad thing. Christine's quick nod in agreement with her son told Yolanda that she probably thought the same. The adults all praised the boy's drawing, but Yolanda was glad it would be covered up by the arm sling.

She needed to know more about Hector's shooting before she could pin it on Brian Jacobs, and before she could confirm whether he or Hector had rammed into her. Maybe Oscar Garcia had calmed down by now and could help.

CHAPTER FOURTEEN

"This case is getting bigger and bigger," Yolanda said to Sydney on their way to her car, "and I'm not sure I'm getting any closer to solving Frank Vásquez's murder."

"Well, I hope Mr. Abe can shed more light on that. Maybe you are out of danger if someone else got to that Hector guy. But I hope he wasn't the target. I don't think you need more to investigate right now."

"I agree," Yolanda said, glancing at her watch, "but we have more time. How about we go see Oscar Garcia? He may know more about his brother's accident if he's been in touch with the first responders."

"Are you sure you're up to it?"

"Sure," Yolanda said, straightening her back before bending to get into Sydney's car. The painkillers seemed to be doing their job. "I want to call Gamaliel too. Let's go."

On their way to San Gabriel, Yolanda called Gamaliel on speaker.

"You know that white truck we saw in the video from the house on Evergreen?"

"Yeah."

"Just learned about a guy who bought one recently but who drove an old red SUV before then. Ever see anyone driving something like that getting together with Frank?"

"Hmm." Gamaliel paused to think. "Saw a red Suburban last night and maybe about a month ago. First time I saw it, a white dude with a beard was talking to Frank outside the store. Noticed them only because he drove up with a noisy engine, like it needed oil or something. Suburbans will last forever, but you gotta take care of them. And Saturday night, when we were closing, I heard a really loud engine and looked around the corner. That same Suburban was making a three-point turn on Malabar to head up Evergreen. He stopped across the street, and I thought he might be looking for Frank, so I started to walk over, but he drove off. I yelled after him, but he was on his phone and probably couldn't hear me over his engine."

"Anything you can tell me about him? Did you get a good look?"

"Not really. He never got out of the car. But I think he had blond hair and a darker beard. Don't see too many white people around here unless they're going up to El Tepeyac for lunch, but both times it was after dark, so the blond hair kinda stood out."

"Could you tell if he was wearing a sleeveless T-shirt?" Yolanda asked, thinking of Turi's description of the man she suspected was Brian Jacobs.

"Sorry, don't remember. But maybe. When I saw him with Frank they fist-bumped before he drove away. I don't remember any long-sleeve shirt, though. Why? Who is he? You think he went after Frank?"

"Don't know. Just trying to piece things together, but the guy may have been blackmailing Hector. Now I wonder if Frank was in on it too."

"Holy shit. Who is he?"

"A guy whose sister-in-law worked with Hector."

"What was he blackmailing him for? The cocaine stuff? No one really cares about that unless he was selling. And if he was, that's some dangerous shit to blackmail someone for."

"I was thinking embezzlement, but the drug angle is definitely something worth considering. Thanks for the info. I'll keep digging, but you should know that Hector was killed in a drive-by up in Eagle Rock last night. I'm wondering if the guy you describe has anything to do with it."

"Oh, shit."

"Please let me know if you see him around again. And stay away from him if you do."

"Damn. What was he doing around here last night?"

"I'm thinking he was trying to establish an alibi for the shooting. Be careful, okay?"

Yolanda hadn't thought of a drug dealer angle but considered it could be another possibility. Gamaliel was right—blackmailing a drug dealer was dangerous business. However, she wasn't sure Frank would blackmail Hector for that and lose his cocaine supply. And she wasn't sure that Hector would be a dealer either. Still, she knew she couldn't rule it out. Desperate people did desperate things, but her money was on the blackmail over embezzlement angle. It tied in Brian Jacobs more neatly.

But what did it mean that Frank Vásquez and Brian Jacobs knew each other? Had they shared information about Hector other than information on possible embezzlement? Did Brian give Frank a cut of the blackmail proceeds to keep tabs on Hector? With both Frank and Hector dead now, she may never know that either.

When Yolanda and Sydney arrived at Oscar Garcia's house, they ran into a woman who rushed a preschooler and a preteen into a Lexus SUV in the driveway.

"Are you Yolanda Ávila?" the harried woman asked, pulling stray hair behind her ear, the rest of it in a rushed ponytail. For a moment, Yolanda wondered if the woman in jeans was the kids' nanny. She wouldn't have expected Oscar Garcia's wife to leave the house dressed so casually, without makeup. But when she looked closer, she noticed a wedding ring with a huge diamond. "I'm Eva Garcia. Oscar's wife."

Yolanda introduced Sydney, and both expressed condolences.

"Thanks," Eva said with a frown, a touch of annoyance in her voice. Yolanda wasn't sure if it meant she was in a rush or didn't care much for her now deceased brother-in-law.

"Is Oscar home?" she asked.

"The family's getting together at my father-in-law's," she said. "He's over there now. I should get going too."

"I hope they don't mind a visit from me," Yolanda said.

"Might be a good distraction," the woman offered. After confirming that Yolanda knew the address, Eva drove off.

Yolanda wasn't looking forward to seeing the entire family, especially the father, but she didn't have any choice. She needed to find out where Hector had been last night, what he was driving, and what he was up to before the shooting. She tried to hide her growing exhaustion walking back to Sydney's car.

"You're starting to look tired," Sydney said. So much for hiding it.

"I'm good," Yolanda lied. "At least I'm not any more sore than this morning. Moving around helps." She tried doing a jig before getting into the car and regretted it immediately. "When do I get to take another pill?" she asked, moving more slowly into her seat.

"Not for a few hours. Maybe after you see Mr. Abe, assuming you're up to it after visiting this family. Before then if it's really bad. Tell me about the Garcias."

A younger Yolanda would have taken the change of subject as avoidance of a conversation about meds, but she knew now that Sydney always wanted to help. She wouldn't advocate against an early dose if Yolanda really needed it. And she wouldn't try to stop her from taking it if she wanted to.

Yolanda filled her wife in on the Garcias: Rolando's activist history, the company's focus on low-income housing, and their steady rise to market-rate housing when the real estate market took off. She shared her thoughts on his children and the likelihood of a second marriage explaining the age difference between Oscar and the younger Hector and Lisa. She mentioned that she hoped to catch the immediate family alone but wasn't sure she'd be able to, not with the obvious number of visitors. Unlike her last visit, several cars parked along the curb on both sides of the street. Sydney had to park down the block. When they walked back to the Garcia house, Sydney let out a low whistle.

"Some digs," she said. Yolanda agreed. They made their way to the open front door. Oscar's preschooler hung onto the doorknobs, swinging with the door. Eva Garcia rushed from beyond the foyer to her son.

"Oh," she said, seeing Yolanda and Sydney approaching the front step. "Come on in." She held the door to let them enter. They donned their masks in anticipation of the crowd inside while the woman grabbed her son's arm. "Rolando, your grandpa won't be happy if you break his door." The boy named after his grandfather stood and ran into the house while his mother closed the door. "No running," she called after him before turning to the two women. "Sorry. You'll want to see my husband, I take it. Why don't you wait in here, away from the crowd?" She indicated a door off the foyer and let them in before heading to the low buzz of conversations in the kitchen and other parts of the house.

Neither Yolanda nor Sydney said a word. They both stared around the interior of the room, a beautiful home office and library, done up with cherry-wood paneling. Yolanda walked past a coffee table framed by two leather armchairs and a matching love seat. She admired a large cherry-wood desk. Sydney walked to the bookshelves lining one of the walls from floor to ceiling. Yolanda went to her and looked over her shoulder, recognizing books she'd read in Chicano Studies courses and others that she didn't recognize but assumed covered similar subjects. Those and the Howard Zinn and the Angela Davis books seemed out of place here, but the James Baldwin hardbacks elicited some grace from Yolanda, even if they looked untouched.

On another wall, old textbooks filled the lower shelves. The upper shelves held fiction by Frank Villaseñor, Julia Alvarez, Richard Rodríguez, Isabel Allende, and Yolanda's favorite, Carlos Ruiz Zafón. Those and a smattering of other popular fiction made the formal office seem a little more homey. Yolanda thought the textbooks might belong to the Garcia children. She looked around the room and tried to imagine herself studying in this space, a far cry from the Formica-topped tables where she and her brother had done their homework. Both women turned when the door opened.

Oscar Garcia entered with a tray of Perrier and what Yolanda assumed was a bottle of still water, accompanied by four highball glasses. If he'd been dressed in something more formal than chinos and a polo shirt, he could have been taken for a butler. The tray had taken some time to put together, Yolanda thought. She welcomed what she interpreted as an invitation to talk for a while. After introductions, and expressions of condolences, Oscar spread out his arms, indicating the women should sit wherever they'd like. Sydney chose an armchair and extended her arm toward the other one, suggesting to Yolanda that it would be more comfortable than the love seat in her condition.

Oscar asked after her injuries while he poured still water for them and a bubbly water for himself. He took leather coasters from a wooden box on the coffee table and placed two on the small side table between the women. Yolanda noted the fleur-de-lis embossed on the coasters, similar to the ones in Oscar's home. He placed his own glass on a coaster on the coffee table. They confirmed their vaccinations, but Sydney suggested it might be prudent to stay masked given the family gathering. Oscar agreed.

"Thank you for coming," he said. "Sorry I was short with you on the phone."

"I'm sorry I was short too," Yolanda said.

"I hope you can help us figure out what happened."

"And I hope you can do the same," Yolanda said. "Please tell me what you know about the shooting. Have you heard anything from the first responders?"

"LAPD has the case. They think it was gang-related, maybe mistaken identity because Hector was in no gang. But they think all drive-bys are gang-related. We know it's not—not after hearing from you yesterday. And now I don't know if it's connected to his friend's murder or some other trouble he got himself into."

Yolanda noted that he seemed calmer than he had on the phone. Time to think and reflect would do that. So would being in shock.

"Tell me what happened," she said.

The man shook his head. He continued, almost as if talking to himself.

"My dad called around midnight. The LAPD had called him because the BMW was registered in his name, and Hector had listed him as his emergency contact in his wallet. I picked up my dad and we headed out there. The coroner took forever, so Hector was still in the car. They had a plastic sheet over the driver's side." Oscar paused and shook his head, staring at his water before continuing, "They wouldn't let us approach him, not until they called me over to identify the body." He cringed and shook his head at the memory. "Clean shot to the head." He shook his head again and turned his face up toward the ceiling, his eyes shut, trying not to cry.

Yolanda felt for him but let him continue. He cleared his throat before he did.

"The car had run into the building on the corner. There weren't any skid marks, so at least it looks like he died instantly."

"I'm so sorry," Yolanda said. "Did the cops say anything about any suspects or any video nearby?"

"Just that they'd need to canvas the area for that."

Yolanda reached for her water and took a drink to give herself time to think. Brian Jacobs could have been in the vicinity. She'd need to connect with LAPD Homicide and suggest looking for a white pickup truck or a red SUV, but she didn't think she could share this with Oscar without discussing her conversations with Christine and Eric. Something told her she should keep them out of this. They all looked up when the door opened. A grieving, angry, maskless Rolando Garcia walked straight toward Yolanda, pointing an accusatory finger at her.

"You! Who else did you talk to? Who else did you tell Hector was stealing money?"

"Dad," Oscar said, coming to his side and putting an arm around him. He tried to steer him toward the love seat. Yolanda and Sydney stood but did not step away from their chairs.

"This woman has something to do with Hector's accident." The older man continued to point at Yolanda. She wondered why he'd called it an accident.

"Dad, let's sit." The younger Garcia calmed his father, rubbing his arm and guiding him to the love seat. "She's going to help us find out what happened." Rolando looked at his son, frowning in confusion while his son continued to soothe. "Let's sit." When they did, Yolanda and Sydney sat as well.

Rolando looked from Yolanda to Sydney as if seeing them for the first time. The man seemed to be in greater shock than his son. His gaze landed on Sydney.

"Are you with the police?"

"No," his son said. "This is Sydney Garrett. She's Ms. Ávila's wife. As you can see, Ms. Ávila has been in an accident herself." Yolanda lifted her cast but said nothing, letting it register with the older man.

"What?" he asked, still confused. "You were in an accident too? Same as Hector?"

"No," Yolanda said. "Separate accident, earlier last night. I was run off the road, but I couldn't see the car that hit me."

"But you lived." Rolando seemed to come to his senses, taking in the information before turning to his son. "She lived. My Hector didn't." Oscar held his father in a one-armed hug and squeezed.

"She may be able to help us find out what happened, Dad. She's a private investigator. Remember?"

"Of course," the man said, but Yolanda wasn't sure he remembered, not in his state. The way Oscar talked to his father made her think the man may have memory issues, but she didn't ask. Instead, she focused on the accident.

"Do you have the LAPD detective's information? Maybe I can make contact."

"Yes," Oscar said, reaching for his wallet. Sydney came to his side to take a card and showed it to Yolanda, who snapped a picture with her phone. Sydney returned the card, her eyes on the older man.

"Hector's gone," he said, a vacant look coming over his face.

Sydney bent to say something in Oscar's ear.

"That might be a good idea," Oscar said. He turned to his father. "Dad, Sydney's a doctor. She's going to talk to you a bit, okay?"

Oscar and Sydney switched places. Rolando Garcia gave her a blank stare. She introduced herself and he automatically shook her hand. She held his with both of hers while she talked to him. Oscar whispered to Yolanda.

"The stress is getting to him, but sitting here is better than being with the crowd back there." He gestured with his thumb toward the back of the house. "Too much stimulation."

"Is he okay?"

"Early-onset Alzheimer's. Kinda comes and goes. He's mostly okay, but it gets bad with lots of stress. I shouldn't have taken him to the scene last night. When he forgets, we tell him it was an accident." Oscar looked at his father with empathy. Yolanda felt for him. His father was a very different man today than the one she'd seen the day before.

"I'm sorry," she said. "That's a lot to shoulder." She meant it. Sydney's mom had looked after her own mother with dementia for several years. Yolanda and Sydney relieved her whenever they could, but, even with a team of caregivers, the work was daunting. Whatever she thought of their business practices, this was still a family that cared for each other.

"Thanks," Oscar said, tearing his eyes away from Sydney and his father in deep conversation. "Do you think you can help figure out who killed my brother?"

"I don't know, but I can try." She looked at the photo of the detective's business card on her phone. Carrie Lan. Yolanda recalled that Detective Lan had helped her once and hoped she would help again. She was glad that Rios hadn't caught this case. "Any chance I can talk to your sister?"

Oscar looked surprised for a second but stood and told her he'd go get her. While he was gone, Yolanda observed Sydney and Rolando. They seemed to have established a rapport, but no longer held hands. His vacant look was gone, and he seemed calmer, if still a bit disoriented. When his daughter entered ahead of her brother, Rolando smiled broadly.

"Mija! Come meet this nice lady. She knows all about Angela Davis. Did you know Angela Davis grew up almost neighbors with Condoleezza Rice in Birmingham, Alabama?"

Lisa, dressed in black goth, glanced at her brother, who gave her a knowing look before the young woman introduced herself to Sydney, then Yolanda. Oscar turned to his sister.

"She has some questions for you," he said. "Why don't we move over here?" He walked toward the desk and the women followed, leaving Sydney and Rolando on the small sofa. Yolanda welcomed the chance to stand and walk. She felt Sydney's eyes on her, monitoring her gait.

Yolanda leaned on the end of the large desk while brother and sister stood facing her.

"Oscar tells me that Hector asked you to take his car to him in Highland Park. Can you tell me where and what time?"

"Like I told the detective, a bar on Fig near Avenue 60," Lisa said. "Sometime after eight. Why?"

Yolanda ignored the question, thinking the young woman had overdone her makeup.

"Do you know what he drove to get there?"

Lisa looked from Yolanda to her brother as if to say, *Duh*, but she turned back to Yolanda when Oscar pointed his chin at the investigator, urging his sister to respond.

"He wasn't driving anything. That's why he asked me to take him his car."

"Do you know how he got there?"

"Uber, I guess." The woman turned up her palms in another *Duh* gesture. Yolanda ignored it.

"How did he seem when you saw him?"

"Like, what do you mean?"

"Like, was he agitated? Calm? Same as usual? Different?"

The woman frowned, thinking.

"Now that you mention it, his hands were shaking a little. But he seemed the same otherwise." She looked a question at her brother, who looked back to Yolanda.

"Did he get like that when he did cocaine?"

"No." Lisa looked back at her brother again. "What is this?"

"Answer the questions," Oscar said. "She's trying to help."

"He couldn't sit still when he did cocaine, but I don't know if his hands shook. He seemed calm last night. Maybe a little pissed. Maybe he got dumped. Whatever it was, he didn't wanna talk about it."

"By the way, did he deal in cocaine, or just use it?"

"What?" The woman frowned and scrunched her nose as if smelling something bad at the thought of her brother dealing cocaine. "Look, he used. Who doesn't? But he wouldn't be so stupid as to sell the stuff."

Yolanda wasn't so sure but didn't respond. She changed the subject instead.

"Did he say where he'd been?"

"No. He didn't say much."

"Which bar, by the way?"

"Some dive called Las Adelitas."

Yolanda tried to contain her excitement, keeping her voice even. If Hector had walked or driven down from her hill after ramming her car, the first bar he'd get to on Figueroa Street would be Mel's. She'd have to go talk to Mel and Brissa. They'd be happy with the "dive" comment. To them, the term meant a welcoming place for regulars, not trendy like other bars that came and went. Mel thought trendy meant temporary.

"What happened after that?"

Lisa described the much cooler bar Hector drove her to in Eagle Rock. Hector had said he was going home. She Ubered home herself.

"Did you happen to see a white pickup truck, or a red SUV, anywhere near you when you met Hector?"

"I don't think so." Lisa frowned again, thinking, but she shook her head. Then, looking at Yolanda's cast, she asked, "What happened to you?"

"Someone rammed into me and ran me off the road up the hill from that bar where you met your brother."

The young woman's jaw dropped. She looked from Yolanda to her brother and back. Oscar frowned and shook his head slightly.

"So, you still think it was him?" he asked.

"Yes," Yolanda said without hesitation. "I still need to talk to the LAPD investigator, but it would help if we knew what else he may have been driving if not his BMW."

"But wait," Lisa said, glancing faster between the two. "Hector's the one who got killed. Why do you think he had anything to do with your accident?"

"You picked him up after my accident but before he was shot. I told your dad and Oscar about some things Hector may have been doing that would have gotten him in trouble. He maybe didn't like me looking into those things."

"What are you talking about?" Lisa said. "I mean, the cocaine, okay, but that's not something to kill over."

"How about embezzlement?" Oscar said. He filled in his sister on Yolanda's suspicions.

"Wait. Like, is that why Christine hasn't given me his accounts yet?" She turned back to Yolanda.

"I wouldn't know about that," Yolanda lied. "But tell me something else. Do you know if anyone was bothering him? Asking him for money? Was he associating with anyone he normally wouldn't associate with?"

Lisa thought some more, bringing a finger to her mouth. She tapped her lower teeth with a black-polished fingernail. After a moment, she answered.

"Well, I don't know if it's all that odd, but a few weeks ago a man came to the office saying he was Christine's brother-in-law. I was going to get her, but he said he actually wanted to talk to Hector. I was, like, 'Okay, whatever.' But when Hector saw him, he rushed him out of the office. I asked him about it when he came back, but he just said he was working on a business lead with him. I didn't think anything of it. He got leads all over the place, so it never came up again."

"Do you remember when that was?"

"I don't know. Maybe like three weeks ago? A month? I don't remember."

"This is all very helpful," Yolanda said, thinking the timeline aligned with Christine's father-in-law overhearing her concerns about Hector's accounts. She'd have to mention it to Detective Lan. "Thank you." She looked at Oscar. "Do you know if Hector rented cars anywhere?"

Oscar and Lisa shook their heads. Yolanda was disappointed that she might not be able to prove Hector had run her off the road, but at least she had a lead on a connection between Brian and Hector. She looked at her watch and realized she had to hurry to get to Kinji Abe. Yolanda and Sydney said their goodbyes, and Sydney promised the bemused Rolando Garcia that she'd return to chat some more.

On their way out, Yolanda considered what this could mean. If Brian Jacobs was blackmailing Hector, he could have spotted him with Frank and approached Frank to keep tabs on his friend, maybe give him a cut. If Hector gave Brian enough to buy a new truck, he may have given him enough to pay Frank for information to squeeze him some more. The fist-bump Gamaliel described meant Frank and Brian were at least cordial. Had something come up? Had Brian tried to cut Frank off from his share? Had Frank refused to turn on his friend? If Brian had gone after Hector, what happened? Had Hector's cash dried up? Had it dawned on Brian that the person who ran his father off the road could have been Hector? Had it been Hector?

She'd have to come back to all of that. Right now, she needed to speak with Kinji and see if she could get him to share what he had discussed with the LAPD before he'd been arrested. She needed to know what else Rios might have on the elderly man.

CHAPTER FIFTEEN

They moved as fast as Yolanda could without triggering more pain. On their way to the county jail, Yolanda's phone buzzed. Her friend Clara's caller ID came up on the screen. That meant she might have news from the morgue.

"Hey, mujer," Yolanda said in greeting. "I'm with Sydney. Putting you on speaker."

"Hey. Hey, Syd. Got a call from my buddy at the morgue. Don't have much, and he says this is all still preliminary, but looks like the cause of death for the grocery store guy may have been a cut and tear to his aorta, near the right clavicle. They're thinking the cut barely nicked the aorta because they couldn't see a clean cut like the one they saw on the skin. They think further irritation from rubbing, and maybe running, caused it to tear. That's not an official finding, just my friend's assessment. The victim would not have been able to avoid bleeding out. And this is more speculation, but they think a blade sliced from directly in front and maybe slightly below. Means it was possibly by someone shorter than the victim, but they can't tell if the attacker would have been right- or left-handed. And this isn't official either, but his guess is that, if the person were right-handed, it could be a defensive move. If the person were left-handed, it could be a more aggressive, offensive move. But that's just a guess on his part, and they wouldn't testify to that or put it in a report. He also says the cops are looking at fibers on the victim's clothing and body. Probably routine. They don't have the blood test results to confirm drugs yet, but I hope this helps."

"Thanks. You never know if the information may be helpful down the line."

"No problem," Clara said. "See you Friday at Mel's." They ended the call.

Yolanda didn't wait to call Kinji's attorney but stopped when Sydney put a hand on her knee.

"You know," she said, "that sounded like a lot of speculation to me. Clara's friend is playing detective. Be careful with that info."

"Got it," Yolanda said. She called the attorney.

"Wait," José Herrera said after receiving Clara's information. "This could be very helpful. Mr. Abe is a tall man. What? Six two, six three? How tall was the victim?"

"I don't know for sure, but if he was as tall as his cousin, he'd be closer to five-eight or five-nine. I'll find out. But, José, my wife's a doctor. Her take is that Clara's friend may be playing detective because that was a lot of speculation." She turned to her wife, who focused on looking for a parking spot near the jail.

"Got it, but it can still help in trial. Also, Mr. Abe told me something about giving his throw blanket to, let's see…" Yolanda heard paper rustling, probably José looking through his notes.

"Gamaliel. Yes, I think I remember something like that too," she said.

"Yes, to cover the body of the victim. Do you know if he did? That would explain fibers from Mr. Abe's clothes, maybe even his hair, on the victim. We'll need to know if he placed the blanket on him."

"I'll find out from Gamaliel. Will talk to you after I meet with Kinji."

When they parked, Yolanda reminded Sydney that she wouldn't be able to go in with her under the Covid restrictions.

"That's probably a good thing," Sydney said. "I'll walk you in and come back and wait in the car. I just hope you get enough information to end this case sooner than later."

"Me too, love. Me too."

In the visitor room, Yolanda watched Kinji Abe approach his chair with a slow gait. Yolanda wondered if he was taller than Clara's friend suspected but had to remind herself that speculation by a worker at the morgue did not amount to evidence. She also wondered if her own gait looked like Kinji's. His upright posture, now bent, made him look like a very different man than when they'd first met. The dark circles under his eyes had grown darker. She hoped he wasn't being mistreated or bullied by other prisoners. She noted that his orange prison overalls looked as neat on him as his civilian clothes had at the grocery store, even with newly hunched shoulders. He just had a way about him, she supposed. His tired look seemed to brighten when he saw her.

"Good afternoon," he said with a small smile. "Thanks for visiting." His eyes stopped at her cast. Concern etched across his face, deepening wrinkles Yolanda had not noticed before. "Are you okay?"

"Oh, just a minor fracture," Yolanda said, looking at her arm. "Nothing serious." She hoped the rest of her looked okay and wouldn't be too distracting for the elderly man. "Kinji, I'm so sorry you're in here. Are they treating you well?"

"They don't treat anyone well here, but I'm okay," he said with a wave of his hand. "What happened to you?"

"Slipped in the shower. Kinda embarrassing. Can we not talk about it?" Yolanda hoped her white lie would help him refocus. She also hoped her face didn't register her back pain.

"Okay," he said, frowning. He asked about Gumer and Gamaliel. Yolanda gave him an update, informing him that everyone was worried about him and knew he was innocent. Then she focused the conversation on him.

"Are they making special accommodations for you given your age?"

"That would require them to have special accommodations," he said with a slight laugh. "But don't worry about me. Saw two guys from the hood last night. Guero and Chicali. They were never very good car thieves. They made sure the others didn't bother me."

Yolanda breathed a sigh of relief.

"That's good to hear. But hopefully we can get you out soon. I know you spoke with Mr. Herrera, the attorney Gamaliel got for you. He said you asked him about what the cops know, but he really needs to know what you told the cops at the store if he's going to defend you. No detail is too insignificant. Can you go over the conversation with me?"

Kinji looked off to the side, distracted.

"Kinji?"

"Gamaliel really shouldn't have bothered with an attorney."

"No, Kinji, we need to get you out of here and find out who killed Frank."

Kinji turned pensive but said nothing.

"You do want to go home, don't you?"

"You know, I'm an old man. I've lived a good life. And I don't have much more to go, so if I stay here, or another prison, I'm okay with that."

Yolanda did not disguise her surprise.

"Wait, what are you saying? You can't do time for what someone else did, and I'm going to help you get out. We already have some leads on a couple of other suspects." She paused. "Or is there something you're not telling me?" Why would this man not be eager to get out if he was innocent? "We just need to know what the cops have on you so that we can fight back. We need to know what you discussed with them."

Kinji stared into space, pensive again before responding.

"You know, my brother did time too. Our parents would die all over again from the shame of knowing I'm in here." Kinji shook his head, his eyes downcast. "Masaru's imprisonment nearly killed them more than it did him."

"Your brother died in prison?"

"No, but his spirit did."

Yolanda waited for him to continue. She wasn't sure how to approach his change in demeanor from the last time they'd met.

"He was older than me. Got drafted at the Heart Mountain concentration camp. I was just a kid, but now that I think of it, so was he. He was one of the boys who ended up in Leavenworth and on some island prison up in Washington. Only a few of them left. Some consider them heroes now, but not like the Go For Broke guys who signed up and kicked ass in Europe. Those guys were badass. My brother and those other boys resisted the draft as long as any of us Japanese Americans remained imprisoned in the camps. But back then, and for a long time after, it was a real source of shame. Even after President Truman pardoned them. The shame was pretty intense. So much so that Masaru moved up to the Bay Area, away from our family, to spare our parents." Kinji shook his head again. "Damn, what he must have gone through. The prison was probably not as bad as what all of us put him through." He slammed his fist on the table, drawing the attention of a deputy who went about his business once he saw that it was an older inmate. "Shit, I was such a stupid kid, falling for all the traitor and coward talk. I wanted to be just like him until the day he refused to respond to the draft notice. It was even worse when he ended up getting arrested and put on trial. I was too young, and too dumb, to know he was standing up against injustice."

Yolanda recalled reading something about the Heart Mountain resisters on a trip to Manzanar back when the only vacations she and Sydney could afford were road trips. They'd stopped there on their way to a campsite near Mammoth, a much more affordable trip in the summer than during the winter ski season. They'd never met anyone close to the young resisters, but, after that visit, they understood why they were called concentration camps, much to the chagrin of Americans who thought the term applied only to the Nazis. Their first reaction had been anger at the mass incarceration of more than 120,000 people for no reason other than their ethnicity. Their next reaction had been to admire the indefatigable spirit of the

Japanese Americans prisoners. It had not escaped them that the political rhetoric of that time so closely mirrored that of the present, with fascism alive and well in national politics.

"Kinji, are you telling me that you staying here is somehow making up for what your brother went through? You don't need to suffer like he did to make up for whatever happened in the past."

"No, it's not that." Kinji paused before continuing, "But it doesn't make any difference anymore. I can handle this place." Then he snorted an ironic laugh again. "Heck, Guero and Chicali even want to give me my own placa. You know, a gang name. El Samurai, they say. But that hits too close to home. You know, my dad claimed to be a descendant of samurai. That's why he kept the swords. But all his talk about samurai honor is part of what drove my brother away. God, how he must have suffered. Losing his freedom, then his family, and I suspect, a good amount of his pride too. No, Yolanda, pride is something even this place can't take away. I'll be fine here or wherever they end up putting me. Shikata ga nai."

"What does that mean?"

"It can't be helped. Can't do anything about it. Don't dwell on it. Used to piss me off when my parents said it about my brother, but it made sense at the camps. You can't erase life, but you can choose how to deal with it. When it can't be helped, you just move on."

His fatalism stunned Yolanda.

"Wait, this is crazy talk. You did not kill Frank, and we have to find out who did! Or am I missing something?"

"Listen, I'll talk to the lawyer again at my arraignment tomorrow. Maybe get some leniency for self-defense, or old age, or something."

Yolanda was more confused than ever. She shook her head, not believing what she was hearing.

"Okay, let's just stop a moment. Tell me what the cops say they have on you that makes you think you can't beat the charge."

"It's pretty cut-and-dried. I have no alibi. The sword had blood on it."

"Gamaliel told me of a time years ago when Frank cut himself. Could the blood be from back then?"

Kinji cocked his head to the side as if trying to remember.

"I'd almost forgotten about that." He turned pensive again. "I cleaned the sword pretty well back then. And I definitely didn't use bleach on the hilt." Kinji looked directly at Yolanda now. "Can you believe it? Bleach!" Then he seemed to pull back as if forgetting himself. "And I'm the only one who handled the swords. That's it."

Yolanda caught his misstep.

"Wait. Are you telling me the cops say someone cleaned the sword with bleach but it's not something you would use?"

"No. Well, maybe."

"Kinji, you're a bad liar. Who are you covering for? And why?"

"I'm not covering for anyone. Just let me talk to the lawyer, and don't worry about any more investigation. Tell Gamaliel I'll be okay."

"Time's up!" The guard approached to take Kinji back to what Yolanda hoped was a safe cell instead of the open, dangerous holding area. He left a befuddled Yolanda alone with her thoughts. What was going on here? Why would Kinji be willing to take the rap? Unless maybe Gamaliel was indeed guilty and Kinji was trying to cover for him. She couldn't bring herself to believe he'd do that for T, or Turi, or Hector, or anyone else, for that matter. Or…wait. Maybe one other person.

Yolanda could not leave the Twin Towers fast enough. She hobbled as fast as she could to Sydney's car, trying not to trigger another back spasm.

"We gotta go to my nina's," Yolanda said, speaking over Sydney's question about how the visit had gone.

"Hold up. Slow down. What happened?"

Yolanda relayed the conversation with Kinji while giving Sydney directions to her godmother's house. They zipped around the MTA tower and the old Denny's on their way to the Fourth Street bridge before turning onto Soto Street and stopping at a familiar yellow duplex across from Hollenbeck Junior High. Yolanda knocked on the back door that everyone treated as the front door, Sydney at her side.

"Ay vengo," Nina Mercedes shouted from somewhere inside. She unbolted the door and opened it enough to see who it was. Yolanda saw a huge smile of recognition come across a face framed in white hair.

"Mija!" Nina Mercedes said, closing the door again to undo the chain lock.

A part of Yolanda was glad that her godmother, her nina, took care to be safe at home. Another part of her wished she'd hurry.

"Ven aquí," Nina Mercedes said, wiping her hands on one of her ever-present smock aprons. She opened her arms wide to welcome Yolanda with a full-body embrace.

"Buenas tardes," Yolanda said, savoring the embrace. Her nina gave the best hugs.

"Y esto?" she asked, laying a gentle hand on Yolanda's cast. "Oh, you too, Sydney," she said, noticing her for the first time. "How good to see you, too." Nina Mercedes enveloped Sydney in a warm hug as well.

"You can take off the masks, if you want," the older woman said.

"That's okay," Sydney said, considering the older woman's age. "Better to be safe."

Yolanda smelled something steaming on the stove, even through the mask. It could be a tea or some medicinal potion for all she knew. Her curandera godmother used all kinds of herbs to help heal people of their physical, and sometimes spiritual, ills.

"What is this?" Nina Mercedes asked again, motioning to the cast and giving Yolanda a once-over with her eyes—a quick exam, Yolanda thought. The twinkle in her eyes never left her face, but the intense focus made Yolanda squirm.

"It was just a small accident," Yolanda said. "I'm okay. I don't need any healing today, just some information."

"Okay, sit. Sit," her godmother said, a doubtful frown on her face. She pulled out two of the four chairs at the small kitchen table and motioned them to sit. She smiled, again seemingly happy for the company, but the worried look on her face did not completely go away. "What kind of accident?" Nina Mercedes asked, pointing at the cast with her chin.

"A car accident, but believe me, I look much better than my car."

That did not seem to allay her godmother's concerns, so Sydney gave it a try.

"Two small fractures that should heal well," she said. "She'll be good as new in no time." She smiled, patting Yolanda's shoulder.

Who is this woman? Yolanda thought, appreciating Sydney's attempt to put her godmother at ease. It seemed to work.

"Okay, but let me get you a pomada," Nina Mercedes said. "A car accident means your muscles are sore. They will be sore for a while."

Yolanda could not refuse the offer, knowing from experience that her nina's ointments worked miracles. Her godmother ambled to the dining room where Yolanda knew she kept her potions and lotions on shelves next to a treatment bed. Next to that, her mother's picture sat among others on an altar. The ache in her chest felt a bit duller than it used to at the thought of her mother, but it was still there. She knew she'd visit the altar before leaving.

While she waited for her godmother to return, Yolanda took in the retro kitchen with its white O'Keefe Merritt stove and Felix the Cat clock. It wasn't designed to be retro as much as it was simply well-preserved. Yolanda had spent many days doing homework at this very table, its Formica top now covered with an embroidered tablecloth and a clear plastic covering. The avocado-green phone on the wall had long ago been replaced by a digital phone, but it remained on the wall because it matched the green refrigerator that could probably use updating as well. Everything was otherwise pristine, if a little worn.

"Aqui tienes," Nina Mercedes said, returning to the kitchen and handing her what looked like a waxy, off-white cream in a small glass jar with a mayonnaise lid. The only way not to confuse the two was the fact that the label had been removed. Yolanda knew better than to ask what was in it or risk having her godmother and Sydney get into a very detailed discussion of all the ingredients and their medicinal properties. But she was grateful for her godmother's medicine and said so. In her experience, it always worked better than anything from a pharmacy.

Nina Mercedes smiled, happy to be of assistance. She turned to the refrigerator and pulled out a pitcher of her signature cucumber limeade, pouring each of them a glass. Yolanda couldn't resist the fresh, sweet scent and took a quick sip before putting the glass down.

"Okay, so what kind of information do you need?" Nina Mercedes asked, taking the chair across from Sydney. Yolanda noted her godmother's switch to English, as she always did when Sydney was around, even though Sydney understood most Spanish.

"Well, I'm trying to help a family over on Evergreen. I think the mother goes to your church. Gumercinda Campamoche. Do you know her?"

"Gumer? Yes. Very nice lady."

"Yes, I agree. I'll tell you why I'm asking these questions in a bit. But can you tell me if she was at your church on Thursday?"

"Thursday? Yes, I think so."

"Please think. Can you tell me what time she arrived and what time she left?"

"Why do you ask?" Nina Mercedes frowned as if not sure why Yolanda would be asking.

"I'll tell you in a bit. But can you tell me what time she arrived and left?"

"Well, she sometimes comes a little late because she works at a tiendita that closes late."

"What time is a little late?"

"After eight, sometimes eight thirty."

"Now, please try to remember. What time did she arrive on Thursday?"

Nina Mercedes stopped to think.

"On Thursday she was on time. Not late. We start at eight p.m. She is on time when the owner or her son close the store."

"Did she seem upset?"

"Upset? I do not think so. Why?"

"What time did she leave?"

"The usual time, I think, nine-thirty? Why, mija? Is she in trouble? Are you helping her?"

"I'm trying to help her family," Yolanda said, thinking that thirty minutes to get back home on the bus sounded about right. She wasn't sure how much she should divulge. "Her nephew was killed Thursday night outside the tiendita."

"Dios mío!" Nina Mercedes made the sign of the cross and looked expectantly at Yolanda for more information. "How?"

"It looks like he was stabbed. I don't know much more than that. The police arrested Gumer's son, Gamaliel, but he was taking pictures at a protest down the street here at Mariachi Plaza." Yolanda motioned with her hand in the direction of the plaza. "They released him late in the day on Friday. But then they arrested the owner of the store, Kinji Abe."

"Como? That is not possible. He is such a nice man. He gives Gumer fruit to bring to us before it spoils. Y Gamaliel. He is a good son."

"That's what I think too. I don't think either of them did it. But Mr. Abe seems to be protecting someone. I wonder if that someone is Gumer."

"Oh, no. Impossible! She could not kill anyone—especially not family."

"Sometimes that's how it happens. Sometimes it's an accident. Did she ever say anything about problems with Frank?"

"Frank? That is the name of her sobrino? Wait." The older woman looked up toward the ceiling, thinking. "When we were putting things away after the service, she said her sobrino told her he would call La Migra if the owner did not sell the store. She said that the owner did not want to sell. She hopes he will not. Where will she and Gamaliel live? Where will they find work? But on Thursday, let me think." Nina Mercedes stared into the limeade between her hands for a moment.

Yolanda noted the bulging knuckles, early signs of arthritis. She had never considered her nina's white hair as a sign of aging because she'd never seen it any other color, but her heart sank a little knowing that this ageless woman was, in fact, aging. Her voice brought Yolanda back from the thought.

"Gumer was not upset. She said she scared the boy away, and that was that. She was, how do you say? Annoying?"

"Annoyed."

"Eso, but not upset."

"Did she say how she scared him? With a knife, maybe?"

"She did not say. Pero Madre de Dios. Que horrible." Nina Mercedes shook her head and stared at the table, apparently not wanting to believe her friend capable of murder. "No. She could not act normal if she knew she was responsible for a death. No. Someone else killed her sobrino. Not Gumer." Nina Mercedes crossed her arms, adamant.

Yolanda and Sydney sipped their limeade in silence, each with their own thoughts for a moment, before Nina Mercedes spoke up again.

"How did the boy die?"

"He was stabbed and bled to death. The police think it was with one of the Japanese swords that Mr. Abe keeps in the store as decoration. They're very sharp. I don't know more yet."

"Ay, Dios mío," Nina Mercedes said, shaking her head again.

"You know, Nina, the police may come to suspect her as I do, but I'll still try to help her. I think it may have been an accident or self-defense, especially if she thinks she only scared him off."

"Why do you think she did it if the police arrested the owner of the store?"

"He said some things that don't make sense. And all of a sudden, he doesn't want to defend himself. Like he's covering up for someone. Since Gamaliel was not near the store when it happened, Gumer is the only other person I can think Mr. Abe would be protecting. Maybe it was an accident. People do not say very nice things about Frank."

"If an accident, or like you say, self-defense, do you want me to ask her about it?"

"No. Let me do that. But we will need to get her a lawyer. And a lawyer may want to ask you to sign a statement repeating what you've told me. That will help." Yolanda waited for the woman to nod her assent before continuing, "Thank you. It will be best if Gumer talks only to the lawyer. So please do not ask her about it. But she may want to pray with you."

"Pray. That I can do. Thank you for helping her."

Nina Mercedes made the sign of the cross again and offered Yolanda a blessing before she left. The three women walked to the dining room, where the older woman dipped her fingers in holy water at the altar and blessed both Yolanda and Sydney. Yolanda touched her own fingers to her lips and to her mother's picture on her nina's altar. She loved that picture—the one she'd taken at a party with her mother in open-mouthed laughter. Below her mother's picture, another one showed a young Uncle Bobby strutting down what was then called Brooklyn Avenue. The Cesar Chavez Avenue of today did not look much different. She silently thanked them both for keeping her safe and alive. She felt a tingle up her arm when she touched her mother's picture and thought it might have been a twitch from her injuries, but then she smelled onion. What the hell was that? She mentioned it and the dream with the smell of onions to her godmother.

"Listen to your mother and your Tío Bobby," Nina Mercedes said. "They are always with you and will always help you. But you must listen."

"Listen to what? Maybe not buying tacos with onions? I don't get it?"

"Maybe if you listen more, you will understand more. But if something happens, like smell of onion like in your dream, pay attention. Be careful."

"That's it?"

"Sometimes it is that simple."

Yolanda shook her head. Nina Mercedes hugged each of the woman goodbye. She held onto Sydney and whispered in her ear.

"Thank you for taking care of her."

Yolanda now understood the mark written in blood. Frank had written a T after all. He'd tried to write "Tía" for his Tía Gumer before he died. Now they needed to get to Gumercinda Campamoche.

CHAPTER SIXTEEN

"I don't get it," Yolanda said on their way to the Abe Grocery. "I can't believe the juju's back."

"Please promise me you'll pay attention to it this time," Sydney said.

"I guess I'll have to, I just don't get it."

"What I don't get is, if you think this lady did it, why do you think the real estate guy Hector went after you? The embezzlement? Totally separate from Frank's death?"

"Precisely."

"Wait. Do you think Christine's brother-in-law went after Hector?"

"Better him than Christine's husband, I think. I hope it wasn't Eric. It might be totally unrelated to Frank Vazquez's death, but I'll need to find out to make sure no one else gets hurt. Who knows what else a desperate Brian might do."

Yolanda and Sydney looked at each other in sad silence before Yolanda spoke again.

"Let me call José before we go in. He needs to know what we just learned."

The attorney asked about her meeting with Mr. Abe, and Yolanda hesitated. She wasn't sure why. Maybe because she felt sorry for Gumer. Heck, she felt sorry for the whole family. She took a deep breath and updated the lawyer on her strange conversation with Kinji, then shared what she had learned from her godmother. José Herrera paused for a long moment. Yolanda thought the call had dropped and looked at her phone before he finally spoke.

"Well, well," he said. "Did I say you were good? You are exceptional."

"Well, thanks for saying that, but this poor woman was probably defending herself from her nephew, and now we have to help her too."

"Mr. Abe is my client. This may be enough to exonerate him, but we'd need a confession from her. I can't represent both simultaneously unless they both agree. I don't think Mr. Abe would object, but she might."

"Let me talk to her. Can you get Kinji's consent in the meantime?"

"Sounds good. It's too late to get in to see him on a Sunday. I'll speak with him at his arraignment tomorrow. The timing may be tricky, but I think I can get him released. I'll need to inform the DA of a possible confession by this woman, but please tell her not to talk to the cops before she talks to me. I should be present when she confesses. I can head over there tonight if she agrees to representation."

After she ended the call, Yolanda's heart went out to Gumer. She understood now why she didn't want to speak to the police. It wasn't her fear of deportation; it was her fear of being arrested for murder. But how could she have let her son and Kinji be arrested? Did she think they'd both just fight it? Had she been willing to let her son and the old man go to prison?

When they arrived, Sydney helped her wife step out of the car. She'd parked away from the curb so that Yolanda wouldn't have to lift her body more than necessary. Yolanda appreciated the gesture, thinking the painkillers were starting to wear off. She mentioned it to her wife.

"You can take the next dose now," Sydney said. "Let's get you some water in the store. And after we're done here, you're going home to rest. No objections."

"No argument from me, love."

Inside the store, Gamaliel sat at the register while his mother busied herself across the way cleaning behind the deli case. Yolanda noted that she held a blender glass with her left hand and dried it with a cloth in her right hand. The woman's son greeted Yolanda with a hug and a concerned look at her cast. He shook hands with Sydney and introduced himself before asking about it.

"Sydney can tell you all about it while I speak with your mom," Yolanda said.

The three walked over to Gumer. The woman looked like she hadn't slept in a few days. Yolanda noted a paler complexion with dark, puffy bags under her eyes, more pronounced than on Friday. Yolanda thought the contrast with the light-blue surgical mask accentuated the sickly look. Like Kinji, she looked older. Yolanda wasn't sure, but new wrinkles seemed to appear on her forehead as well. After introducing her wife, Yolanda asked the woman if they could talk in private.

"What gives?" Gamaliel asked.

Neither Yolanda nor Sydney answered, but Gumer put down the blender glass and looked at Yolanda with resignation in her eyes. They told her that the woman knew that Yolanda knew. She took off her apron and shuffled to the back of the store.

"What gives?" Gamaliel repeated, following them.

"Yolanda needs to ask your mom about something," Sydney offered. "Let's give them some space."

Yolanda was grateful for her wife's intervention. Gamaliel stopped following them, but she wasn't sure if was because some customers had entered the store. When Gumer motioned to the stairs that led to the apartment upstairs, Yolanda asked if they could sit on Kinji's porch instead. She wasn't sure she could manage descending the stairs without pain. The woman agreed and seemed to notice Yolanda's cast for the first time. She asked her about it, but Yolanda mentioned only that she had been in an accident and was okay.

When they reached the porch, Sydney caught up to them with a couple of water bottles. She took some tissues from her pocket and handed them to Yolanda before heading back to the store. Damn, she loved her.

Yolanda took her water and handed the other to Gumer. Both removed their masks. Yolanda noted that the older woman's face seemed thinner, wrinkles running deeper on the sides of her mouth. She probably hadn't had much appetite since before this ordeal. They sat on chairs facing the oak tree in the small front yard. A dusty loquat tree stood off to the left. The street beyond was quiet, without traffic. They both stared at the oak tree while Yolanda opened her water. She fished a pill out of her pocket and swallowed. Then she turned to face Gumer for a long moment, but the woman did not avert her gaze from the tree. Yolanda couldn't imagine what was going through the woman's mind, but she seemed much more at peace than she'd seen her since they'd met. Her face relaxed and her jaw dropped. Her mouth opened slightly, making her look younger than a few minutes ago. Steady, deep breathing sounded loud in the silence.

"Gumer, you know what I'm going to ask you, right?"

"Sí," the woman said, suddenly looking more miserable than ever. Yolanda's question had brought her back to reality, and whatever peace she'd felt for a moment had disappeared. Yolanda felt a twinge of guilt for triggering the change. She switched to Spanish to make it easier on her, or as easy as confessing to murder could be. In this case, hopefully it would qualify as involuntary manslaughter.

"Did you use one of the samurai knives on Frank?"

The woman's eyes welled with tears. Her hands grasped the arms of the patio chair, and she looked up to the porch ceiling. She blinked fast in a valiant effort to keep the tears from running down her cheeks. Yolanda offered her the tissue.

"Que desgracia," Gumer said, taking the tissue and shaking her head.

Yes, Yolanda thought, this was a disgrace, but she kept that to herself.

"Tell me how it happened. From the beginning, when Frank arrived."

Gumer spoke in a calm voice just above a whisper. Yolanda likened her tone to what one would use in a confessional. The more the woman talked, the more relief she seemed to feel, her body relaxing steadily. Frank had arrived with lots of nervous energy, like he was on drugs. He said he needed her help to convince Kinji to sell the property. She told him she'd have to be crazy to do that and lose her home. He came around the counter and right up to her face. He said that if she didn't, he'd call La Migra and have her and Gamaliel deported. And Kinji would go to jail for helping them. She wasn't thinking. It just happened automatically. She grabbed the short knife from the display stand and held it up to scare him. He laughed and told her he could report her to the cops for that too. He moved closer to her—she didn't know if to grab the knife or to grab her wrist, but she defended herself. She made a motion as if holding the knife across her chest. She hadn't meant to stab him. He kind of jumped into the knife and he started bleeding almost immediately. He called her a crazy bitch, holding the wound, and ran out of the store. She figured he'd left and wouldn't come back. She went to the restroom at the back of the store and cleaned the knife with bleach before putting it back. She was nervous but didn't worry about it, because the boy had run out and hadn't come back. She didn't want Kinji to know she'd touched one of his knives, so she didn't mention anything when he came over from his house to lock up. He told her to go on to her church meeting because he'd seen her bus coming. She got on the bus at the stop in front of the store, and that was it. When she came back, she saw the crowd and the police, but she still didn't think the small cut would have killed Frank. She'd barely touched him with the knife. She was sure someone else had killed him. Her small cut could not have been fatal. And when Gamaliel was arrested, she didn't know what to do.

"Jesse said you would help. He was innocent. They could not keep him in jail."

"And when Kinji was arrested?"

"I don't know. I was scared. I still thought someone else had done it. I still can't believe the small cut was enough. Kinji is innocent too. You can help him too, no?"

The woman seemed relieved to have told someone, but Yolanda wasn't sure she'd like what she had to say.

"The best way to help Kinji is to confess that it was you and not him. The police will find fiber from Kinji's clothes, and maybe his hair, on Frank because Gamaliel took one of his blankets to cover him. Kinji's lawyer can help you because it sounds like it was self-defense. You did not mean to kill him. But you need to confess so that Kinji can go free. Here's the thing. You may still go to jail, but at least an innocent man won't."

Gumer's chin dropped to her chest. It bobbed up and down with her sobs. Yolanda's heart went out to her.

"Yes, he must come home," Gumer said, regaining control of her tears. She looked up at Yolanda. "Will I be deported?"

"I don't know," Yolanda said. "Would you like me to call Kinji's lawyer? He can represent you if you agree, even though he represents Kinji. Telling a judge that you will confess is in Kinji's interest, so he needs your permission to say that and to represent you too."

"Yes, please call him," she said. "We need to bring Kinji home."

Gumer seemed to deflate. Her shoulders sank and she slumped in her chair. Yolanda worried that the woman had fainted, but color had returned to her face. The weight of her secret seemed to leave her, and she straightened her shoulders when Gamaliel came running to her, Sydney in his wake.

"No, 'amá. You did not kill Frank."

His mother stood and hugged him. She seemed stronger than Yolanda had seen her throughout this ordeal. Confessions sometimes did that.

"Kinji's lawyer said he'd come over to help with her confession," Yolanda said. "It was self-defense."

"No!" Gamaliel said.

"Sí, mijo," Gumer said. "We need to end this." She held him tighter. "I need to end this and bring Kinji home."

Gamaliel dissolved into tears. He went from being a man to being her baby in the span of a few seconds. He bent at the knees and slid to the floor, his arms around his mother's legs, his back racked with sobs. His mother shed tears again, but without sobbing. They fell silently down her cheeks while she kept her hands on her son's shoulders.

Yolanda got up and walked away from the porch to call José Herrera. Sydney followed her.

"I tried to hold him back, but after I told him about your accident, I told him about your conversations with Mr. Abe and your godmother, and the reason we'd come back here."

"Thank you for holding him off. I think she's ready to talk to the lawyer now."

Yolanda called José and filled him in. He told her he'd be there within the hour.

After he had recovered, Gamaliel went to close the store and take his mother upstairs. Yolanda and Sydney waited for the lawyer on Kinji's porch. They sat in silence, both feeling for the woman and the tragedy that had befallen this family.

When José Herrera arrived, Yolanda pointed upstairs, but Gumer must have seen him from the window because she and Gamaliel came downstairs to Kinji's porch. After introductions in Spanish, Yolanda and Sydney excused themselves. Yolanda promised to be back the next day, before Gumer turned herself in. José suggested she wait until after Kinji's arraignment. He'd communicate whatever he arranged with the prosecutor. Yolanda hoped her friend Celine would indulge some flexibility.

Yolanda gave Gumer a hug before departing. Other than holding onto the younger woman a little longer than would be normal, Gumer showed no sign of regretting her confession.

On their way to Sydney's car, Yolanda glanced at the growing sidewalk memorial for Frank. She shook her head at the tragedy of it all. Then a back spasm had her thoughts returning to Hector. What did he do? Why had he not been driving his own car? Had he driven another car to crash into hers? Had someone else crashed into her? Why would anyone else go after her other than Hector? She didn't see Turi's truck across the street on Malabar but figured it was still in the shop to fix the taillights. She told Sydney she'd be back in a moment and walked across the street. Rather than object, her wife took a deep breath and sighed before accompanying her.

Killer and Baby announced their arrival on the property with loud barking as soon as they opened the gate.

"Hey, Killer. Hey, Baby," Yolanda said at the front door. The pit bull stopped barking, but the Chihuahua continued. "That's Killer," Yolanda said to Sydney.

"Hey, Killer," Sydney said with a laugh, bending down at the screen door. To Yolanda's surprise, Killer stopped barking. It surprised Emilio "T" Luna too.

"Well, that's a first," he said from behind the screen door. He opened it to let them in. "You must have good energy," he said to Sydney. "He doesn't let anyone pet him like that except us." Killer had flipped onto his back to let Sydney scratch his belly.

"Wow, do you want him?" Turi laughed, entering the living room. His father pretended to be insulted, snapping the dish towel in his hand at his son. But Yolanda could see where his son might want some relief from the yappy dog. Yolanda made the introductions.

"We have to stop meeting like this," Turi said.

"What happened to you?" T asked, pointing to Yolanda's cast.

"Got run off the road last night." In response to their looks of concern, she added, "Doing much better than my car."

"Who was it?" T asked.

"Dunno," Yolanda said.

"Well, in your line of work, somebody might have it in for you," he said. "Any idea who?"

"That's what I hope you can help me with," she said, turning to Turi.

"Wait," T said. "This sounds like good chisme." He offered the women some quesadillas or something to drink, but Yolanda declined, even though she was tempted to have a quesadilla. She didn't want to keep them from their dinner but needed to know more about Hector. When T rushed to the kitchen, probably to turn off the stove, Turi offered the women a seat on the couch.

"We won't keep you from your dinner," Yolanda said. "Just need to know something more about Hector."

"Shoot," Turi said, sitting on the recliner. His father, having returned from the kitchen, propped an arm on the back of the chair.

"Ever see Hector drive anything other than his BMW and that Ferrari?"

"You think he did it?" T asked.

"I may have discovered that he was embezzling money from his family's business, not something he'd want me to pursue."

"Oh, shit," the father and son said in unison.

"I met with him and his father yesterday. Last night I talked to his brother. On the way home, I got run off the road near our house. Later, his sister took him his car nearby. That's why I figure he was driving something else." Yolanda left out the part about Hector dying in a drive-by shooting.

"Hmm." Turi thought for a moment. "Can't say that I've ever seen him drive anything else."

Yolanda had figured it was a long shot but was glad she'd tried anyway. Sitting on the couch had made her back ache, so she was glad to stand, Sydney standing with her.

"Wait," Turi said, motioning with his hands to have them sit again. Yolanda stayed standing, rubbing her lower back with her good hand. Sydney remained standing as well, both with their eyes on Turi.

"Haven't seen him driving another car, but I seen him in another car."

"I'm gonna stand a bit," Yolanda said, "but please continue."

Turi stood as well and put his arm on the other side of the recliner from his father.

"He's been slumming with this artist he picked up a couple months ago at a show at Self Help Graphics," he said, referring to the popular community art center on First Street. "Bought a bunch of her stuff and they left together. Seen them going from Xela's to Eastside Luv once. Don't know if they're still together, but that night they rode in her old pickup."

"What make and what color?" Yolanda said, pulling out her small notebook and pencil from her shirt pocket.

"Light blue. An old Chevy. A classic, but kind of a clunker. We tease her about it at the Self Help workshops because it's all banged up. She said her father left it to her and doesn't wanna fix it. Turns down offers from guys in lowrider clubs who want to restore it. Says the beat-up look and the stick shift are the perfect anti-theft devices. Can't argue with that." Neither could Yolanda. Most people drove automatic transmissions nowadays.

"Do you have her contact information, by any chance?"

"I think I have her number," Turi said, pulling his phone out of his pocket and scrolling through his contacts. When he'd texted the contact, Yolanda looked at the name. Xochitl. No last name, no address. Just a number.

"Do you know if this is her real name or her artist's name?"

"Both, I think. Pronounces it in Nahuatl." When Yolanda and Sydney gave him a curious look, he explained. "Sh□-chee-TL," he said, emphasizing the TL fricative. "Not 'SŌ-cheel' like most people say it. Don't know her last name, though. Might be Flores, but I'm not sure."

"Do you think they're still together?"

"Dunno. Lots of guys—and some women—try picking up artists at those shows, but I haven't seen none of those relationships last. They're all just having fun."

"Any idea where she lives?"

"I dropped her off once when her truck broke down," he said, thinking. "Somewhere off Indiana, on the other side of the cemetery." Yolanda knew he referred to Evergreen Cemetery. "At the border between Boyle Heights and East LA, near the Mercadito, but I don't remember which street. I can find out if you'd like."

Yolanda thanked him. If he didn't get the information, she might have enough to try and track down this Xochitl, but it would be faster if he remembered. She and Sydney said their goodbyes to the two men, and Killer too. He wagged his tail at Sydney the whole time and didn't bark again until they'd closed the gate at the sidewalk.

"You're not working on this anymore," Sydney said. "You're going home and getting some rest." Her tone told Yolanda that she had no other option.

"Can we stop to visit the people who helped me last night? Really want to thank them properly for saving my life."

"I'll call them and set up a time to meet tomorrow," Sydney said. "Tonight, you rest."

It wasn't even dark yet, but Yolanda had to agree. Her body ached more than it had in the morning. Sitting on their sofa to remove her shoes took considerable effort. Yolanda wasn't sure she'd be able to get up the stairs without significant pain. Sydney suggested she try because the sofa would not be as comfortable as their bed. She helped her get ready for bed and offered her a muscle relaxant before tucking her in. Yolanda slept soundly while her wife read in a chair a few feet from their bed.

It was fully dark when Yolanda awakened at 3:23 a.m., her heart pumping. Here we go again, she thought. She rubbed her eyes, trying to remember the images. A fast-moving car, a handgun, and Kinji and Gamaliel. Was someone threatening them? Where? Kinji had yet to be released from jail. Was he safer there? She'd have to confirm his release with José Herrera. She thought she'd been quiet, but apparently she'd been talking to herself and woke Sydney.

"Again?" Sydney asked, propping herself up on her elbows and looking between the alarm clock and Yolanda.

"Yup." She told her wife about the images.

"But not you? Just Kinji and Gamaliel?"

"Right. That's never happened before. Usually, they're warning dreams about me being in danger."

"I wouldn't assume you're out of danger too, but you may want to warn those two. Be careful today, okay?"

"I will. Go back to sleep. Sorry I woke you."

"Sleep," Sydney said, tapping Yolanda's shoulder before rolling over and doing just that herself.

Yolanda stared at the silhouette of the ceiling fan, thinking of Kinji and Gamaliel. Why would they be in any danger? Thanks to the muscle relaxant she'd taken earlier, sleep overtook her before she could ponder the question any longer.

CHAPTER SEVENTEEN

Monday

The next morning, Yolanda felt much better. Still sore, but much better. She convinced Sydney to drive her to the car rental place where she picked up a compact SUV that was easy to get in and out of with a sore back. Sydney seemed reluctant but also relieved because she was on call at the hospital and couldn't play taxi all day again. After a disappointing breakfast of oatmeal and berries, Yolanda was ready to get back to work.

"Nothing physically strenuous today," Sydney warned.

"I don't know," Yolanda said. "I can get used to huevos con chorizo for breakfast."

"Could be that or something out of *Whatever Happened to Baby Jane*," Sydney said without looking up from her laptop.

"You wouldn't."

"Don't try me." Sydney winked at her wife, but Yolanda got the message. Sydney would never do it, but the image of a demented Bette Davis feeding an incapacitated Joan Crawford a dead rat was enough to convince her to be careful. That and the frightened images of Kinji and Gamaliel in her dream. But she'd have to wait for word of Kinji's arraignment, and hopefully his release, before going to see him. In the meantime, she had to figure out what Hector had been up to.

Yolanda didn't want to be rude, calling Mel at ten o'clock on a Monday. The bar owner would be more useful after some good sleep, she thought. She decided to track down the LAPD investigator assigned to her accident instead. Then she'd check in with José Herrera on Kinji. Her heart still went out to Gumer. She hoped the woman would get off on involuntary manslaughter because she thought she had a good self-defense argument. She especially hoped the woman wouldn't be deported, but deportation was more likely.

After a few calls, Yolanda found a number for the LAPD investigator, Alma Ross. She left a message for her mentioning the possibility of a light-blue truck hitting her. With any luck, she'd hear back from the officer today, then she turned to her wife.

"Hey, love. Any interest in lunch at Mel's? He opens at noon, I think."

"You sure he's open on Mondays?"

"Brissa mentioned last week that they're still trying to make up for the pandemic. She thought they'd go seven days a week for a couple more months. Wanna try?"

"Sure, should be done with this work for the peer review in a few minutes."

Yolanda felt her face flush, embarrassed.

"Oh my god, I'm so sorry. You've been taking care of me and here—"

"No worries." Sydney didn't let her finish. "Almost done. I think we should be okay at the review. Then it'll be a matter of dealing with the lawsuit itself."

"You know, hate to say it, but without Hector's cash now, Brian may be looking at the lawsuit against you to recover money."

"Maybe. But blackmail, extortion, and a possible murder could drive away all but the worst ambulance chasers. And the hospital doesn't settle with those."

Yolanda was glad to see her wife feeling more confident in her case but still felt guilty for needing her help after the accident.

"You sure there's nothing I can do to help?"

"Nah, thanks. Just keep me posted on what happens with Brian. He seems to be the main person pushing the complaint. Don't know how involved his mother is, but from what Christine shared, it sounds like the father was the bigger personality. And Eric is discouraging his mom from going forward with it. We'll see."

"Oh, that's good to hear. Will definitely keep you posted. I'm going to make some more calls and do some social media research in the office. Let me know if you can head out at noon."

Yolanda went into the home office they shared off the kitchen. It was billed as a third bedroom in the real estate brochure, but to Yolanda it seemed more like a converted pantry with an Ikea "closet." The small window let in a modicum of natural light, and their own Ikea desk and chairs did not allow room for anything else. It also meant they worked in the office only when they really needed to concentrate or use the old desktop computer. It might not be as inviting as the Garcias' opulent home office, Yolanda thought, but it was theirs. Sitting at the computer desk was more comfortable for her back than sitting on the sofa with a laptop like Sydney. She turned on the computer and let it cycle through a software update, thinking she needed to call Detective Lan.

First, she logged on and searched for social media accounts for Brian Jacobs and Frank Vásquez. Her phone rang before she got very far. It was Jane Stern, her officemate.

"Hey, stranger," Jane said. "Thought you might want to know that the surveillance videos didn't bear much fruit. No enhancement can capture the license plates."

"Aw, Jane. Thanks so much for trying. Actually, got a confession in that case last night and it was someone else. Sorry I didn't let you know. Been kinda hectic."

"Dang, you're quick, but no worries. Let me know if there's anything else I can do to help."

"Well, now that you mention it…" After updating Jane on the weekend's events, including her injuries, Yolanda detailed the embezzlement she had uncovered and the possible blackmail and extortion. She also mentioned the complaint Brian and his mother had filed against Sydney and the other ER doctor.

"I'm not sure if Brian Jacobs, the guy suing Sydney, was working with Frank Vásquez, the guy killed at the grocery store, to get at Hector Garcia, the real estate agent, but with Brian the only survivor among them, and with his father now gone, I'm worried he might get more desperate for money. According to his sister-in-law, he falls for conspiracy theories and is susceptible to fits of anger due to an old head injury. I want to make sure he's put away if he's responsible for Hector's death. Don't want him anywhere near Sydney."

"Just say the word," Jane said. "Anything for Sydney." Yolanda thanked her and ended the call.

"So that's what you're really worried about," Sydney said, leaning against the doorframe, her arms folded across her chest.

"Well, that and Kinji and Gamaliel," a sheepish Yolanda said.

"Come here," Sydney said. Yolanda stepped into a grateful embrace. "Okay, let's head to Mel's, but in separate cars. I need to get to the hospital this afternoon."

On the way to Mel's, José Herrera called. Kinji had been released and the charges dropped. Yolanda gave a "Whoop" but quickly asked about Gumer. The attorney had been given another twenty-four hours to have Gumer turn herself in.

"That's pretty generous, given that she's undocumented," he said. "The DA usually considers undocumented defendants a flight risk. Your friendship with Ms. Cueva may have helped there. I told her that you'd solved the case and secured the confession. I'm revising it now. Ms. Campamoche's coming to my office this afternoon to finalize it before we have her turn herself in tomorrow. Told her to get her affairs in order at her home, so she should be there tonight."

"Thanks for letting me know. I'll drop by. Want to see Kinji too."

When Yolanda and Sydney arrived at Mel's, they already had their first customers. Mel's green chile pozole always drew a group of regulars for lunch. The women ordered some for themselves too. When Brissa asked about Yolanda's arm, she told her she'd tell her and Mel all about it as soon as they had a chance to join her and Sydney. Brissa gave her a curious look but went on to finish serving other customers. After serving drinks, mostly beers or soda, the couple joined their friends at a corner booth with bowls of pozole.

"What's cooking?" Mel asked, sitting down. "Whoa, what happened to you?"

"Got run off the road up on Via Marisol," Yolanda said.

"Two fractures and a herniated disc," Sydney added, "but if she doesn't push it, she should heal fine."

"Damn," Brissa said.

"Well, don't push it," Mel added.

"Don't plan to," Yolanda said. "But I think the guy who did it may have come here Saturday night."

Her friends opened their eyes wide. Mel raised an eyebrow. "Description?"

"Tall, good-looking, light-skinned Latino. No facial hair. Last I saw him that day, he was wearing a fitted long-sleeved T-shirt, white, and dark-blue dress shorts. Also, Reef flip-flops. Looks like he works out."

Both shook their heads, but Brissa stopped and looked at Mel.

"Wait, there was that cute guy who created that scene Saturday night. Or his girlfriend did." She turned back to Yolanda. "He was wearing a fitted long-sleeved T-shirt, but black. Black pants too, and black sneakers—those Onitsuka Mexico 66 shoes that are hard to get now." Mel turned to his partner.

"You caught all that?"

"Been looking online for those shoes," Brissa said with a shrug.

"What kind of scene?" Yolanda asked.

"Straight out of a Mexican novela," Mel said. "Lots of drama." He turned to Brissa, who took the cue and launched into her story.

"So, cute guy comes in, kinda out of breath. Kinda hyped up. Orders a beer and keeps looking from his phone to the door. Nothing unusual about that. Figure he's nervous about a date. The date turns out to be a woman who looks like Rox. You know, petite, artsy type. Latina, shoulder-length dark hair, nice makeup, hoop earrings, jeans, cute boots, off-the-shoulder top." Mel looked at Brissa like he didn't know her.

"You caught all that too?"

Brissa smiled, touching her own hoop earrings, and continued, leaving Yolanda thinking she'd make a good witness for any crime.

"Anyway, right away they get into this argument. She says, 'What do you mean, stolen?' The place quiets down to hear the chisme, you know? He kinda apologizes, but she doesn't let it go. Yells at him, 'That was my father's truck!' And then, pácatelas!" Brissa slapped one hand with the other. "She slaps him. Hard. Those who hadn't stopped talking, stop right there. You could hear a pin drop. Then she slaps him again." She shook her head, still amazed by the scene.

"And that's when I stepped in," Mel said. "Can't have violence in my place."

"Yeah, Mel goes all Humphrey Bogart," Brissa said, imitating Mel. "'Sorry for the barullo, folks.'" She elbowed Mel in the ribs, laughing before continuing, "So artsy girl storms off and he just sits there. Don't think he saw that coming. But he asks for another beer and gets on his phone. A while later, he pays his tab, nice tip, and takes off. Of course, I had to see if the woman wasn't still out there, so I went to the door. Dude gets picked up by this black BMW. I thought it was an Uber at first, but then some goth woman gets out and he gets in the driver's seat. Then they drive off. Fin." Brissa punctuated the end of her story with a poking motion of her index finger, but then continued, "If you ask me, Rox's look-alike is better off without the dude if he's seeing goth woman too."

"Wow," Sydney said. "And I thought we had all the excitement with Yolanda's rollover."

"You rolled over?" Mel asked Yolanda.

"Pushed off the hill and down the embankment." Yolanda motioned in the direction with her good arm. "Now I wonder if it was with a light-blue truck. Maybe that woman's."

"So," Mel said, "the guy loses the woman's truck to a thief who rams your Jeep. Gotta find whoever stole it."

"My theory is that the guy you saw last night drove the truck into me and then claimed it was stolen. He's the one who had a motive. Found out he might be embezzling from his family's business. The goth woman was his sister."

"Damn," Brissa said. "Gotta find him, then."

"He's dead," Yolanda said. "Drive-by shooting up the street in Eagle Rock."

"Oh shit," Mel said. "Who went after him? Not the woman who slapped him, I think. He left her without a car."

"No, I think it's someone who thinks your cute guy ran his father off the road and killed him some weeks back. He and the father may have been blackmailing cute guy. The surviving blackmailer is very much alive and might have some anger issues."

Mel let out a low whistle.

"Dang, that's twisted. Hope he doesn't come around here."

"Me too," Sydney said. "He's the guy who filed a complaint against me."

"Say what?" Mel said. He shook his head vigorously, like he couldn't believe it. Then he turned to Yolanda. "Dang, woman. How do you keep track of all this shit? You gotta find that guy."

"I'm on it," Yolanda said, taking the last spoonful of her pozole.

"In the meantime," Sydney said after finishing her own, "I gotta get to the hospital." She turned to Yolanda and gave her a quick peck on the cheek. "Let me know if you're good to take your rescuers to a nice dinner tomorrow night."

"Oh, right. Yes, definitely."

Yolanda stayed for a while to share more details with Mel and Brissa before they had to get back to their other customers. Mel brought her a mocktail on the house. She savored the fresh watermelon juice and mint concoction, thinking that recapping the weekend's events helped her get her head around the related and unrelated cases. One step at a time, she thought. She decided to call Detective Lan and try to track down the LAPD accident investigator before heading over to see Kinji and, hopefully, Gumer.

"Well, aren't you a blast from the past," the detective said.

"Congratulations on making it to Homicide," Yolanda said.

"Thanks, but why do I have the feeling that you're calling about a homicide?"

"Because you're a great detective."

Lan laughed at that. Yolanda pictured the tall woman's sober expression changing with her laugh, looking younger.

"Well," Yolanda said, "now that you mention it."

"I knew it. Probably can't help you, but tell me about it and I'll let you know."

"Hopefully we can help each other. I'm calling about a hit-and-run and a drive-by on Saturday night. My Jeep and I got pushed down an embankment near my house, and the guy I suspect got shot in a drive-by later up the street in Eagle Rock. Your case, I believe."

"Dang, you take revenge seriously," Lan deadpanned.

"As much as I'd like vengeance, I'd rather not take on the bad karma. I think the guy was targeted by the son of someone else he may have run off the road. I'm glad you caught the case instead of Rios."

"Okay, start at the beginning." Detective Lan was all business now.

Yolanda recounted the accident and what she suspected of the drive-by shooting. While she was at it, she relayed the Frank Vásquez case and took some pleasure in reporting that Rios had been wrong, again, arresting two innocent people in succession.

"So, let me see if I have this right," Lan said. "You and Rios catch a homicide that turns out to be all in the family, but in your investigation, you track down a developer who's embezzling from his own family. He goes after you in what you suspect may be his now ex-girlfriend's blue pickup. Then, some neo-Nazi type whose sister-in-law works for the developer, and who you suspect had been blackmailing said developer, goes after him with a gun in either a new white pickup or an old red Suburban."

"You got it." Yolanda smiled. Finally, someone in authority who believed her understood the entire story. "Oh, and hey, Alma Ross is working my hit-and-run. Do you think you can get her to track Hector's whereabouts? Maybe through cell phone data? Would like to get closure on that."

"That happens mostly on TV and in cases with more resources, but I'll see what I can do. What I don't get is why would this"—Lan paused as if reading her notes—"this Brian Jacobs kill off his source of money?"

"Because he's all worked up thinking that Hector ran his dad off the road and killed him to stop the blackmail. He never accepted that his father's crash was an accident. Said he was too good a motorcyclist, especially with his grandson on the bike at the time. And he may think Hector might come after him next."

"Why would he suspect Hector?"

"Because…" Yolanda thought a moment. "Oh, shit."

"What?"

"I don't know. The only people I talked to about Hector's possible involvement in the motorcycle accident were Brian's brother and sister-in-law, Eric and Christine Jacobs. It was their son, Jack, who was riding on the motorcycle when his grandfather was killed. He got hurt really bad—skin grafts, concussion, internal bleeding…Brian has a motive, but so does Eric. I don't know how Brian would suspect Hector unless Eric shared the suspicion."

"Or Brian puts two and two together on his own, given the extortion. Or maybe he didn't, and this Eric guy took matters into his own hands."

"Damn. That's a possibility. I asked Eric whether Brian owned a gun, and he confirmed his dad had owned a rifle and a Glock, but I didn't ask Eric if he owned a gun. He said his dad and Brian used to go to the shooting range all the time. I don't know if it was a family thing, but maybe Eric used to do the same with them or his dad." Yolanda stared at her now empty glass, hoping Eric was not involved. "You know, he also said something about Brian doing them all a favor if he did go after Hector."

"And like you said, his son got banged up too. Do you know what Eric drives?"

"I don't, but he's a construction contractor, probably a truck too. When he's not working, he and Christine spend all their time in the hospital with Jack. Oh, wait, they mentioned he's being released today, so they'll be home later if they're not already there. Jack will need lots of physical therapy and more care at home, so I'm sure they'll be with him as much as they were at the hospital. You know, Carrie, for Jack's sake, I really hope Eric didn't do it. He needs both of his parents right now. Can you keep me posted?"

"Well, this gives me plenty to go on," Detective Lan said. "Can't promise to divulge what I find but can let you know when we make an arrest. You may learn about that from the family in any case."

When she ended the call, Yolanda sat, the otherwise delicious pozole sitting heavy in her stomach. She wiped down the table with a napkin and took her glass to the bar.

"Something the matter?" Mel asked.

"Nah, just feeling sorry for the little nephew of the guy who filed the complaint against Sydney. His father may have gone after your cute guy from Saturday night. I keep thinking it was his brother, but both brothers would have a motive to go after the man they think killed their father. Just talked to the detective. Hopefully she can figure it out."

"Sorry, mujer, I got nothing for you. But don't stress. Come by when you need to get away from all your crime fighting. I'll fix you a good cocktail."

"Thanks, I know you will." Yolanda appreciated Mel's friendship. Sober himself, he was always ready with a cocktail for his friends. But she was still in a sad mood. Maybe visiting the newly freed Kinji would help.

CHAPTER EIGHTEEN

At Abe's Grocery, only a masked Kinji sat at the register. Yolanda donned her own mask and came around the counter to give the man a hug. He seemed to welcome it, holding on a bit longer than Yolanda expected.

"Are Gumer and Gamaliel upstairs?"

"No. Your brother gave them a ride to see the lawyer to finalize her confession. They should be back soon, but they'll probably head upstairs to take care of whatever Gumer needs to take care of before turning herself in tomorrow." He stopped talking, his eyes filling with tears. To give him a moment, Yolanda walked the few steps across the store and brought over one of the stools from in front of the deli case and sat on it. She was glad Jesse had given them a ride. She couldn't imagine the emotional toll they were experiencing.

Kinji dabbed his eyes and blew his nose with a real handkerchief. Had anyone else done that, it would have seemed like an affectation, but it seemed to suit a man of Kinji's age. He probably had plenty of handkerchiefs.

"I'm so sorry," Yolanda said.

"It never should have come to this," Kinji said when he regained his composure. "They would have put me in the prison hospital eventually anyway. Gumer and her son would be together. I could have handled it. I owe them at least that much."

"What do you mean, hospital?"

"I have something wrong with one of my arteries. My heart doesn't get enough blood, so it makes me tired sometimes. Not too bad, but it's gonna get worse. Myocardial something or other."

"I'm sure a good cardiologist could take care of that," Yolanda said, thinking that this confirmed what Hector said Frank had told him about Kinji's health.

"No. The doctors have done all they can—angiograms, stents—I'm done with it." He shook his head. "No. The Campamoches could have lived off the store. You know, I'm leaving it all to Gamaliel anyway."

"That's very generous of you," Yolanda said, pointing at the framed deed he had shown her a few days ago. "But I thought when you showed me the deed and that affidavit that you'd planned to keep the property in the family." Yolanda noticed for the first time that Kinji had other Japanese and Mexican keepsakes on the shelves, including a grape boycott flyer and what looked like a letter signed by Cesar Chavez, leader of the United Farm Workers union. Both documents sat in frames on either side of several dog-eared books.

"No," Kinji said. "But I'm glad we can talk about this instead." He sat on his stool and leaned against the counter with the register, more at ease now. "I have two nephews in New York," Kinji said, "but I think they'd just sell the place since they don't really have any ties to LA except for me. And they never visit."

Yolanda's eyes turned to the books on a shelf, not wanting to see the hurt in his eyes. She turned back to Kinji when he chuckled.

"I don't blame them. Their mother didn't want much to do with California or the Midwest after Santa Anita and Heart Mountain. Amiko—Amy—married her concentration camp sweetheart and moved with him to start a new life in New York. After she and her husband passed, the boys and I kinda lost touch. Well, they're middle-aged men now, busy with their own families. Ona didn't move away, but she and her husband didn't have any kids before they passed. And, of course, my brother, Masaru, like me, never married." Kinji gave a wistful glance upward. "I like to think he had an otherwise happy life up in the Bay Area." He shook his head in what Yolanda read as a gesture full of regrets.

"No, my family is here, with Gumer and Gamaliel, and Chata and Frank. Well, just Chata, his mother, now. Their family saved the store when the government shipped us off to Heart Mountain."

"How'd they do that?"

"My father had a part-time employee, Ricardo Vásquez. He and his family fixed up the apartment upstairs that we used for storage and moved in when we got shipped out. My parents had planned for me or my brother to use it when we married, but…" He motioned with his hand, palm up, and let it fall again, not finishing the thought before continuing, "Anyway, my mom told us the story of how Ricardo and his wife, Amelia, ran the store all those years we were at Heart Mountain. One of my earliest memories was the excitement around a Christmas shipment of rice and oranges they sent one year. I don't know where they got so much rice during the war years, but man, everyone in camp wanted some!" Kinji smiled at the memory. "When we came back, Ricardo and Amelia were still living upstairs with their son, Fernando. He was my age, six years old. Our house was spotless. Amelia had kept our house dust-free and ready for our return. Ricardo had painted a silhouette of Abraham Lincoln over the store's name. I guess to make it sound American instead of Japanese. But all the locals still pronounced it in Japanese because the vowels sound the same in Spanish.

"My parents were forever grateful to the Vásquez family," Kinji said. "They even saved the income from the store after taking their salaries and paying the utilities and mortgage. Property taxes too. Didn't even give themselves a raise. Meant we could order real winter clothes from a catalogue for Heart Mountain. Didn't have to rely on our lighter California clothes like so many others. I don't remember if from Sears or Montgomery Ward, but man, those coats and long johns and boots really saved us.

"Anyway, my mother couldn't get over our luck coming home to everything in its place and an operating business. Everyone else had such a hard time picking up the pieces after the concentration camps. She made my father promise to let them live rent-free for as long as they wanted. Fernando was my best friend until the day he died of a stroke. I don't know how my parents avoided losing the property when the state went after families with ownership arrangements like ours. I think Ricardo and Amelia running the place may have helped. They hid things like the samurai swords and some Japanese books and magazines at their place before we shipped out and before moving in upstairs."

"These books?" Yolanda pointed to the ones on a shelf. She thought the elderly man seemed reinvigorated by these recollections and tried to encourage more.

"Oh, no, those are too fragile now. They're in the house. These are newer books. If you want to learn more about that time, these here are pretty good. Your brother and Gamaliel and I have read all of them. The boys indulge my interest with a kind of informal book club." He pulled down four of the books and Yolanda read the titles on the bindings: *Fred Korematsu Speaks Up*; *Life After Manzanar*; *Nisei Naysayer: The Memoir of Militant Japanese American Journalist Jimmie Omura*; and *Beyond the Betrayal*. "The other ones offer more human-interest stories from the camps, but these hit home more to me because they helped me understand what my family went through. I wish they'd been written when I was a youngster instead of an old man, but at least they're out there now."

"Do you remember much about what the adults went through?"

"No. That's just it. I was just a little kid. Playing marbles and running around the camp made it feel like an exciting experience. The adults all tried to make it fun for us. My only disappointment was that I was too young for the Boy Scouts. I think I saw my mom cry only once during the entire ordeal. And after, like many others, my parents didn't want to talk about it. It wasn't until I was older that I realized how much people suffered."

"You know," Yolanda said, "before I visited Manzanar, I had no idea that there'd been a real, active resistance from within the camps. And I'd never met anyone close to any of the resisters until I met you."

"Jesse says I should write the story of my family and the Vásquez family because there aren't enough published accounts of what happened and what we all went through. Gamaliel started pushing me to do it more after the 2016 election. All the political rhetoric now certainly sounds like back then, but I'm no writer."

"Maybe one of these authors or someone they know would be interested," Yolanda said, placing the books back on the shelf. "May I borrow one?"

Kinji seemed to brighten at that, smiling.

"You can borrow as many as you'd like. And keep coming back for more."

His face suddenly turned serious, and Yolanda followed his gaze to the store entrance. Gamaliel and Gumer entered with the weight of the world visible in their downcast expressions, Jesse behind them. Mother and son had red-rimmed eyes from crying. Whatever relief Kinji had felt from his conversation with Yolanda had disappeared from his expression. He stepped quickly toward Gumer and held her in a tight embrace. Yolanda noted that both seemed a bit more stooped than the prior week. Had it been only three days ago that they'd met? Both seemed to have aged too. When Gumer started to cry again, Gamaliel tried to soothe her, rubbing her back. Kinji took another handkerchief from his pocket and wiped her tears above her mask. None of them said anything. They didn't have to. Yolanda and Jesse stood back to give them space to express their grief.

Finally, Gumer pulled away and straightened her back. She seemed to notice Yolanda for the first time and walked to her. To Yolanda's surprise, she received a hug as well.

"Por favor prométeme," Gumer said, pleading. "Promise me that you will help my son so that they do not deport him."

"Por supuesto," Yolanda said. Of course. She had no idea how she'd do that but felt compelled to promise the woman.

"Tengo que alistar mis cosas," Gumer said, excusing herself to take care of her things, whatever they were. Yolanda and the men watched her go to the back door. Gamaliel called after her, saying he'd be up in a few minutes. When she'd gone, Kinji turned to Gamaliel.

"What did the lawyer say?"

"He's going to argue self-defense," Gamaliel said. Turning to Yolanda, he added, "Your godmother can help describe Mom's state of mind because she thought she'd only scared Frank."

"She'll be happy to help," Yolanda said. "Did he say anything about bail or pleading to a lesser charge?"

"He said bail may be tough because she didn't come forward right away, but he thought involuntary manslaughter might be the most lenient charge. He needs to discuss it with the DA."

Yolanda wondered how her friend would respond if she put in a good word for Gumer. She didn't really know the woman, but Gumer had no other place to go. Even Mexico would be foreign to her after all this time in the US. Yolanda didn't want to get Gamaliel's hopes up, so she made only a mental note of connecting with Celine Cueva. She'd have to speak with José Herrera first, so as not to screw up any of his negotiations on the plea.

"Yo, Yabai!" a voice shouted from the store entrance.

"Guero, Chicali," Kinji said. "You guys got sprung too?"

"Special treatment for those who get caught in the act," the shorter, fair-skinned man said with a huge smile and his hands in the air, pantomiming his arrest.

"They're still trying to keep the jail population down cuz of the Rona," the taller, dark-skinned one said.

They all put on or adjusted their masks at the reminder. Kinji introduced the shorter man as Guero and the taller one as Chicali.

"Yabai?" Gamaliel asked.

"My placa, ese." Kinji tried a pachuco pose with both hands in his pockets, much to the amusement of Kinji's jail buddies.

"Means he's a badass," Guero said. "'Member, dude? Called him that way back when he went after that pendejo who tried to rob the store. Pinche vato never came back into our hood."

Gamaliel half-smiled, presumably at the recollection of Kinji wielding the katana to scare the man away. The half-smile told Yolanda that he welcomed the distraction, but a look toward the back of the store told her he was still focused on his mother and the very different outcome from her use of one of the swords. Yolanda didn't think that Kinji would display them again if the police returned them. Guero and Chicali grabbed a case of beer and brought it to the register.

"Gonna celebrate with the homies," Guero said.

"It's on the house," Kinji said. "Thanks for looking out for me in la pinta." He laughed again, using the slang term for prison. He slapped the two men on the back, walking them out of the store.

"Sorry," he said to Gamaliel when the men were gone. Yolanda thought Kinji regretted joking about his freedom with Gamaliel's mother going to jail. The younger man turned up a corner of his mouth and gave a one-shouldered shrug. No harm done.

"How are you doing?" Yolanda asked while Jesse grabbed a couple more stools for himself and his friend. Gamaliel didn't sit but leaned on his with one hand. He took a moment to respond.

"You know, I don't know that I could resent Frank any more than I do right now. My Tía Chata is dealing with the funeral arrangements. On Saturday she asked for help with them, but that was before she knew my mom had anything to do with him dying. I don't think she'd want any help from us now anyway, but I kinda feel relief at that." He covered his face with his hands and rubbed his eyes, shaking his head. "Fucking Frank." He slumped on his stool and looked at the others one by one. "Thanks for all your help. All of you."

"Is there anything else we can do?" Jesse asked.

Gamaliel shook his head before responding. "Anything you can think of to keep my mom in the country would be great, but I think I need to contact relatives in Chihuahua in case she needs to go soon. Mr. Herrera said one option for a suspended sentence was to self-deport. He thought it was more likely she'd serve time and then be deported, but we'll see."

Yolanda had never heard of a self-deportation option. She thought they shouldn't get their hopes up about it, not with a manslaughter charge.

"Let's hope she doesn't have to do much time," Yolanda said.

"We'll need to deal with it," Gamaliel said.

"And we'll provide whatever help we can," Jesse said before pointing at Yolanda's cast, changing the subject. "Anything we can do to help you find out who did that to you?"

"I don't know. Right now, I'm thinking it was Hector Garcia, but he's dead."

After the three men expressed their shock, speaking over each other to ask how, Yolanda regretted springing the surprise on them.

"I thought you said you'd fallen in the shower," Kinji said.

"Sorry, Kinji." Yolanda blushed, her lie exposed. "When I visited you yesterday, I didn't want you to get distracted by everything else going on. But why don't you sit, I'll fill you in."

She proceeded to tell them all about her suspicion that Hector was embezzling from the family business, and that Kyle and Brian Jacobs likely were blackmailing Hector over it after Kyle overheard his daughter-in-law mention it to his other son, Eric. She confirmed for Gamaliel that she thought Frank and Brian were possibly sharing information about Hector, and maybe his blackmail payments too, but no way of proving it. She also mentioned Brian's suspicion that someone, maybe Hector, had run his father off the road in the motorcycle accident that killed Kyle and hospitalized his grandson. She told them about her meetings with the Garcias and Turi's information about Hector's girlfriend driving a blue truck that Hector claimed had been stolen when she met him at Mel's, and about Hector's death in a drive-by shooting a short time later. She mentioned that she needed to confirm blue paint markings on her car and maybe find the girlfriend, but that she was more worried about finding out who had killed Hector. When she mentioned a new white truck or an old red SUV, Gamaliel perked up.

"Wait," he said. "This happened Saturday night?"

"Yes," Yolanda said. "Any of this ring a bell?"

"Well, remember when you called yesterday, I mentioned that I'd seen the red SUV on Saturday night? Thought it was the guy I'd seen with Frank, maybe looking for him. I thought maybe he didn't know about Frank, but if he did, what would he be doing around here again?"

Yolanda recalled Eric and Christine telling her that Brian had called from near Evergreen Cemetery. To set up an alibi, she'd thought.

"Should we be worried?" Kinji asked.

"My recommendation is that if you see him or that red Suburban or a new white pickup around here again, stay away from it. I don't know what he and Frank were up to, but if he shot Hector, he's not someone you want to mess with. Here, let me give you a number to call if you see him around here again." Yolanda pulled up the contacts app on her phone and shared Detective Lan's number. "Call her and let her know I asked you to call her if you spotted him again. Don't hesitate. He likes sleeveless shirts and has a tattoo of a white pickup on his biceps. Swastikas too."

She didn't mention her dream about a frightened Kinji and Gamaliel but was glad she was able to tell them to be careful. She considered sharing that Brian had also filed a complaint against Sydney but let that go for now. These people had enough on their minds.

"Damn," Gamaliel said, rubbing his face with his hands again, as exhausted as the day she'd met him. That had been on Friday, after his Thursday arrest and subsequent release. Here they were on Monday with Kinji, who'd been arrested and released after him. But now Gamaliel's mother would turn herself in the next day. A roller coaster of emotions over these days would be an understatement. He had to be more than exhausted, his whole world falling apart around him. Yolanda didn't want to burden him with any more details of her investigation and was glad her brother was at his friend's side, supporting him.

"Why don't you head on up to your mom?" she said. "No need to worry about this other stuff right now." She stood and placed a hand on his back. He turned his face into her shoulder and sobbed. Jesse and Kinji came to him, and the four of them stood in a group hug for what seemed like a long time. Kinji broke the silence.

"Go on up to your mom, son. I'll come up after I close the store. Let's take your mom to dinner."

Yolanda and Jesse looked at their watches. That would be in another three hours. Jesse offered to sit with Kinji. The elderly man protested but allowed it once Jesse had offered to make sandwiches in the deli for them and for the Campamoches upstairs. He offered to make one for Yolanda too. She declined but signaled with her head to have him follow her out of the store. After thanking Kinji for the book she'd borrowed, she walked out with Jesse.

"What's up?" he asked.

"The dreams are back."

"Mom and Uncle Bobby warning you again?"

"Well, I think they sent a warning dream regarding my accident, but it wasn't a very clear one." She mentioned the smell of onion and cilantro in her dream and the same smell at her accident after having bought tacos on her way home. "But that was a warning for me. Last night I had a dream of a car chase, a handgun, and a very frightened Kinji and Gamaliel. Never had dreams warning me about someone else before."

"Oh, shit. Maybe it's a warning to you by proximity. Wait. Didn't you once get a warning dream about Sydney?"

"Oh, you're right," she said, recalling her wife's stalker a couple of years ago. "Back then, I thought it was just for me and my loved ones. But this time it could include people around me, in my proximity, like you say." Both paused to think about that before Yolanda continued, "Glad you're sticking around here, but please be on the lookout. And if you see the guy I described, don't hesitate to call 911 and Detective Lan."

Jesse assured her he would. She needed to find out more about Brian and track him down as well. If he'd killed Hector, maybe he thought that he could get money from his lawsuit against Sydney and her hospital. If he'd been brazen enough to shoot Hector, could he go after Sydney too?

CHAPTER NINETEEN

Yolanda wasn't sure where to start, but she always felt most confident in her detective skills back at her office.

"Didn't think I'd see you today," Jane said, looking her up and down, her eyes landing on the arm sling and cast. "At least you don't have a mean shiner this time."

Yolanda had to smile at that.

"I'd prefer a black eye to a herniated disc any day," she said.

"Need any other help?"

"Not yet, but thanks. Gonna run a background check on Brian Jacobs. See what that turns up. Need to find his address in any case."

The background check turned up only minor infractions and one arrest for disorderly conduct at a bar near his home. That arrest also included possession of methamphetamine, but not enough to charge him with a felony. She noted the arrest in Riverside County and thought of her PI friend from the Inland Empire, an aspirational name if Yolanda had ever heard one. No one seemed to question whether the moniker fit the desert counties east of Los Angeles. They weren't any poorer than

Los Angeles County, but a smaller population and less business meant fewer tax revenues and more limited services, at least in the poor, rural areas. Sheila Robinson had moved there with her preteen children from Birmingham, Alabama by way of a "way too cold" Chicago. "On the tail end of the tail end of the Great Migration," she liked to say. Her kids were not kids anymore, likely hitting their twenties soon.

"Robinson. If you lost it, I can find it. How can I help you?"

Yolanda had to smile at Sheila's signature greeting. They'd met and hit it off some years back when they'd both worked on a housing discrimination case for the Fair Housing Coalition in the desert county. Yolanda was ever grateful for her friendship and for Sheila's tip to her on the office in the Bradbury Building. A board member of the Coalition had been a private investigator with Jane Stern's father and had retired around the time that Yolanda was looking for an office. Every time Yolanda looked around her yet-to-be-decorated digs, she couldn't help but wonder what it had been like for Hirschel "H" Stern and Harold Winston working on cases to fight McCarthyism and help the Black Panthers. With names like that, the building owner probably thought they were jewelers, an easy mistake in the middle of the Jewelry District. Instead, they were a Jewish and Black team that the LAPD would not have back then. Instead, they settled for doing some sleuthing on their own. Yolanda had met Harold Winston a few times and loved to hear his stories.

"Hey, Sheila. It's Yolie."

"Hey, girl. What's cooking?"

"Have a question for you but wanted to ask about Mr. Winston too. Haven't heard from him in a bit."

"I think he's still living it up in Henderson," Sheila said, referring to the Nevada town that drew many California retirees. "Slowing down a bit physically, but he's still as sharp as ever. Saw him about a month ago on my way to Vegas."

"Ah, that's great to hear. Please give him my regards. Tell him I love his old office. I'm calling from there now."

"Will do. And you say 'Hey' to that badass wife of yours. What can I do you for?"

Yolanda filled her in on the developments over the last few days.

"Dang, girl. Sounds like you and that grocery store family need one of your godmother's limpias."

"You may be right," Yolanda said. "A spiritual cleansing could do us all a lot of good. But I'm afraid it won't keep Gumer from being deported. I just hope that she and Gamaliel and Kinji come to no harm."

"Why would they if the bad guy you're after got the guy who came after you?"

"Well, remember those dreams I told you about when you helped me get this office?"

"The juju's back?"

"I'll say. Had a dream about a gun, a car chase, and a very frightened Kinji and Gamaliel."

"Girl, like I told you back then. Listen to the juju. You know we all got some of it. You just got an extra helping."

"Don't I know it. Plan to keep my eye on those two, but I want to find Brian Jacobs before he's up to any more mischief. Keep an eye on him too."

"Well, you know how to find his address, what do you need me from me?"

"Thought maybe your contacts would know something more about him, so I know what I'm up against. I mean, besides the racism and the conspiracy theories. If the LAPD doesn't have enough to get him for the drive-by, he'll be running around, maybe thinking he can get away with anything. Makes those types bolder, I think."

"I agree. My contacts and I stay away from those types, as you call them, but lord knows there are plenty of them all over the desert. We keep our distance, but we keep an eye out too. I'll call you with anything I find."

"Thanks," Yolanda said, feeling relief that someone else was involved in bringing Brian Jacobs to justice. "And let me know whenever you want to use the office. You still have the key, right?"

"Sure do. Thanks."

When they'd ended the call, Yolanda considered her next steps, but she was feeling tired again.

"You going home any time soon?" Jane, asked, peeking her head into Yolanda's office.

"You read my mind. I'm exhausted and in need of some more of those anti-inflammatories Sydney recommended."

"Let's head on out, then."

The two women walked to the garage where they kept their cars. The attendant with an aesthetic similar to Jane's commented on Jane's shoes, Fluevogs that Yolanda now found too heavy. The attendant and Jane both wore buttoned vests that Yolanda didn't think she could pull off like they did. When they parted ways, Jane reminded Yolanda to be careful and get some rest.

"Rest would be great," Yolanda said, thinking that there'd be time for that after she found Brian Jacobs. For now, a good night's sleep would do.

CHAPTER TWENTY

Tuesday

On Tuesday morning, Yolanda awoke from a dreamless sleep close to 10:00 a.m. Her body wasn't as sore as it had been, except for the pain from the herniated disc, which seemed to abate somewhat. Most of the soreness she felt now was more likely due to the awkward sleeping position required by the cast on her arm. Sleeping in didn't help either. She glanced at Sydney's side of the bed only to find it empty. It prompted her to get up herself. She made slow progress washing up but felt accomplished at having done it on her own.

On the kitchen island, Sydney had left a note: *Off to work. Peer review today. Love you. S.*

"Shit." Sydney had mentioned the formal meeting the night before, but Yolanda was so tired that it had slipped her mind. She dressed as quickly as she could, which wasn't very quick in her condition. She wolfed down a protein bar with her coffee instead of a decent breakfast.

At the door, Yolanda remembered the image of Kinji and Gamaliel's frightened faces in her recent dream. There was a gun in the dream too. She stopped and headed back upstairs. She put on her shoulder holster with greater ease than she'd thought possible and thanked the goddess for having the cast end just above her elbow. She checked her Glock and confirmed the safety. When she tried to aim with it, she found the cast too restricting. If she had to use her gun, she'd have to brace it awkwardly or with something other than her left hand.

By the time Yolanda arrived at the hospital, it was almost 11:30 a.m. When she walked from the visitor parking garage, she spotted an old red Suburban without license plates at the red curb outside the emergency room. She hadn't noticed it when she'd pulled into the garage, so it likely had just arrived. She walked faster, feeling for her gun and careful not to strain her back. Inside, she heard a man's loud voice beyond the reception area.

"I'm offering you a good deal," a man shouted. "You'll regret it if you don't take it."

"That man is threatening Dr. Garrett," Yolanda screamed at the two security guards at the entrance. They had already stood up upon hearing the shouting and moved faster at Yolanda's statement. She walked around the metal detector and followed the security guards into the emergency room area. One of them got on his radio to request assistance. Yolanda hobbled behind them, staying close. In the center of the vast room, Sydney walked slowly away from behind a circular workstation, trying to draw the man away from the nurses and other hospital workers in the area.

"I can't speak with you," Sydney said to the man in a calm voice that seemed to irritate him more.

"It's the best offer you're gonna get," the man said in a lower voice at the sight of the approaching security guards.

"Have your lawyer speak with mine," Sydney said. "That's the right way to do this."

Yolanda noted Sydney's stance, ready to defend herself or any of her staff.

"Fuck you," the man said in a very calm almost whisper. The sound of it sent chills up Yolanda's back and increased her adrenaline. She walked up to him ahead of the security guards, one of whom pulled at her good arm and asked her to back away. The other guard addressed the man.

"Come on, sir, you can't be in here."

"Right," the man said. "I'm outta here."

He turned and walked out of the emergency room as if he had all the time in the world. He never turned back but waved a raised middle finger in their direction, one of the guards on his heels. Three more security guards ran into the reception area, and all four escorted him out.

The other guard and Yolanda went to Sydney and asked if she was okay.

"I'm fine," she said, leaning against the wall in a back corridor. Turning to Yolanda, she added, "I could have defended myself, you know."

"I have no doubt," Yolanda said, thinking of her wife's second-degree black belt in tae kwon do. "But what did he want?"

"Money. Ten thousand dollars cash, to be exact."

"To settle his lawsuit?" Yolanda asked. "Doesn't seem like much for a wrongful death case."

"Right," Sydney said, but she raised an eyebrow at her wife.

"I mean, just saying." Yolanda gave her an apologetic smile.

"Damn," the security guard said. "You sure you're okay, Dr. Garrett?"

"I'm fine, Gerardo. Let the chief know everything's fine, will you?"

"I'll need to file a report."

"Please do," Yolanda said to the man. She turned to Sydney, "No objections."

"Fine," she said. "Thanks, Gerardo. My wife and I will talk over here." Sydney indicated the on-call room down the corridor. Once they entered, they checked to make sure they weren't disturbing any sleeping residents or interns on any of the cots. The place was empty.

"I'm so sorry," Yolanda said. "Totally forgot today was your peer review meeting. Tell me how it went, then tell me what happened with this guy."

"The meeting went very well," Sydney said with a huge smile. "Just like we thought it would. We're mostly off the hook. Now the hospital will deal with the lawsuit, assuming that guy continues to have representation."

"Mostly?"

"Well, it's not over till it's over. The lawsuit, I mean."

Yolanda gave her wife as tight a hug as she could with her cast on one arm, followed by a kiss that lasted almost as long as the hug.

"I'm so glad to hear it. Congratulations. So, what else did Brian Jacobs say?"

"Well, first he came up to the nurses' station and creeped out Sylvia. You know her, she can handle anything on this floor, but he creeped her out with a maniacal smile. She tried to keep him occupied while another nurse went to warn me. Before he did, I walked up behind them not knowing what was going on. Sylvia looked at me with a scared look on her face, and he started talking to me. Introduced himself as Brian Jacobs and said he had an offer I wouldn't want to refuse, giving me this weird-ass smile the whole time."

"Like a bad imitation of *The Godfather*?" Yolanda shook her head. "Really?"

"Yup. Sylvia told him to stop being a creep and leave. He insisted I hear him out. He offered to withdraw his complaint if I paid him ten thousand dollars in cash. I tried to walk him away from the others, and I think you heard the rest."

"That's some crazy shit, but I'm glad you're okay."

"You just make sure you're careful with that gun," Sydney said, patting the bulge under Yolanda's unbuttoned shirt. When Yolanda looked at her without responding, Sydney added, "You don't think I felt it with that hug?" She smiled and shook her head.

"Whatever. Let me see what else your security guys get out of him. I'm sure the chief will want to file a report with the Pasadena PD."

"Go on. I'll be fine. But stay away from that guy. He's either high or psychotic. Gonna go check on my people."

When Yolanda walked out to the reception area she saw only one security guard. She exited the building, thinking the others would be outside, but there was no one out there, and the red SUV was gone. She almost ran back to the guard inside, but a back spasm slowed her down to walking with a limp.

"You guys let him go?"

"We were gonna hold him, but once he got outside, he ran to his car and took off. We couldn't stop him. Gerardo is writing his report back at the office."

"You've got to be kidding me!" Yolanda couldn't believe it. She headed back to the security office to speak with Gerardo and the chief of security. She caught Chief Johnson coming out of his office when she stepped into the security room full of video and computer equipment. He gave Yolanda a warm smile and went over to shake her hand in greeting. The former Pasadena Police Captain looked as dapper as ever in a dark-blue suit. He'd lost some weight but looked younger instead of older as some men do when they get in shape.

"What brings you here?" he asked.

"The disturbance just now in the ER," Yolanda said, pointing with her chin to the security guard at a computer screen. "I think Gerardo's writing the report now, but looks like the guy got away after threatening Sydney."

"What?" Chief Johnson asked. His raised eyebrows wrinkled his forehead and a good portion of his bald head too.

The security guard turned from the computer screen and relayed what happened.

"He got away?" the chief asked, his smile gone.

"We called in a report to the PD, but we couldn't chase him. And his vehicle didn't have a license plate."

"But we know who he is," Yolanda said, interrupting what she was sure would have been a dressing down of the security guard. The chief turned to her, and she continued, "He filed a complaint against Sydney and Connor a few weeks ago when his father didn't make it after a motorcycle accident. Sydney saved his nephew, though. The guy's also a suspect in a drive-by shooting that killed a man on Saturday night."

The security guard's eyes could not have gotten bigger.

"Please have a seat," Chief Johnson said. "Fill us in."

Yolanda gave an abbreviated version of the weekend's events, concentrating on Brian Jacobs's background and presumed whereabouts. The chief turned to the security guard.

"Get Ng in here. See if he can pull up a video screenshot with a good image of the man, and make sure all stations in the hospital get a copy with an APB."

Yolanda remembered Duc "Duke" Ng, the young security guard who once had a crush on Sydney. She hoped his feelings for her wife would help ensure he did his job well.

"You know," Chief Johnson said, turning back to Yolanda. "We have to stop meeting like this. At least we know more about this guy than the last one. Any chance we can keep Dr. Garrett from being chased by these nefarious characters in the future?"

"This one came through your hospital before he came across my case," Yolanda said, sounding more defensive than she'd intended. "But I do have an address for him out in Jurupa Valley. Maybe someone can pay him a visit. His car didn't have plates, but I found them in a background check last night. He also drives a newer white pickup truck. If he's driving the old SUV, I'm concerned he is definitely up to something." Yolanda checked the small notebook in her shirt pocket and looked for the information she'd jotted down the night before. Chief Johnson handed her a sticky note from one of the computer desks, and she provided Brian Jacobs's address, phone number, and license plate numbers. She also provided contact information that she'd found for his mother, who lived at the same address.

"Damn, you're good," Gerardo said. Chief Johnson nodded in agreement.

"I'm sure your legal team would have provided the same, given his claim against Sydney," Yolanda said. Her phone buzzed in her back pocket, and she excused herself. In the hallway, she answered a call from Sheila Robinson.

"Please tell me you have good information for me," Yolanda said without a greeting. "I just chased the guy out of Sydney's hospital. He came to ask for a cash settlement of his complaint against her, but he took off in his dad's car. Took off the license plates. Means he's up to no good."

"Wow," Sheila said. "Glad I called. Is Sydney okay?"

"You know her. Not even fazed. Figures she can defend herself, and I'm sure she can. She was more concerned about her coworkers. The guy sounded irrational, maybe high, but was a bit creepy too. Scared one of the supervising nurses who's not easy to scare."

"Maybe he was high," Sheila said. "Heard that he's mostly a loner, but more recently he's been hanging out with some meth heads in Jurupa Valley and near Palmdale."

"Palmdale?" Yolanda said. "Meth capital of Southern California?"

"It's a nice town, but yes, the outskirts have lots of meth labs. Jurupa's nice too, but some of the rundown areas have the same, just like most towns nowadays."

"Agreed. But that's quite a hike between the two."

"Not sure how he made a connection way out in Palmdale. Probably for meth. But some of his contacts out there are running an extortion racket. His acquaintances in Jurupa don't seem to be involved in any dealing. Mostly using. Maybe he's acting as their meth connection. Who knows?"

"What kind of extortion in Palmdale?"

"Mostly quick money stuff, going after people with money or stable jobs who've gotten hooked on meth and whose employers or families would not approve. Only a couple of the extortionists have done time, so I figure it's a new enterprise, enriched by prison education. My contact at the sheriff's says they only started to look into them a couple of months ago. Seems they expanded from fencing stolen goods for sale online to selling meth last year. This year's business growth is focused on extortion. Not sure yet if they're involved in meth production, but it's probably just a matter of time. My take is that your guy wasn't involved in any extortion because his contact with them seems limited, but he may have learned a few things from them and may be moving in that direction on his own."

"Well, if he was blackmailing Hector, that's certainly an indication. And based on the proposal he made to Sydney, he seems hard up for cash."

"Means he's desperate. And desperate people on meth can be dangerous."

"Don't I know it." Yolanda paused, thinking. "Oh, shit."

"What?"

"The Abe Grocery. Remember the dream I told you about? He may be going after Kinji or Gamaliel. Frank had threatened Gamaliel's mother with a call to ICE about their undocumented status. Maybe Brian is looking to pick up where Frank left off. Damn, I gotta get over there." Yolanda barely heard Sheila's warning to be careful before ending the call and heading to her car.

CHAPTER TWENTY-ONE

Kinji tried not to feel sorry for the young man he thought of as a grandson. Both sat behind the cash register, neither saying a word. What was there to say? Kinji certainly wasn't about to pull out the shikata ga nai saying that his parents did during and after Heart Mountain. Accepting and moving on from Gumer's arrest wouldn't be easy for either of them, but it would be especially hard for Gamaliel. Shikata ga nai helped Kinji and his family during and after the war. They couldn't do anything about their situation, had to move on. But these were different times. He looked over at a dejected Gamaliel, hunched on his stool, head bent over hands clasped between his knees. The elderly man thought of another concept that might be more fitting. One that Gamaliel had lived with all his life.

"Gaman," Kinji said.

"What's that?" Gamaliel turned to him, slowly coming out of his own inner thoughts.

"Gaman," Kinji repeated. "Means what you would call 'aguante.'" When Gamaliel squinted at him in confusion, he added, "Perseverance, endurance, but I think the Spanish *aguante* captures it better."

"What about it?" Gamaliel said, straightening and turning toward Kinji with his full attention now.

"You've lived with it all your life, and the universe just tossed more *gaman* at you."

"No shit. I don't know about the universe, but fucking Frank sure did."

Kinji could feel his anger from a few feet away. He let Gamaliel take a few breaths while he dispatched a kid who'd come in for a quart of milk. When he turned back to Gamaliel, the young man was staring into midspace, shaking his head.

"That fucker," he said, tightening his lips until they turned white before continuing, "He had all the advantages of citizenship, and he threw it all away. What I wouldn't have done…What my mom wouldn't have done…" Gamaliel took a deep breath without finishing the thought. Kinji waited for him to continue. "I'm no saint, I know, but I never had…I was never…" He dropped the thought, fighting back tears.

"You're entitled to your anger at him," Kinji said, "but be careful that it doesn't eat you up. Remember what I used to tell you as kid about how not to think of yourself?"

"I remember." Gamaliel quoted from memory, "'If you define yourself by what you are not or by what you do not have, you will always want and will always be wanting.'"

"Right. Guy at the post office used to say that. Grew up in the South. Serious hard knocks, but it was his personal code. Still holds true for anyone. He was a good man. And so are you, Gamaliel. Never forget that. Heck, you embody *kaizen* better than any corporate guru ever did."

"What's *kaizen*?"

"It's a way to embrace personal improvement," Kinji said, thinking that the events of the last few days had him drawing on things his brother had tried to teach him. "Corporate types call it continuous improvement in those business books you like to read. But it's more than that. It comes from right here," Kinji said, drawing the fingertips of his right hand together and tapping his sternum with them. "You, son, have lived it in your everyday life, since you were a kid, even while resenting Frank. Maybe that resentment has helped you embrace kaizen. You've never wanted to be like your cousin. You've wanted to be better."

"That hasn't been hard to do," Gamaliel said with an ironic chuckle.

"Maybe not, but not everyone does it like you did. I think my brother used similar motivation. Masaru didn't want to be like our dad, self-righteous and clinging to a samurai family past that may or may not have been real. Didn't like being told that we were named after some famous samurai. Masaru just lived doing the right thing." It was Kinji's turn to stare into midspace and shake his head at the memory of his brother. "Me? I just ran from it all. That's why I went to work for the postal service, to be away from my dad, be something other than him. But you and Masaru took a better path, not just being something other, but being better. Better men. Damn, I wish I'd gotten to know my brother more. Could have learned so much from him."

"Well, aren't we a sorry pair," Gamaliel said. Kinji took it as an effort to cheer him up. "Any Japanese concepts besides gaman and kaizen to get us both out of this funk?"

"We are a sorry pair, aren't we?" Kinji had to chuckle along with Gamaliel, glad they both were able to laugh at themselves. He glanced up to the bookshelf. "I can order a book on Japanese concepts," he said, returning his gaze to Gamaliel. "You know, my brother used to talk about ikigai. Used to tell me we all have a purpose in life and that I would find mine, just like he'd found his. I don't know if I believed that his purpose in life was to fight the injustice of military conscription. Said it was the right thing to do while we were still imprisoned only for looking like the enemy, but I think it helped him move forward. He worked for some civil rights organization in the Bay Area and with the United Farm Workers too. God, I wish we'd been closer in age. Would have made for a closer relationship."

"Is that why you say you grew up as an only child?"

"Pretty much. I think I was an oops baby. Everyone else moved away soon after we got back from Heart Mountain."

"I guess the only-child thing is something we both have in common," Gamaliel said, looking at the older man with so much raw affection that Kinji had to look away. But he could not deny that he loved the young man as if he were his own.

Both men looked up at the sound of loud footsteps on the linoleum floor. They glanced at each other in recognition of the man meeting the description that Yolanda had provided. Kinji silently opened a drawer that used to hold a knife, but he closed it, pursing his lips in disappointment. The police had confiscated all the knives they'd found in the store. He looked wide-eyed at Gamaliel, who stood and placed his stool in front of him. He leaned on it with both arms, grasping the seat with his hands, as if ready to use it as a weapon. Kinji nodded to him in acknowledgment.

"Ah, just the people I need to see." A bearded man in a tank top that showed off impressive but offensive sleeves of tattoos stopped at the counter, smiling as if he was in on a secret the others weren't. Kinji found the smile and tone of voice unnerving but tried not to show it. "Actually," he said. "Thought I'd catch Frank here too. Saw his car across the street, is he around?"

"Frank's dead," Kinji said, surprising himself at the calm in his voice.

"Whoa, what's that you say?"

"You heard the man," Gamaliel said, standing to his full height, shorter than the man but stockier. Kinji looked from the man to Gamaliel and back, thinking he and Gamaliel could take him. He didn't want this to become a fight, but he stood off his stool to be at the ready just in case. His six-foot-three frame seemed to surprise the bearded man, his smile going away.

"Well, I guess that just leaves me, then. I'm Brian." He tried smiling again and stuck his hand across the counter, but neither man took it.

"What do you want?" Kinji asked, trying to keep his voice even.

"Well, we're all businessmen," Brian said, leaning on the counter. "I'll cut to the chase. I have a proposition." When neither man responded he continued, pointing to each of them in turn, "You own the store and you're undocumented. Be a shame if someone called ICE to report both of you. I can prevent that from happening for a small fee, maybe even on a monthly payment plan."

Kinji glanced at Gamaliel, whose jaw clenched and eyes narrowed in anger. The older man held up a finger to let him know he'd respond for them. Kinji leaned on the counter until he was eye to eye with Brian. He spoke slowly in a low, deep voice that often worked with youngsters caught shoplifting.

"Frank tried some of that business here the other day, and now he's dead. I don't think you want to go there."

Gamaliel looked at Kinji, his eyes as wide as Brian's, but Brian recovered first, holding up his hands, the sick smile back.

"Whoa, old man. Think about it. Ten K up front and another K every month should do it. Don't say no until you see that I can keep my end of the bargain." He stroked his beard as if thinking. "Course, missed payments mean interest, and multiple missed payments could mean more than a call to ICE." He looked around the store. "Not many windows here, but that door's pretty wide. Wide enough for some bullets to come through. Wouldn't you say?"

Kinji's own jaw tightened now. He spoke in the same voice but through his teeth this time.

"Get the hell out of here, and don't let me ever see your face again."

"I'll give you until Friday," Brian said, sure of himself. "That's my payday. And don't be surprised by any messages before then—messages just to show you I mean business."

"You heard the man," Gamaliel said, adopting the same tone as Kinji. "Get the hell out."

Brian turned on his heel and walked out slowly, as if to tell them that he was not afraid of them and that they should fear him instead. Before he was out the door, Gamaliel dialed Detective Lan.

* * *

On the way to her car, Yolanda thought of the woman who would have turned herself in to custody that morning. José had told her that he'd pick up Gumer and Gamaliel early in the morning. Yolanda had meant to visit Gamaliel when he got back anyway, and now she figured he'd been back for a few hours. Jesse had class at Cal State LA, so Yolanda knew he wouldn't be there for his friend until later. She thought she'd make it to the Abe Grocery in no time until she hit rare early-afternoon traffic on the Pasadena Freeway. Must be an accident, she thought. She maneuvered to an exit and took the streets. She wound her way through South Pasadena, El Sereno, and finally into Boyle Heights, taking the street that ran by General Hospital up to Evergreen Avenue. She wondered if this had been the route Hector had taken on the night Frank had died.

She zigzagged her way across Wabash Avenue to the street that led to the historic cemetery. Before she reached El Tepeyac, she heard gunshots up ahead. She counted three rapid shots and sped up, hearing three more before seeing the old red SUV in the middle of the street. She steered with her cast, reaching for her gun with her good arm while Brian Jacobs fired three more rounds at the Abe Grocery and took off, heading north, barely missing a head-on collision with Yolanda. She swerved and gunned it, braking hard in front of the store and lowering her passenger window before shouting, "Anyone hurt in there?"

She saw Gamaliel come around the counter, his cell phone to his ear.

"We're good. Have Detective Lan on the phone."

"Gonna follow him," Yolanda said, giving Gamaliel a thumbs-up. She managed a fast U-turn, grateful for the wide street, and followed the big SUV, honking as she went to alert pedestrians. Brian Jacobs zigzagged back up the way Yolanda had arrived, but on Marengo Street he made a sharp turn onto the 10 freeway, heading east. Her phone rang in the passenger seat. She glanced at it and saw Detective Lan's caller ID. She cursed the lack of Bluetooth in the rental car and tried steering with her cast again while putting the phone on speaker. She interrupted the detective before she could finish asking where she was.

"Ten freeway east. Number two lane. Just passing the 710. Eighty miles an hour and speeding up. Red Suburban. No plates. Get a chopper."

"You know you're not supposed to be chasing this guy."

"I'll pull back as soon as I see a chopper or the CHP on his tail."

"Okay, back off. Chopper's on the way. Gotta go radio the CHP."

"Got it," Yolanda said with no intention of ending the chase. "But know that the Riverside sheriffs will have a bead on this guy in Jurupa Valley. He lives somewhere around Jurupa but may get his meth from near Palmdale."

"Thanks," Detective Lan said. "Will pass it along. Gotta go."

A couple of minutes later, Yolanda saw the helicopter overhead but didn't see any flashing lights behind her until several miles farther into West Covina. As soon as she heard the sirens, she pulled off to the right and the exit. She swung around and got back on the westbound lanes to return to the grocery store. The CHP would take care of Brian Jacobs.

When she arrived, she saw two patrol cars parked at odd angles in front of the store. A bit dramatic, Yolanda thought, given that the suspect was leading a car chase now. She turned onto Malabar Street and parked alongside the store. The memorial to Frank Vásquez had stopped growing but sat undisturbed. The officers had not bothered to block off the store entrance with yellow crime scene tape, but they had several cones on the street and the sidewalk, likely marking shell casings and bullets.

"Where'd he go?" Gamaliel asked when he saw Yolanda.

"Eastbound on the 10," she said. "CHP and choppers are on him. Don't think he'll get too far in that old heap. You okay? Kinji okay?"

"I'm fine," Kinji said, coming up one of the store aisles with a broom and a dustpan. "I think we're still missing a bullet." He looked up and down the shelves and then back at the floor, zeroing in on one shelf. "Here we go," he shouted to an officer at the door. "Looks like the only bullet that made it inside hit this bag of flour."

"Were you guys behind the counter at the time?" Yolanda asked.

"Yup," Kinji said. "Took cover back there. But he wasn't a very good shot if this is the only bullet that made it inside."

The three of them walked back out to the front of the store, where Yolanda studied the bullet holes.

"No, guys," she said, pointing at the bullet holes around the frame of the door. "He meant this as a message. Look at the pattern. I heard nine shots. Look where they hit. Three on each side of the door, and three above. This one in the middle on the left is the only one that made it inside. Splintered the doorframe. That's the shot that missed. He meant it to be an inch or more from the doorframe."

"Holy cow," Kinji said, his jaw dropping.

"Damn," Gamaliel said. "He's a damned good shot, then. Hope they get him."

"So do I," Yolanda said. "But I think he may stay away from here for a bit. Did he say anything before he opened fire?"

"Did he ever," Kinji said. "Come inside, we'll fill you in."

Once inside, Gamaliel offered Yolanda a sandwich from the deli. She declined, thinking that people sometimes resorted to basic courtesies like hospitality when their nerves ached for a return to normalcy. Kinji and Gamaliel relayed what happened when Brian came into the store. She didn't know if the creepy smile was meth-related, but she didn't like how unsettling it felt hearing about it from Sydney and now from these two men.

"I know you don't need this on top of everything else," Yolanda said to Gamaliel. "How'd your mom do this morning?"

Gamaliel gave her a one-shouldered shrug and turned up one side of his mouth in what Yolanda read as an effort to hold back tears.

"She tried to be strong. We'll be okay," he said, trying to be strong himself.

Before Yolanda could respond, Maya Luna, Turi's wife, stuck her head in the door.

"You guys okay?" She continued when she saw both men standing by the flour on the floor. "Gotta get back to my kids, but you should check out the car chase on TV," she said. "It's on all the channels."

Kinji thanked her, and Gamaliel went over to the deli to turn on the television mounted high in the corner. He seemed to welcome the distraction.

"Put it on Channel 5," Kinji said. "They're the best on car chases." Gamaliel acquiesced. Everyone in Southern California who followed car chases had a favorite car chase channel. Some had real-time speed and direction meters, others had multiple screens with maps, and others had map overlays with video coverage. Yolanda sometimes thought that the coverage had become as specialized as the weather, but more interesting and variable than the weather in LA. Sydney always shook her head at the fascination with car chases but understood why her team in the ER monitored them when they approached the hospital's service area. Rox was always the first to alert their group chat about a new chase, the freeway involved, and the direction. Yolanda appreciated the updates when driving because it helped anticipate the bottlenecks but didn't follow them otherwise.

The television coverage did not disappoint. Even the police officers waiting for the detectives came in to watch. A couple of customers stopped to watch as well.

"What's he doing?" Kinji asked. "Is this one of those slow-speed chases?"

"Certainly doesn't seem to be speeding," Gamaliel said.

"Maybe he's running out of gas," a customer offered.

"That thing has a huge gas tank," Kinji said. "He can go on forever on half a tank."

"Okay, guys," Yolanda said, shaking her head at one of Southern California's favorite pastimes. "Gotta go. Will check in with you tomorrow." She had agreed to meet Sydney at home so that they could drive together to dinner with the people who had helped her get out of her banged-up car on Saturday night.

They barely heard her. She shook her head again. Like Sydney, she didn't understand the fascination and didn't get why suspects did it. They always got caught. She could think of only one or two times when suspects got away, once near LAX where the air traffic impeded helicopters, and another where the original infraction was not serious and police stopped the chase for the safety of the public. They'd probably apprehended that suspect later unless he'd stolen the car. In this case, Brian Jacobs was toast. Just a matter of time, she thought. In her car, she thought that Brian's expert marksmanship made him a stronger suspect in the drive-by shooting that killed Hector Garcia.

At home, Yolanda turned on the TV to see if Brian had been caught.

"A car chase?" Sydney asked, coming down the stairs. "Really?"

"You'll be interested in this one. It's Brian Jacobs." When Sydney looked at her with raised eyebrows, she patted the cushion next to her. "Come sit, I'll fill you in." Once she did, Sydney sank back into the sofa.

"You mean he had a gun the whole time he was in the hospital?"

"Don't know. Could have had it in the car. If he went around the metal detector like I did, he could have had it with him."

"Damn."

Yolanda patted her wife's knee, and they watched the chase for a while. It looked like Brian was going off and on the freeway but continuing to head east. Spike strips didn't seem to be working. He either drove around them, or the officers tossing them in his way missed their mark. Yolanda wasn't sure why they hadn't tried a pit maneuver, bumping his rear fender to make him crash, but then she realized there were too many other cars around. The police would not want to endanger other drivers.

"So, where's dinner?" she asked Sydney while they continued to watch.

"Some place called Casa Fina. Hugo Montes said he and his wife had been meaning to try it since the owners changed."

"Casa Fina? You mean the former Serenata?"

"I don't know. It's on First Street in Boyle Heights. Is that the one?"

"You don't remember, do you?"

"Remember what?"

"I got banged in the head with a metal pipe in the parking lot behind it," Yolanda said, recalling an older attempt to keep her from investigating a case.

"Oh, shit. You okay going back there?"

"Sure. I think so," Yolanda said, hoping so.

"How about we park on the street instead of the lot?"

Yolanda gave her a thumbs-up.

When they arrived at the restaurant, Yolanda noted that La Serenata's white tablecloths were gone, but Casa Fina seemed to have a welcoming, casual vibe. They even had used books by Latina authors on shelves near the back door, a kind of lending library. At the bar, all eyes were on the television above the liquor bottles.

"Is that chase still going on?" Yolanda asked no one in particular.

"Can't see much of it now," a waiter said. "He's near the Ontario airport. The helicopters can't get close."

"Looks like he's heading to the mall near the airport," a bartender said.

A woman at the bar pointed at the TV.

"Look, he ran into the mall," she said.

"Oh, damn," the bartender said. "They're going to lose him." The television channel broke for a commercial but continued to show the video on a small screen on the lower right. Sydney shook her head.

"You've got to be kidding me," she said. At first, Yolanda thought she was referring to the station's efforts to keep their viewers from changing channels to another live feed, but then she realized she was thinking of Brian Jacobs. "They're really gonna let him get away? I can't believe it."

"Hi." A stocky, bearded Latino tapped Sydney on the shoulder. Her demeanor changed almost immediately. She gave the man one of her signature smiles and a warm embrace. When she went to hug the two women with him, the man turned to Yolanda, pointing to her cast.

"You must be Yolanda Ávila. So glad you didn't get hurt more than that."

"Hugo Montes, I am so happy to be able to give you a hug," Yolanda said and did just that. She did the same with his wife, a similarly stocky Jenny, and his sister Beatriz, a younger, female version of Hugo. "I don't think that I can thank you enough for saving my life." Her three rescuers blushed and protested that anyone would have done what they did, and that it wasn't that big a deal.

"Well, if not her life," Sydney said, "you certainly saved her from far greater and lasting injuries. Come on, let's sit." She signaled a waiter, who showed them to a table on the other side of the room. Yolanda sat with her back to the wall and with a full view of the television over the bar.

"Sydney's right," Yolanda said after they'd ordered drinks. "I'm lucky this broken arm and a sore back is all I got out of it. She's told me, but I'd like to hear from you how you did it."

Yolanda thought the family was eager to share their story, and she wanted to hear it. They did not disappoint. The three launched into an animated tale of how Beatriz first heard the crunch of metal and how Hugo and Jenny ran out of their house in time to see Yolanda's Jeep hurl down the embankment. Jenny saw something fly out a window and went to retrieve it while Hugo kicked in the front windshield. He and Beatriz helped Yolanda get out of the vehicle. They had no idea how close in time they'd been to the ensuing fireball. Jenny praised Yolanda for having a label with Sydney's phone number as her emergency contact on the back of her driver's license.

Yolanda listened intently, but they paused while the waiter brought their drinks, cocktails as good as Mel's and a cucumber agua fresca for the underaged Beatriz. She glanced at the television while the waiter took their food order. The sound was on low, and she was too far away to make out the captions on the screen. All she could see was an aerial shot of the mall where Brian had abandoned his car. She worried that, as unlikely as it seemed, he might get away. She wondered if he'd parked his white pickup nearby. When the waiter left, she focused on her rescuers again.

"I only remember you, Hugo. Beatriz, I had no idea that you helped get me out of the car too." She placed a hand on the young woman's hand. "Thank you."

The young woman blushed again, but a proud smile lit up her face. She sipped her agua fresca, seemingly embarrassed by the focus on her. They continued to talk about the accident, Sydney's response, and the paramedics' response. When their food arrived, Hugo savored his enchiladas de mole, saying that the food was as good as La Serenata's had been. The others agreed, diving into their own plates.

The conversation turned to the Montes family and their history growing up in Boyle Heights. They'd moved around different parts of East Los Angeles before landing at the bottom of Monterey Hills. Their grandparents had been displaced by freeway construction that tore through the community like spider veins. This family had been displaced by ever-soaring rents. They mentioned growing up LA sports fans. Yolanda and Sydney looked quickly at each other, both likely thinking the same thing: The family would love some Dodger tickets before the end of the season, maybe Fan Appreciation Day, and maybe some Rams and Lakers tickets after that.

Yolanda glanced at the television from time to time, but nothing seemed to have changed. Their conversation had moved on to schools they'd attended and work. Jenny described her job as a home care worker and her interest in nursing school, which Sydney encouraged. Yolanda had asked Beatriz about her community college classes when they heard a commotion at the bar.

"You're shitting me," a man at the bar said. The diners all turned to the television. The bartender raised his hands in exasperation.

"He got away?" he asked no one in particular. "No way!"

Yolanda and Sydney rose from their seats and walked closer to the television, napkins in hand. They read the closed captions and turned to each other, then returned to their seats in silence.

"What's the deal?" Hugo asked.

"He got away. I can't believe he got away," Sydney said, her eyes downcast.

"What?" Beatriz asked. "Do you know him?"

Sydney let Yolanda respond.

"It's a long story," Yolanda said. "We think he shot and killed the guy who rammed my car and threw me into your hands."

"Dang," Hugo said. "That's some serious revenge."

"No," Yolanda said. "They had a running beef. But he also happens to be a guy who filed a complaint against Sydney and one of her colleagues." Yolanda told them of the efforts to save Kyle Jacobs and Jack Jacobs after their motorcycle accident. The Montes family sat in silence along with Sydney and Yolanda, shaking their heads at the turn of events. Yolanda excused herself and stepped outside to call Chief Johnson at the hospital and the Abe Grocery. Chief Johnson committed to keeping his security personnel on alert.

"You think he'll be back?" Gamaliel asked.

"I don't know," Yolanda said. "I wouldn't think so, but people on meth aren't predictable. Who knows what's going through his head? Is there any place you and Kinji can go for a couple of days?"

"And close the store?" Gamaliel asked. "No way."

"Well, it's near closing time for you anyway, isn't it? I suggest you sleep at Kinji's house tonight so you can look out for each other." Yolanda hoped they wouldn't have reason to, but she couldn't shake the thought of Brian going back.

CHAPTER TWENTY-TWO

Wednesday

After a restless night, Yolanda woke up early. She'd wanted to visit Eric and Christine Jacobs to ask about Brian after dinner the night before, but Sydney convinced her it was best not to drive the thirty miles to Chino after having three drinks. Her headache reminded her of another reason why she shouldn't have had them. She'd taken advantage because she'd stopped taking pain medication, but now she regretted that some of the back pain had returned. She moved slowly to get up without waking Sydney but then realized her wife had gotten up already. In the kitchen, Yolanda welcomed the smell of fresh-brewed coffee. Sydney leaned her back on the counter, sipping from a mug. She turned to pour another and handed it to a grateful Yolanda, along with two aspirins. Yolanda took them, embarrassed. She looked back up at her wife.

"How'd you know?"

"You mixed your alcohol last night. A margarita, a mojito, and an old-fashioned. Tequila, rum, and bourbon. Not hard to tell what was coming."

"Damn. Sorry, love. Why didn't you stop me?"

"After the news of Brian Jacobs getting away, I had an old-fashioned myself."

The two women moved to sit on stools at the kitchen island, both looking into their mugs in silence. Yolanda regretted not going to the Jacobs' after dinner. Sydney had made the right call in getting her to stay home, but she should not have had three drinks in any case. Sydney never drank more than one cocktail at a sitting anymore. It had helped Yolanda cut down right when her own body had started telling her to do the same. Sleepless, restless nights would do that.

"Okay, no more three-drink nights, okay?" Yolanda brought her mug up in a toast, and Sydney responded in turn.

"What's your plan today?" Sydney asked.

"Gotta visit Eric and Christine to see if they have any clue about Brian's whereabouts."

"Want me to come with?"

"Nah…" Yolanda said, before stopping herself. "You want to see the kid, don't you?" When Sydney nodded, she continued, "Thanks. Might be good to back each other up in case it was Eric who shot Hector instead of Brian. You think you're up to that if necessary?"

"Absolutely."

They got dressed and headed out to Chino, the poor cousin of its neighbor Chino Hills. Yolanda shook the chain-link gate to make sure there was no dog in the well-kept yard. Eric's truck in the driveway surprised her. She'd thought he'd be at work. Eric answered the door and did not seem surprised to see them.

"Glad you're both home," Yolanda said after the two couples exchanged greetings in the tidy living room. Sydney immediately asked about Jack, and Christine took her to his bedroom. In the living room, Yolanda sat on the couch while Eric took what she assumed was his chair, both facing a fifty-five-inch television screen.

"I'm sure you can guess why I'm here," Yolanda said.

"I'm sure I can. But I have no idea where he is or where he could have gone."

"I take it you weren't as close as he and your dad were."

Eric looked away at the mention of his deceased father. Or was it at the mention of his brother? Would he tell Yolanda where he was if he knew?

"Have the cops come around yet?"

Eric didn't hide his surprise at the question, turning quickly back to Yolanda.

"Why would they come around here?"

"Same reason I'm here. You're family. You might have an idea where he would go."

"I don't."

"Listen, Eric. He probably killed Hector in that drive-by, then fired on a business after trying to extort money from them, then led the cops on a wild chase. What is he driving now, his white truck? Unless he switches to something else, it's only a matter of time before he's caught. What does your mother drive, by the way?"

"Leave my mother out of this," Eric said, bringing his hands together as if pleading. "Look, I don't know where he is. I'm telling you that, and I'd tell the cops that too."

"Let me ask you something else, then. I forgot to ask last time we spoke. Do you own a gun? Are you as good a marksman as your brother?"

Eric's eyes opened wide at that but didn't say anything.

"Come on, Eric. You had as much of a motive to go after Hector as your brother did. Maybe more. He lost his father. So did you, but you almost lost your son too. Doesn't matter that there's no proof of Hector's involvement."

"Look," Eric said, standing. "I gotta get to a worksite."

Yolanda stood as well, unsure how she'd keep him talking. She wondered why he was being circumspect. Was he trying to protect his brother? She noted that he hadn't answered her question about his mother's car and wondered if he was protecting her too. Or was he trying to protect himself because he'd been the one who killed Hector? Had speculation and conspiracy theorizing convinced either—or both—of the brothers that Hector had run their father off the road?

Yolanda was about to ask for his opinion of Hector when she heard Christine call her husband from a back room. He turned and walked to the sound of his wife's voice. Yolanda followed. At Jack's room, she hung back at the door while Jack demonstrated his use of a pulley system that Eric had apparently set up that morning to help his son pull himself up and sit up in bed. His parents and Sydney clapped at his success. Yolanda did too but stepped into the hallway when her phone buzzed in her pocket. When she saw Detective Lan's caller ID, she continued to walk out to the front porch.

"Hey, Ávila," Lan said. "A couple of items for you."

"Shoot."

"Cell tower readings place Hector Garcia on your hill around the time of your accident. We found the so-called stolen truck in a drugstore parking lot off Figueroa. Lots of front-end damage, but I guess it kept running. A newer truck would have been totaled. They don't make 'em like they used to."

"Damn, thanks for confirming," Yolanda said, not sure if she felt any relief. "What's the second thing?"

"More important matter. Any chance a woman could have shot Hector Garcia?"

"What? I don't…" Yolanda paused. "Oh, shit." How could she have not suspected her? She stared at the front lawn, mentally kicking herself. "You thinking Christine Jacobs?"

"Don't know. Was calling to ask for a current description. No sign of Brian Jacobs anywhere near the shooting in Eagle Rock. No white truck and no red SUV. But a woman with a ponytail sticking out of a dark baseball cap follows Garcia's car for a while in San Marino. It's dark out, but she's wearing sunglasses and a Covid mask. Too dark to make out hair color. Surveillance video captures her again in Eagle Rock near the shooting but not at the exact corner. No cameras there. Dark-colored SUV. Could be a RAV4. Missing license plates. Looks like premeditation to me."

Yolanda glanced at the driveway. In front of Eric's truck sat a charcoal-gray RAV4 SUV not missing its license plates.

"Oh, god," she said, sinking against the wall next to the door. "Could be her. What kind of gun?"

"Not sure, but it's a nine millimeter."

"I can see what kinds of guns they have. I'm at their house now."

"What the hell?" Lan raised her voice. "Get the hell out of there. I don't want you interfering with this case."

"Hey, you called me to ask for help. I'm helping. Gotta go." Yolanda ended the call before Lan could object. How had she missed the timing? Here she thought Eric could have done it, but it was Christine who had gone home to shower, returning to the hospital later Saturday night. Plenty of time to head to San Marino, follow Lisa in Hector's car, and then follow Hector after he dropped off Lisa in Eagle Rock. Shit.

Back inside, Yolanda walked to Jack's bedroom. She couldn't help but feel for the boy upon hearing his mother could very well go to prison. She'd felt the same toward Gamaliel, but a grown man could handle it better than a kid, she thought.

"All right, little man," Christine said. "That's enough excitement for today. We'll do more physical therapy later."

Yolanda caught Sydney's eye and motioned with her head toward the living room. Both sat on the couch, Yolanda filling her in on Lan's call in a whisper. Sydney closed her eyes and shook her head at the additional tragedy to strike this family.

"We stand when they come back," Yolanda said. "Near the door." Sydney pressed her lips together as if mentally preparing herself. When Jack's parents came back to the living room, Yolanda noticed a somber look on both faces. Christine's turned into a smile as soon as she saw the two women. The smile didn't reach her eyes. Yolanda and Sydney stood and moved in front of the door.

"I take it you've told Christine about my questions," Yolanda said to Eric. Neither responded, but Christine's smile turned into a frown. "What kinds of guns do you guys own? And are they here in the house?"

"What are you talking about?" Christine asked. Eric placed his hand on his wife's arm.

"Look," he said. "We don't know where Brian is. He has no access to our firearms. We're not answering your questions. If the cops want to ask, they can come here with a warrant."

"We don't have anything to hide," Christine said, patting her husband's arm. "We have two guns—a Taurus handgun and an old Ruger rifle that Eric's dad gave us." Eric stared wide-eyed at his wife but didn't say anything. Yolanda wasn't sure what to make of Eric's reaction. Was he surprised that his wife responded? Or was he surprised at the content of her response?

"Christine," Yolanda said, "where did you go after you went home to shower Saturday night?"

"What?" Christine asked. "I went back to the hospital. Where else was I going to go?"

"Maybe to San Marino to scope out Hector's car. Maybe follow Lisa until she picked him up in Highland Park, and maybe to Eagle Rock where he dropped off Lisa, and finally to Figueroa and Colorado, where you shot him before getting on the freeway to go back to the hospital."

"Are you fuckin' crazy?" Christine asked, mad now. Yolanda felt Sydney spread her feet and go into an alert stance. Christine's reaction would be normal for someone who was innocent, but also for someone who was guilty but a good actor, or in denial. Perps sometimes convinced themselves of their innocence regardless of damning evidence.

"No, Christine, a woman driving an SUV like yours was spotted on surveillance cameras along the way. Don't deny it." Yolanda was careful not to mention the baseball cap. Detective Lan needed to keep that confidential so that she could do a proper search of the house. Christine had not worn one at the hospital, but that didn't mean that she didn't have one. Christine was indignant now, something normal for an innocent person as well.

"How could you even think that? My only focus is my son. How could you think I'd do something that stupid? Risk being taken away from my son? From my husband?" She shook her head and addressed Sydney. "You can't possibly believe this."

"I don't know," Sydney said and left it at that.

"Please leave," Eric said, his arm around his wife now.

"I'm sorry," Yolanda said. "I'm sorry for the tragedy that has befallen your family, but call me if you want help talking to the police."

The couple did not respond, both shaking their heads. Yolanda didn't think they'd call.

At Sydney's car, Yolanda shook her head too. She called Detective Lan when they'd driven away.

"All of her responses were appropriate for an innocent person, or for a very calculated or delusional killer," Yolanda said.

"And how much did you tell her?" Lan asked. "I swear, if you compromised this investigation—"

"No worries," Yolanda said, cutting her off. "I only said she'd been caught on video surveillance and didn't mention the baseball cap. But there's something you may want to look into. I asked them how many guns they had, and she mentioned a Taurus handgun and an old Ruger rifle. A Taurus makes sense for affordable home defense, especially for women, but here's the thing. Eric seemed surprised at his wife's response. I don't know if because she responded after he told us they wouldn't answer any questions, or because maybe she left out a gun she may have used. May be worth checking out gun registrations, assuming they registered their guns."

"Maybe," Lan said. "Now, will you please walk away from this and let me deal with it?"

"Okay," Yolanda said. "I'll try."

"Do. Don't try," Lan deadpanned her version of Yoda from *Star Wars*. She ended the call.

Turning to Sydney, Yolanda hoped she'd seen the same thing.

"What do you think? Do you read it the same way I do?"

Sydney thought a moment before answering, turning onto the westbound freeway.

"I think I saw a lot of anger and rage. Kind of blew me away. At first, I thought it was aimed at you for accusing her, but there's more there. The woman has been through a lot, so I kind of understand it. I don't know if she did it, but Eric is the one who confuses me. I can't tell if he's protecting his wife or himself. He kind of shut down. I caught the same thing you did when Christine mentioned the guns. He shut down even more after that."

"Thanks for the validation. My heart still goes out to them, and I hope Hector pissed off some other woman, but I don't know. Feel for the kid."

The women rode home in silence. When they arrived, they heated up some leftovers from the restaurant for a late lunch. They were about halfway through eating when Yolanda's phone buzzed.

"They found him," Gamaliel said. "They arrested Brian Jacobs!"

CHAPTER TWENTY-THREE

On her way to Gamaliel and the Abe Grocery, Yolanda called Detective Lan to get more details on Brian Jacobs's arrest. She didn't answer. Yolanda considered that she was ignoring her for having spoken with Christine and Eric.

At the store, she spoke with Gamaliel and a much-relieved Kinji. They didn't know much about the arrest but said that one of the detectives would call them with more information as soon as they could. All they knew was that he'd been arrested last night near the Nevada border. Yolanda would have to wait. She hated waiting, but while she did, she welcomed the opportunity to speak with Kinji. He seemed more tired and a bit more pale than after being released from jail. Yolanda hoped the emotional toll and excitement of the last few days had not put a strain on his heart. She sat with him while Gamaliel stocked shelves and took inventory.

"How are you doing, Kinji? You look a little tired."

"I'm fine," he said with a wave of his hand. "Just getting old."

Gamaliel looked up from his clipboard, concern in his eyes.

"Why don't you go rest your eyes?" he said. "I'll cover things here."

Kinji ignored his suggestion and turned to Yolanda.

"Sometimes he thinks he's the boss of me, like the kids say." Kinji chuckled at his own joke, then turned to Gamaliel. "We're gonna need help soon, son. Why don't you ask that young woman you've been eyeing if she'd like to work here?"

Yolanda saw Gamaliel's neck flush, but he kept his eyes on his clipboard and responded without looking up.

"Eliana already has a job. She's a social worker for the county."

"Well," Kinji said, "maybe her younger sister."

"Could work," Gamaliel said, still not looking up. "Izel's a barista. Might be good at working the deli too." Then he looked up at Kinji. "And if we get that espresso machine, we can add fancy coffees to the menu."

"That's my boy, always thinking." The older man smiled broadly with undisguised pride in the younger man. "But about Eliana…"

Gamaliel held the clipboard to his side and tapped it against his thigh before turning and walking to the register opposite Kinji.

"You're not going to let this go, are you?"

"Nope." Kinji smiled, a mischievous twinkle in his eyes.

Yolanda enjoyed their easy banter and understood why her brother liked to hang out with them.

"Well, she's not interested, so let it go."

"How can you be so sure?"

"Come on. She went to college and graduate school."

"And?"

"And she wouldn't be interested in me."

"I wouldn't be so sure. I mean, she comes in a lot on weekends, sometimes multiple times a day. Comes in on days she's working from home too. I'd say she has a crush on you."

Gamaliel's neck flushed again before spreading up his jaw and reaching his cheeks and temples. If he'd been lighter skinned, he'd be bright pink. His darker complexion offered him some grace and made him look like he had a deep tan instead. His eyes had turned toward the door, and Yolanda saw what had precipitated his blushing—or, rather, who. A young woman and a younger girl entered, classic beauties with olive skin and long, pitch-black hair. The woman wore it loose, while the girl wore French braids.

"Hi," the woman said. A flustered Gamaliel simply stared rather than give a verbal response. The girl looked between the two and shook her head.

"Yo, dudes, customer here." She raised her arms in exasperation. "Can a girl get a torta already?"

"Gamaliel," Kinji said to the young man still staring at the woman. He didn't move until Kinji cleared his throat and signaled with his hand that he should go to the deli.

"Oh, um, sure."

While Gamaliel scampered away, Kinji gave a hearty laugh.

"What did I tell you?" he said to Yolanda. The woman hadn't seen Yolanda behind the counter and turned to Kinji, thinking he'd addressed her.

"Excuse me?"

"Why don't you ask the boy out already?" Kinji said. This time, the woman blushed almost as much as Gamaliel had. Yolanda didn't want to laugh but couldn't hold back a broad smile.

"Oh, hi," the woman said, noticing Yolanda for the first time.

"Hi," Yolanda said, offering her hand. "I'm Yolanda Ávila."

"Eliana Gomez," the woman said, shaking her hand. Then she turned to Kinji. "Wanted to check on you guys. Heard what happened yesterday. How awful. I was out in the field. Um, yesterday. But I'm working from home today. Thought I'd come by."

Yolanda smiled again, noting the woman's nervous chatter.

"Well, thanks for checking on us. We're good. Yolanda here's been helping us. She's a private eye."

"Really? The one asking all the questions about Frank the other day?" Yolanda noted that the gossip network was alive and well. She thought of neighborhood gossip as a sign of a healthy community, people looking out for each other as much as to get the latest news about each other. New residents sometimes found it off-putting, but, like small-town America, it kept people close. She didn't think she could say the same for the suburbs, where many people didn't even know their neighbors. She hoped the closeness wouldn't go away with housing becoming less affordable and changing the demographics of the neighborhood.

"Yup," Yolanda said. "I was hoping for help from the chisme network and was not disappointed." She then changed the subject. "So, Gamaliel tells us you're a social worker."

"With two college degrees," Kinji said.

"Yeah," Eliana said. "Went to Oxy. But that was back when they recruited and embraced Latino students more." Yolanda knew she was referring to the exclusive Occidental College in Eagle Rock. Its claim to fame was Barack Obama's attendance for a couple of years. "Well, glad to see you guys are okay. Gonna go get my sandwich for lunch." She pointed to the deli with both thumbs over her left shoulder and walked over to one of the stools there.

"See?" Kinji said.

"Oh, I see," Yolanda said, understanding Kinji's not so subtle matchmaking efforts. Her phone buzzed in her back pocket. The caller ID flashed Detective Lan's name.

"Please tell me you're not still at the Jacobs house or at the mother's," Lan said.

"I'm not," Yolanda said. "I'm at the Abe Grocery, waiting for word on Brian Jacobs's arrest. I thought you'd be questioning him before questioning Christine. How'd you get him, by the way?"

"Alert gas station attendant saw his picture on the news. He was driving his white pickup. Could have gotten away if he'd driven his mother's car instead. Anyway, we did question him. Claims he had nothing to do with the shooting that killed Hector Garcia. Denies the shooting at the Abe Grocery too, but that's no surprise."

"So why are you calling? Did Christine give up anything?"

"That's just it. Couldn't find anything. No baseball cap. And the Taurus looks like it hasn't been cleaned in a long time, let alone fired. We'll test it anyway. We questioned her at the house because she was alone with her kid. Plan to question the husband separately as soon as we can get to his worksite, hopefully before they can talk too much more. Just wanted to check with you about any other way to connect the woman to the Garcia shooting."

"Only thing I can think of is cell phone data."

"We're checking that but coming up empty. Looks like she left her phone at Children's Hospital."

"Wait. I called her on Saturday to tell her about my conversations with the Garcias."

"Where was she when you called?"

"Oh, shit. Wait." Yolanda paused, thinking. "She didn't answer. I left a message. But if her phone was at the hospital, it was in the room with Eric. He didn't answer it."

"The hospital is the only place it pings on Saturday. She said she saw your call on it when she got back but had kept her phone on silent so as not to disturb the boy."

"Still means she could have acted alone or with her husband's knowledge. Good luck getting him to talk, but you won't be able to force a confession from either of them unless they slip up. Damn. She's either very smart or very lucky."

"The ones that get away are lucky, not smart."

"Holy shit, you really think she can get away with it?"

"We don't have enough to hold her. We're testing for gunpowder residue, but the techs aren't too confident about it. Unless something else comes up…" Lan said without finishing the thought. "Based on what you've said, I'm not sure we'll get much from the husband either. But I take it he was at the hospital while his wife was away. His phone pings there too. Just let me know if you come up with anything. We're gonna keep trying. See if either of them cracks." She ended the call, leaving Yolanda dumbfounded.

Lan was right. Unless Eric knew something and turned in his own wife, which he likely wouldn't do, Christine could get away with it. Damn. The more she thought about it, the more she thought Christine perhaps had tried to set up Brian too. Why else would she have made a point of talking about Brian's strange call from Boyle Heights? Gamaliel had seen him near the store that night, but maybe he wasn't there to create an alibi for Hector's shooting. Maybe he was there because he wanted to work up the nerve to go through with his extortion plan. She looked at Kinji, who watched her expectantly.

"Sometimes, justice isn't fair," she said, shaking her head.

"Don't I know it," Kinji said. "But why do you say that?"

"Looks like the most likely suspect in Hector Garcia's killing is someone I would not have suspected at all. And, unlike Gumer, she may get away with it because there isn't enough evidence to hold her. I don't know if Hector ran that motorcycle off the road, but I know he ran me off the road. Don't think that merits a death sentence, but he certainly got one. The woman gets to raise her young son, and here Gumer will be separated from her own son, maybe for the rest of their lives, only because she tried to defend herself." She shook her head.

"Sometimes the world is not balanced," Kinji said. "What's the Hopi word? Koyaanisqatsi, life out of balance." He stopped and grasped the register's counter with both hands.

"You okay, Kinji?"

"I'm okay. Just got a little vertigo all of a sudden. Maybe Gamaliel is right and I should go lie down for a while."

Concern etched across Yolanda's face. This was not a man who would admit weakness like this unless he was feeling ill.

"Should I call 911?" Yolanda asked. She called over to Gamaliel to let him know that Kinji was not feeling well. He came over right away, wiping his hands on a dish towel, but Kinji continued to protest.

"No, look. I can walk fine. Just need to lie down with my feet elevated. That's what the doctor suggested."

Eliana and Izel had come over, both looking worried. Gamaliel looked over to them and back at Kinji. Yolanda tried to ease his concern.

"Go ahead and take him to the house," she said. "We'll watch the store."

"Yeah, don't worry," Izel said. "I'll finish making our tortas."

"I'll be right back," Gamaliel said, walking behind Kinji, who waved at the women and told them not to worry, that he was just going to take a quick nap.

"You sure he'll be okay?" Eliana asked Yolanda once they'd left. "He looks kind of pale."

"I agree. Let's see what Gamaliel says when he comes back. Meanwhile, I'm going to call my wife. She's a doctor."

Yolanda called Sydney while Izel and Eliana busied themselves behind the deli case. She described Kinji's symptoms and what he had described to her the day before about his heart condition.

"They should take his blood pressure too," Sydney said. "If he's dizzy, he may not be getting enough blood to his brain. I'd call 911 if he doesn't get back to normal after he lies down. But he should get to his primary doctor as soon as he can, in any case. I'll be done with my rounds in a few minutes. Want me to come over?"

"Could you?"

"Okay, let me wrap up. I'll be there within the hour, but call 911 if he doesn't improve. Got it?"

"Got it."

Yolanda ended the call and hoped that Kinji wasn't too sick. She wasn't sure how Gamaliel would handle another blow. She mentioned as much to Eliana, and the woman agreed. She offered to relay Sydney's recommendation and went over to check on both men in Kinji's house. Shortly after, Yolanda's brother arrived. She filled him in on Kinji's condition, and Jesse walked over to the house too, leaving Yolanda and Izel in the store. A couple of customers walked in, and Izel helped Yolanda figure out the register. Fortunately, the items they bought all had price tags, and the customers used their bank cards to tap instead of using cash.

Sydney arrived half an hour later and headed over to Kinji's house with her medical bag. Yolanda had given it to her for her birthday a couple of years ago, but she'd never seen her use it until now.

"He'll be okay," Izel said, reading Yolanda's anxiety about Kinji. "My mom says he's from a hardy generation and that it takes a lot to take them out."

"I hope you're right," Yolanda said.

A few minutes later, Jesse came in through the back door of the store.

"Sydney called 911. Thinks he's having a heart attack. She said it could be a mild one, but with his age and his heart condition, he should go to the ER. At least, that's what she said to convince Kinji."

Yolanda heard the sirens approaching and was glad Sydney had had a chance to evaluate the man.

"Told Gamaliel that I'd stay and help with the store," Jesse said. "Between me and Izel here, I think we can run the place for a couple of hours." He turned to Izel. "Don't you think?"

"Fo' sho," Izel said, grabbing an apron from behind the counter. "I've filled in for Gumer in emergencies before." She rapped her fingers on the counter as if waiting for customers.

"It takes a village," Yolanda said, smiling. She thanked them both. "Let's just make sure the hospital's village is as good as this one."

After the ambulance left with Kinji and Sydney, Gamaliel walked back into the store, his face as drawn and downcast as when he'd returned from the lawyer's office with his mom. Eliana walked in beside him, saying something to him in a low voice. Yolanda assumed she was trying to provide encouragement.

"He was trying to joke the whole time," Gamaliel said to Yolanda and Jesse, "but this is the worst I've seen him since his diagnosis. Thanks for getting Sydney here. I don't think he would have listened to me about going to the hospital."

"Might not be so bad if he's still being stubborn," Jesse offered.

"Right," Yolanda said. "Must be the toll of everything happening over the past few days. It's a good reminder to take care of ourselves. How are you doing?" she asked Gamaliel.

"I'm good," he said, taking a deep breath. "Thanks for all your support, guys. I'm gonna run down to White Memorial. Taking Kinji's car. You guys sure you can hold down the fort?"

They all told him not to worry and to go ahead. He turned to Izel.

"You know how to lock up, right? Can you do that and leave the keys at Kinji's? I can get his house key from you tomorrow. I have an extra set." He handed her a set of keys and turned to leave, but Jesse stopped him with an embrace.

"You got this, bro," Jesse said.

The women hugged him as well. Something told Yolanda that the awkward hug between Gamaliel and Eliana was perhaps their first. Both looked away from each other before he walked out of the store. Yolanda couldn't help but think that a romance could help his immigration status. When the sisters went back to the deli, she asked Jesse about it in a whisper.

"Man's got a lot of pride," Jesse said. "Says he never wants to put that on someone. That and his basic shyness keep him from dating, I think."

"You never know. The events of the last few days have been enough to change anyone. Maybe he'll be ready now."

Jesse gave her a sad smile, likely thinking about his friend.

"Maybe," he said.

Yolanda's phone buzzed with Sydney's caller ID.

"May want to tell Gamaliel that Mr. Abe won't be going home tonight."

"Is it that bad?" Yolanda asked.

"Could've been worse," Sydney said. "I think he'll be okay, but he'll be weaker for a while. They'll know more after they run tests. But they're definitely keeping him overnight to monitor him. I would too."

"Thanks for being there, love. I'll come over in a bit to pick you up. We'll come back for your car."

"Okay, let me give you his room number."

"He already got a room?"

"Membership has its privileges," Sydney said, referring to the courtesy extended to her as a doctor. "At least when they have rooms available." Yolanda heard a loud, deep voice in the background. It grew louder as Sydney brought the phone to Kinji and apparently handed it to him.

"I was telling your wife to tell you that I'm fine. I'll be fine. No need to make a fuss. Tell Gamaliel I'll be home in no time."

"You can tell him yourself," Yolanda said. "He's already on his way to you. I'll see you soon too."

"Sheesh," the man said. "Okay, in that case, bring me some tacos."

"No," Yolanda and Sydney said in unison.

"He's joking," Sydney said into the phone. "See you soon."

Gamaliel had arrived ahead of Yolanda and was in Kinji's room when she entered. The two men were in deep conversation. Sydney tried to give them some privacy by sitting on the window bench and studying her phone. Yolanda greeted all three. She had to admit that Kinji didn't look any worse than he had earlier in the day.

"You're looking pretty good, Kinji," she said. "Even have more color on your cheeks."

"It's whatever life force they're pumping into me with all these tubes," he said, pointing to his saline drip. "I'll be younger when I get out." His laugh, more than the joke, made the others chuckle too. Yolanda welcomed the relief they all seemed to feel.

"Telling the young fella, here," Kinji continued, "that he should hire the sister of that woman he likes. Make it easier to date her." He winked at Gamaliel, whose neck flushed red again. "Go on. Your mom would be happy for you, and it'll give you more to talk about when you visit her."

Gamaliel took a deep breath. The stress of the last few days compounded by Kinji's health scare clearly weighed on him. He spoke in a soft, tired voice.

"Gonna try to see Mom tomorrow but won't tell her about you being here."

"Good idea. Tell her I'll be over to visit her as soon as we coordinate our schedules. She'll want to see you more anyway."

They chatted some more about the logistics of jail visits and running the store before Gamaliel walked the women out. He turned back to tell Kinji that he'd walk them to the garage, and Kinji blew them all a kiss.

"I'm so glad he looks better than this afternoon," Yolanda said.

"He'll need rest when he gets home," Sydney said. "He may not admit it, but he'll need naps to gain some strength back. You may notice that he's weaker," she said to Gamaliel. "May be good to get him a cane to reduce any risk of falling. Tell him he'll need naps until he can walk from his house to the store without feeling winded."

"I'll tell him he'll need them until he can walk around the block without being winded." They all stopped at Yolanda's car, Gamaliel with his hands in his pockets, shuffling his feet.

"What's on your mind?" Yolanda asked. He looked her in the eye.

"Mr. Herrera called on my way here. He confirmed that Mom will get six months, less if she gets off for good behavior. He thinks that means three months. But she'll be deported right away when she completes her sentence."

"I'm so sorry, Gamaliel," Yolanda said. Sydney echoed her sympathy. Yolanda didn't say so but thought that Gumer's sentence was a generous one, even with a self-defense claim. Celine may never tell her, but she wondered if her own involvement had helped with the plea bargain.

"We'll make the best of it," Gamaliel said. "At least I'll be able to send her money." He paused, shaking his head. "You know, when she was going through her things yesterday, she showed me a bag at the bottom of her knitting basket. It had thirty-three thousand dollars in it. Cash. Can you believe it?" Both women raised their eyebrows. "I need to put it somewhere so I can wire it to an account as soon as she sets one up in Mexico." He continued to shake his head. "Wanted me to get a car with it, but I don't need one, especially since I use Kinji's. Still can't believe it. Must've saved a thousand dollars a year for thirty-three years." He shook his head in amazement.

"That'll give her a nice start in Mexico," Yolanda said. "I'm glad you're not telling her about Kinji yet. She doesn't need that added stress. Plus, it looks like he'll be okay."

Gamaliel agreed and thanked the women again before they left.

In the car, Sydney provided Yolanda more details on Kinji's condition.

"He's not going to get much better," she said. "Has a rare condition with a damaged artery. Not something that a bypass or other intervention can cure. Already has early signs of something called cardiac cachexia. It's a condition caused by low blood flow to the heart. You see it often in cancer patients. Means his heart is weakening and he'll slowly waste away. He'll need to eat often. Small meals. I told Gamaliel all of this, and he said he'd noticed some weight loss over the last year and especially over the last few months, so that kind of confirms it. Said Kinji claimed he was exercising."

"Damn. He looked so healthy to me last week. How much time do you think he has left?"

"Hard to tell. Depends on how well he takes care of himself, but his age will make it harder to slow it down. I've seen younger people last a long time, years even, but older folks often take a more precipitous dive. He'll need to get his affairs in order if he hasn't already. Needs to make some decisions on end-of-life care too. Gamaliel will sit him down when they go home. The doctor working on him has a good bedside manner, but he'll be very clear with him on his prognosis before he leaves."

"How sad." Yolanda shook her head. "And damn, Gamaliel will lose his mother and his only father figure one right after the other. That's gotta suck."

"Gotta feel for the guy."

"I'll let Jesse know so that he can continue to support his friend. Damn, that sucks."

CHAPTER TWENTY-FOUR

Three Months Later

Yolanda and Jesse dropped by the Abe Grocery with Christmas gifts.

"You guys know you shouldn't have, right?" Gamaliel said, taking the packages for him and for Kinji. "I didn't get anything for you guys."

"Friendship," Jesse said.

"You look great, by the way," Yolanda said, noting that he looked more rested than after September's ordeal.

"Yeah, lost some weight. Working out. But Mom's getting worried. I finally told her about Kinji. Had to explain why he doesn't visit. But now she thinks I have the same thing."

"How is she doing?" Yolanda asked.

"Not bad, I think. She lost some weight too, but she's getting out next month. She was happy to hear that I finally asked Eliana out. Actually, she asked me."

So that explained the glow, along with his efforts to get in shape, Yolanda thought. It had to be bittersweet for Gumer, learning about her son dating but not being able to see him happy.

"How's Sydney, by the way?" Gamaliel asked.

"She's well. Pretty happy, actually. Remember the guy who shot up the store?"

"Who could forget?"

"Well, he also filed a lawsuit against Sydney, remember? It got dismissed with prejudice. Guess the guy and his mother couldn't get another lawyer to take their case. Means it's over and she won't have to go to court."

"That's awesome," Gamaliel said. "Tell her I said congratulations."

"Thanks. So back to your mom. Will she be able to spend time at home before being deported?"

"Unfortunately, no. Mr. Herrera said it used to be possible, but the new policy is to have prisoners convicted of felonies go directly from prison once they finish their sentence. We were hoping for before Christmas because they seem eager to keep the prison population down since the pandemic. She could've been with family in Mexico for the holidays but, of course, the paperwork didn't go through fast enough. Now we're hoping by January sixth, you know, Dia de los Reyes. That's the real Christmas in Mexico anyway. We'll see."

"Glad to hear it," Jesse said. "Let us know if you need anything. We all know people visiting Mexico, in case you need to send stuff."

"Appreciate you, bro."

"How's Kinji doing?" Yolanda asked. The last time she'd seen him a few weeks earlier, he had taken a turn for the worst, his body more emaciated, his mind not what it had been.

"He's hanging in there," Gamaliel said. "Good days and bad days. You know the drill. It really hurts to see his mind go, though. When he's lucid he's good, like that day you dropped by last week," he said to Jesse.

"Yeah, he was joking around like old times. Just physically weak."

"Sorry to hear it," Yolanda said. "I know it's gotta be tough."

"It is, but my Tía Chata has been great, coming back to help care for him. She's been managing the caregivers too. Says she'll move in when it gets close to the end to make sure he has family around when he goes.”

“You’ll be there too,” a voice behind them said. Izel Gomez, in her trademark French braids, came over from the deli, wiping her hands on her apron. “And you don’t have to worry. I’ll cover the store.” Gamaliel placed an affectionate arm around her shoulders.

“I know you will. I’m so glad you took the job.”

“How else am I gonna get free tortas? That bread you get for them is bomb.”

Yolanda was glad the young woman lightened the mood as much as she lightened the load on Gamaliel. He had enough to worry about.

“Can we see him now?” Yolanda asked. “Got him a book I think he’d like.”

“You know he can’t read anymore, right?”

“Sure, but thought maybe you could read some of it to him. I met a client in Little Tokyo yesterday and thought I’d check out the Japanese American National Museum across the way. Found this.” She pulled the book out of the gift bag for Gamaliel to see. He read the title aloud.

“*A Rebel’s Outcry: Biography of Issei Civil Rights Leader Sei Fujii (1882-1954).*”

“Has to be the same guy Kinji mentioned when we first met. It’s the lawyer who wrote that brochure on how Japanese immigrants could buy property before World War II. The one who got the Alien Land Act overturned. Came out last year. Thought Kinji would like to add it to his collection.”

“Wow, he’d love this if he could make it out,” Gamaliel said, holding the book in both hands. “Let’s walk over. Can’t guarantee he’ll be awake, though.”

When they entered Kinji’s house, Yolanda noted the telltale smells of a sick person in residence. It smelled similar to Sydney’s grandmother’s house before she passed—house cleaner overlaying a musty body odor that no amount of washing could eliminate. At least the bleach wasn’t overwhelming, Yolanda thought.

"How is he?" Gamaliel asked his aunt, Chata. Yolanda was glad her own son's death had not prevented her from helping the man who'd helped her family so much. Jesse had told her that Chata had offered to help without being asked because she considered Kinji family and thought of him as a second father.

"In and out, but he had a good morning. Good idea to see him now before the sundowning sets in." Yolanda recognized the term. Sydney's grandmother would fade out or become disoriented in the evenings too.

"Hey, old man," Gamaliel said with a smile in his voice.

"Hey, young man," Kinji responded.

"Have some visitors for you." Kinji looked behind Gamaliel and smiled.

"Jesse, good to see you." He squinted at Yolanda. "And you are?"

"Yolanda, Jesse's sister," she said.

"Oh, sure. The private eye. How are you?"

"I'm well. Question is, how are you?"

"One foot in the grave and the other on a banana peel, as they say."

"They keeping you comfortable?" Jesse asked.

"Oh, sure. Nice ladies. But they keep trying to fatten me up. Tell them I can't eat all day, unless it's that lady's mizu yokan." He lowered his voice to a whisper. "Don't tell her it's not as good as old Mrs. Ito's from down the street, but it's still pretty good."

"What's mizu yokan?" Yolanda asked.

"It's like a red bean cajeta," Gamaliel said. "Like a gelatin. A lady who used to live down the street made it all the time years ago." He turned back to Kinji. "Yolanda brought you a book."

"Thank you," Kinji said. "Open it." Gamaliel pulled it out of the gift bag and held it in front of him. Kinji focused on the book cover.

"Hey, that's Mr. Fujii," Kinji said. "I remember him."

"This is a book about him," Gamaliel said.

"Thank you," Kinji said again, turning to Yolanda. "Get one about Mr. Okamoto. Should call it 'Troublemaker at Heart

Mountain.' Pauper's grave at Evergreen now. Check it out." Kinji seemed to tire with every sentence. His effort triggered a coughing fit.

Chata raised his hospital bed with a remote to help him sit up while Gamaliel patted his back and held a tissue to his mouth. Kinji tried waving him away but had a hard time raising his arm. The cough had weakened him. Yolanda was surprised to see how much more weight he'd lost, the tendons in his hands visible under his skin.

"Okay, old man," Gamaliel said. "We gotta go, but you get some rest."

As difficult as it was to see him in this condition, Yolanda was glad they'd caught Kinji on a good day. She wasn't sure when she'd see him again, but she was impressed with how well Chata and Gamaliel and the caregivers looked after him.

Four Months Later

Gamaliel had just finished up with a customer when the phone rang. It startled him. No one called on the landline anymore except "Spam Risk." Most pickup orders came online, but they'd kept the landline because the burglar alarm was connected to it. Only Kinji used it for outgoing calls—or at least used to. Gamaliel stared at it for a couple of rings, distracted.

"You gonna get that?" Izel stopped sweeping and put a hand on her hip, her head tilted to the side.

Gamaliel blinked and reached for the receiver, his eyes still on the kid working that nasty, watermelon-flavored gum in her mouth.

"Abe's Grocery."

"Gamaliel, you have to come see him. He's asking for you," Chata said. Dread pushed a bit of bile up in this throat. He swallowed hard before answering.

"I'll be right there." He turned to Izel removing his apron. "Be right back. Gonna see Kinji."

He walked to Kinji's house at a fast clip but hesitated after climbing the two steps to the porch. Chata opened the door and motioned him in.

"Go to him."

Gamaliel did as instructed, stepping toward Kinji's bedroom. Chata had put a tray table and chair by the door.

"What's that for?" Gamaliel asked, as much for something to say as to avoid looking at the old man in the bed.

"For the hospice nurse," Kinji said with some effort.

"What?" Gamaliel and Chata had arranged for hospice help but he did not know that Kinji knew. He was glad to see that he was lucid and did not have that frightened or vacant look in his eyes that had come and gone frequently for the past few weeks.

"Soon. Not yet." Kinji patted the arm of a chair next to the bed. "Sit."

Gamaliel sat.

"How you doing, old man?"

"Before I go, there's something you need to know."

"You're not going anywhere."

Kinji smiled weakly and continued.

"I have a trust," he said as if trying not to waste effort on words. "This place and store will be all yours. You know where papers are, right?" His clipped speech sounded strange, almost foreign.

"Uh-huh." Gamaliel grunted his assent, his throat tightening too much to speak. Kinji had mentioned his intention years ago, but Gamaliel somehow always thought Kinji's nephews would come first. He was surprised the day Kinji asked him to accompany him to a lawyer's office after his mother's arrest and Kinji's heart attack. Gamaliel had shaken his head at the irony of not being able to work legally for someone else in this country but being able to inherit and own a business. He gathered himself to thank Kinji again properly, his voice cracking.

"I don't know how I can ever thank you for being so generous and good to my family. For giving us so much hope, especially after everything that your own family went through."

Kinji's eyes brightened, and he took a deep breath as if to gather strength to speak.

"They tried to bury us but didn't know we were seeds, eh?"

Gamaliel squeezed his hand and smiled so as not to cry. Kinji had quoted the Mexican activist saying. Jesse had once explained it also had Greek roots.

Kinji closed his eyes tight, wincing in pain.

"Can I get you anything?"

Kinji shook his head slowly and opened his eyes when he heard someone else enter the small room. Chata stepped in with two other women, one a tall Black woman in dark-blue scrubs and the other a short Asian woman in slacks and a copper-colored, knee-length coat. They introduced themselves to Gamaliel and to Kinji with kind eyes. The Asian woman, Hope Ono, asked Gamaliel if there was somewhere they could talk while Rachel Murrell, the hospice nurse, examined Kinji. Gamaliel led Hope to the small dining room table where she explained the hospice process and asked questions about Kinji that he had become accustomed to answering for medical personnel.

"Are you his grandson?" she asked.

"No, but he's been like a grandfather to me," Gamaliel answered, blinking back tears.

"But you are listed as his power of attorney and the person who can make decisions as to his medical care, right?"

"Yes," Gamaliel said, staring at the floor.

"I know this is hard," she said, placing a gentle hand on his knee, "but we'll try to make him as comfortable as possible. Has he been in much pain?"

"Yes, the codeine doesn't seem to do much for him anymore. But at least he hasn't tried pulling out the catheter again."

"Rachel will check that. We're prepared to move him onto morphine if you approve. We just need your signature here," Hope said, indicating the form she placed in front of him.

Gamaliel took the paper and looked at it for a moment before signing.

"Can we ask him anyway? I think he can still decide for himself when he's lucid. And he seemed to be just now."

"Of course. And just so you know, we offer counseling services for the family as well. You don't have to do all of this on your own, you know."

"Thank you. Can we go back to him and ask about the morphine?"

They did that, but Gamaliel knew as soon as he saw the vacant look in Kinji's eyes that he was gone again. He tried sounding upbeat anyway.

"Hey, old man. Nurse Rachel here has some stuff that's better than what we've been giving you for the pain. You okay with morphine?"

Kinji stared at him blankly. Gamaliel took his hand, careful not to disturb the saline tube in his arm, and bent to speak into his ear.

"Okay, we're going to give you something to make the pain go away. You'll feel better."

With that, the nurse stepped forward and placed a dropper under Kinji's tongue. He made a face but did not seem to resist.

"He'll fall asleep for a while," Rachel said. "We should let him rest, and you two should too," she said, turning to Chata and Gamaliel. "I'll be right here until morning. Another nurse will come for the day shift."

"Thank you," they both said.

That was the last time Gamaliel had had a conversation with Kinji. For the next few days, the old man seemed to go between disorientation and morphine-induced sleep. One night, at closing time, Yolanda dropped by to ask after Kinji. Gamaliel invited her to go with him to his bedside. Nurse Rachel encouraged them to sit for a while.

"I haven't given him the morphine yet, but even after I do, you can always talk to him. He'll hear you. I'll be right outside. Stay as long as you'd like."

Gamaliel thanked her for her kindness and held Kinji's hand, sitting on the bedside chair. Yolanda stood at the doorway so as not to intrude.

"Old man, you have no idea how much I love you. How much we all love you," Gamaliel said, his voice cracking. "Thank you for loving us," he choked out before breaking down in tears, his head on the bed. He gathered himself and continued, "Sorry, Kinji. We're all going to be okay. Better than okay. You made sure of that. Thank you. Know that we love you and that we are proud of you." He wasn't sure why he'd said that last part, but it seemed to be something he thought Kinji would want to hear spoken aloud.

Kinji squeezed Gamaliel's hand, opened his eyes, and smiled broadly, staring into midspace. Just as suddenly, his grip loosened, his throat gurgled, and he seemed to fall asleep with his mouth slightly open. The nurse walked in and took his pulse, shaking her head slowly.

"That was beautiful," Yolanda said, placing a gentle hand on Gamaliel's shoulder.

Author's Note

The events in this book are fiction, but the historical background is all too real. The following are a few resources for more information on the plight of Japanese Americans during and after World War II:

https://densho.org/

https://encyclopedia.densho.org/Heart_Mountain_Fair_Play_Committee/

https://www.heartmountain.org/collections-archives/draft-resisters/

A Rebel's Outcry: Biography of Issei Civil Rights Leader Sei Fujii (1882-1954). (Based on Rafu Gigyu Ondo by Kenichi Sato) by Jeffrey Gee Chin and Fumiko Carole Fujita

Beyond the Betrayal by Yoshito Kuromiya edited by Aurthur A. Hansen

Fred Korematsu Speaks Up by Laura Atkins and Stan Yogi illustrated by Yutaka Houlette

Life After Manzanar by Naomi Hirahara and Heather C. Linquist

Nisei Naysayer by James Matsumoto Omura, edited by Arthur A. Hansen

Rebel Lawyer: Wayne Collins and the Defense of Japanese American Rights by Charles Wollenberg

The Eagles of Heart Mountain: A True Story of Football, Incarceration, and Resistance in World War II America by Bradford Pearson

We Hereby Refuse: Japanese American Resistance in Wartime Incarceration by Frank Abe and Tamiko Nimura, artwork by Ross Ishikawa and Matt Sasaki

Resources for Children:

Baseball Saved Us by Ken Mochizuki and Dom Lee
Finding Moon Rabbit by J.C. Kato and J.C.[2]